The Cursed Divination

A Victorian Historical Murder Mystery

Book 5 of
The Field & Greystone Series

Lana Williams

USA Today Bestselling Author

Ebook ISBN: 979-8-9914769-8-0
Print ISBN: 979-8-9914769-9-7

Cover Art by The Killion Group

The Field & Greystone Mystery Series

The Ravenkeeper's Daughter, Book 1 - Also available in Audio

The Mudlark Murders, Book 2 - Also available in Audio

The Gravesend Murder, Book 3 - Also available in Audio

The Rookery Killer, Book 4

The Cursed Divination, Book 5

The Sinister Deception, Book 6

If you'd like to hear about future releases and special promotions, sign up for my newsletter at lanawilliams.net. You can unsubscribe at any time.

Chapter One

London, 1884

THE RAIN PELTING CLARENCE Digby was misery-inducing. The kind of drenching wet that chilled one's bones and prompted daydreams of hunkering down before a warm fire clasping a hot drink.

Clarence snorted at the thought, the motion causing a drip to scuttle down his collar. That wasn't an option when his circumstances grew more dire with each day that passed.

Brushing aside his worries as best he could, he flipped up his tattered jacket collar and forged ahead, careful to avoid the biggest puddles. Never mind that his shoes and socks, both with numerous holes, were already soaked.

Sudden April showers were the worst.

King's Cross railway station emerged from the evening gloom, its square ornate clocktower barely visible through the downpour. Passengers departed the station, many pausing to frown at the sky or wrestle with an umbrella. Just as many entered it, bound for other parts of London or destinations farther north now that the workday had ended for most.

Giving the station an angry glare, Clarence continued around the side of the brick building. His pride still stung from his unexpected dismissal as a railway clerk nearly two weeks prior, any loyalty he'd felt severed that day. Fine, he'd taken some copper wire and brass fittings from a storage shed and sold them to earn a little extra money—but they weren't being used. His mum needed the funds, and he liked to think he was merely tidying up the grounds.

His superior hadn't agreed.

Now Clarence was forced to rely on his resourcefulness in new ways, most of which were illegal, hence the reason he was out in the miserable weather this evening. He might have received his final wages the day he'd been fired, but that didn't end the railway's debt to him. After all, he'd given them nearly six whole months of his twenty years, carefully guarding his secret the entire time. Now Clarence was resigned to do whatever was necessary to support himself and his mum...even if thus far his efforts had been met with somewhat limited success.

Over the past week, he'd found a few more things from the sheds at the railyard to sell, easily avoiding the watchman who guarded the place. It was simple enough to slip into the fenced yard if one knew where and how and when to do so, especially with his slender frame.

More impressively, Clarence had managed to sort through several passenger bags in the luggage compartment early this morning and had taken a few valuables when a porter was otherwise occupied.

The items bounced in his trouser pocket with every step, marking the start of a brighter future if they were worth what he hoped. It hadn't been easy to find the right person willing to buy what he carried. A regular pawnbroker, even one who didn't feel compelled to inquire how Clarence had come to possess the suspect loot, wouldn't do.

The risk was too great.

Clarence's entire body tightened with nerves as the Queen's Slipper came into view. The pub, despite its lofty name, was one of the seedier taverns in the area, an establishment he hadn't dared venture into before now.

If only he looked older and meaner; but his youthful features and thin form didn't lend themselves to the reputation he so desired.

Still, he had a knife tucked in the top of his boot and knew how to use it. Mostly. If whittling counted. Shouldn't be too hard to stick a man if he had to, right? He ignored the way the thought unsettled the meager contents of his stomach.

Clarence straightened his shoulders, narrowed his eyes, and tried for a snarl to dissuade anyone lingering nearby from approaching him, then opened the door.

The pungent scents of fried food, smoke, and unwashed humanity assailed him, but not in equal measures. His nose twitched, mainly from the latter, as he scanned the room to gain his bearings.

Soon I'll move on from here, he told himself. He had lofty goals and refused to lose sight of them. Soon, he'd be frequenting much finer establishments and would at last be able to put the secret, increasingly difficult to keep, behind him.

Clarence edged around the crowd, hat pulled low, nodding at a few strangers as if they were familiar, and continued weaving his way to the stairs. A drink would have to wait until he had money in his pocket rather than stolen trinkets.

Per the instructions he'd received in the scrawled note also in his pocket, Clarence went up the stairs, eager to have the meeting over and done now that he was this close. He reached the second door on the left and paused to wipe his damp palms on his trousers. The secrecy was both invigorating and nerve-wracking.

Soon. Soon this would all be over.

He knocked twice quietly, waited a beat, knocked harder a third time, then entered. A single candle burned on a table in the center of the small room, the rush of air from the door causing it to dance.

"Close the door."

Clarence's heart raced as he quickly did as ordered. His eyes slowly adjusted to the dim interior to find a grizzled middle-aged man wearing a hat and a scowl seated at the table.

"Evenin'," Clarence said, detesting how his voice threatened to squeak. "Are ye Scranton?"

The man only scowled harder. "No names. Do ye 'ave the goods?" He tapped his fingers, encased in ratty fingerless gloves, on the table as if impatient.

"I do." Clarence cleared his throat and pulled out a chair, only to realize it would be easier to retrieve the items from his pocket before he sat. The clandestine behavior felt unfamiliar and awkward, disorienting, unsettling.

He managed to pull forth a handful and took his time spilling the items onto the table, gold and silver gleaming in the candlelight. Feeling rather proud of himself, he repeated the process, adding to the pile, before searching the pocket one last time for the two remaining items.

One in particular never failed to catch his breath—a golden ring with a red stone. Surely it was a genuine ruby, rather than paste, based on the way it sparkled.

"Humph." Scranton, if that was really his name, pulled out a chipped jeweler's loop and studied a few of the pieces, leaving the ruby ring for last.

Clarence sat in the chair and did his best to hide the anticipation gripping him. The risk he'd taken was about to pay off. He felt it in his bones.

The man sorted through the motley collection using a dirty finger with a broken nail. The sight of that finger sent unease crawling down Clarence's spine as the reality of how far he'd lowered himself sank in.

He was as dirty as that finger, fencing treasures he'd stolen from others. Shame heated his face even as he watched the man, his odd grunts impossible to interpret.

His mum wouldn't be happy if she knew...but she'd take the money he sent, all the same.

"I'll give ye seven pounds and five shillin' for the lot of it." The man looked up with a crafty gleam in his eye.

The number was disappointing, given the ruby ring. "That won't do." Clarence shook his head. He might not like what he was doing, but he refused to be taken advantage of. "Them's worth twice that."

"Humph." Scranton sorted some more, adjusting the small piles he'd made. "Nine pounds. Best I can do. Takes work to sell these wivout gainin' notice." He eyed Clarence for a long moment, seeming to see through to his very soul, sending uncomfortable prickles along his skin. "And I don't think you could do better on yer own."

"Twelve pounds an' we have a deal." Clarence thought twice before finally offering his hand to shake, the filth of the other man's giving him pause. The amount was still less than he'd wanted, but arguing was unlikely to get him more.

The man hesitated, and Clarence held his breath. At last, the stranger nodded, grunting in that odd way of his as he shook Clarence's hand. "Very well."

Scranton pushed back from the table and unbuttoned his coat, revealing the butt of a pistol tucked into his trousers.

Clarence stilled at the sight of the weapon, terror rising in the back of his throat.

Was this the moment his life ended?

To his relief, the man reached past the gun into an inside pocket and pulled forth a wad of pound notes, which he carefully counted then placed on the table. "Pleasure doin' business wiv you."

"T-Thank you, good sir." Clarence cleared his throat again and forced himself to slowly reach for the money as if in no hurry to escape the room.

The man studied him from beneath the brim of his hat. "If I were ye, I'd look fer a new line of work. This ain't fer the likes of ye."

Clarence stiffened once again, heart pounding at the worry of his secret being discovered. "For yer information, this is only temp'ry. With luck, ye won't be seein' me again."

The stranger nodded, seeming satisfied with the answer.

Clarence stood and tucked the notes in a pocket, eager to be gone. "Good evenin'." He dipped his head and reached for the door, breathing out a relieved sigh the moment it closed behind him.

He shrugged his shoulders to ease the tension and hurried down the steps, deciding he didn't want a drink after all. Better he leave this place—and the stench of humanity contained in its faded walls—behind.

The cool evening air was welcome, though the depressing rain continued. Clarence hurried along the empty street, skin crawling. Only a few hearty souls braved the rainy night now.

He glanced over his shoulder, certain he felt the weight of someone's stare. Had Scranton decided to follow him? Or had a copper discovered the theft?

Disquiet settled in the pit of his belly as he continued forward, though he hadn't seen anything to cause it. Clarence looked back again, water dripping off the brim of his hat and obscuring his vision of the dimly lit street. A cloaked figure stood across the street, watching him from the shadows of a building, seemingly oblivious to the foul weather.

Clarence proceeded forward, even as he told himself his imagination was getting away from him. "Losin' my mind," he muttered to himself. "Bit o'blunt in my pocket an' I'm suddenly convinced everyone knows and is after it."

Yet even with that reassurance, he couldn't help glancing back again to see the figure trailing him at a steady pace. A hat pulled low and the high collar of a cloak hid most of the stranger's face, but his attention appeared fixated on Clarence.

Fear spread along his flesh, leaving chill bumps in its wake. He quickened his pace, heart pounding, and searched for somewhere to hide. King's Cross—it was just ahead. He might be able to lose himself amidst the passengers in the station he knew so well. But a quick look in that direction showed few people, the evening rush having already passed.

That wouldn't work. Then where?

The iron fence of the railyard came into view. Perfect. He'd stick with what was familiar and would soon lose his pursuer. Not risking a look behind him, he trotted along the fence until he reached the place he'd previously pried open.

Clarence darted inside and was immediately engulfed in darkness. He blinked rapidly, willing his eyes to adjust, and continued toward the crumbling brick wall at the back of the yard. The watchman would be wandering about somewhere and might be of some help, but Clarence couldn't risk searching for him.

He moved around a rusting coal cart and down a slippery slope to where a heavy wooden door hung on sagging hinges, the padlock broken, failing to protect the abandoned train tunnel hidden inside.

As quietly as possible, he pulled on the door. It barely moved. He hadn't ventured inside for some time but knew it would make the perfect hiding place. Even as Clarence paused to listen, wondering if he was overreacting, he heard the rustle of someone approaching in the darkness.

Panic skittered down his spine as he jerked harder on the door using both hands. It creaked open, the sound loud in the quiet of the yard. Blast it all to hell—he'd just given away his location.

Did he hide somewhere else? Or—

Before he could finish the thought the figure stood before him, at least a head taller and broader of shoulder than Clarence, though that said little given his own short stature. The stranger's face was impossible to see in the moonless night, his form barely visible by a lamp post on the nearby street.

"W-What do you w-want?" Clarence demanded, remembering too late about the knife tucked in the top of his boot.

"You." The raspy voice gave no hint as to the person's identity.

"Me?" Clarence couldn't catch his breath, panic grabbing him by the throat as he took a step back, only to come up against the door. "What for?"

"A sacrifice."

Clarence stilled, his blood running cold. "Wh-What? How do you mean—"

The stranger hefted a large wrench in one hand, surely something he'd collected in the railyard as he'd trailed after Clarence in the dark. "You have been chosen. Chosen, to serve a greater purpose."

"I-I don't want to." Clarence's heart threatened to pound free of his chest, the restriction there that helped keep his secret suddenly feeling impossibly tight.

"I must insist." The man's giddy tone clashed with his dark words.

Clarence bent low to grab his knife—only to see the stranger's gloved hand rise, swinging the wrench in his direction.

No!

He attempted to dodge it a moment too late. Stars filled his vision, his ears ringing from the blow. Excruciating pain stabbed his skull and his arms flailed to catch his balance.

This wasn't how his life was supposed to end.

Thoughts of his mum flashed through his mind. She needed the money in his pocket. That damned railway station. He should've had that drink in the pub after all...

Darkness swept over him like a heavy curtain, and Clarence Digby crumpled to the ground.

After a moment's pause, the stranger tossed aside the wrench to heave open the heavy wooden door, revealing a cold, damp, inky blackness. He smiled. It made the perfect place to leave the body. It wouldn't remain there for long. The sacrifice would soon be found, and the first step of the plan taken.

His low chuckle filled the dark night.

Chapter Two

Amelia Greystone studied the houses passing the hansom cab window, unable to set aside the nerves troubling her since the previous evening. The hour was early for calls, but the purpose of this one wasn't exactly social.

"You don't have to do this." Scotland Yard Inspector Henry Field's deep but quiet tone prompted her to look at him, grateful for his presence beside her. "I can speak with her while you wait in the cab."

Though tempted by the kind offer, Amelia shook her head. "Thank you, but I'll be fine. Especially since you are accompanying me." She smiled, a mixture of emotions swirling within her. "I'm actually quite interested in what our Mrs. Nettle has to say."

And why the woman who claimed to be gifted in divination—the practice of gaining knowledge using the supernatural—had contacted her not once, but twice.

The second message from Mary Nettle had come as a surprise, considering Amelia had already declined her initial request for an interview with *London Life*, the periodical which employed Amelia as a special correspondent. Receiving that second note, this one delivered to Amelia's home last evening rather than to her editor, had been even more unsettling.

Mrs. Nettle claimed to know where the body of a missing young lady was.

Luckily Henry had been there when the note arrived. His curiosity and concern matched Amelia's, though doubt had shadowed his brown eyes after she'd told him the identity of the sender.

Amelia didn't blame him. She had some hesitation about the situation as well. Divination was nothing she had ever chosen to learn more about, nor did she care to do so now. It wasn't something her scientific mind, intrigued by chemistry and enjoying her various experiments in her attic-based laboratory, had ever taken seriously. However, there could be no denying that many people were fascinated by the topic. Séances were fairly common, as were other types of divination, including tarot cards, palm readings, and the use of crystal balls.

If not for Henry, she might've simply directed the so-called medium to contact the police with the information, despite the woman's persistent attempt to involve Amelia.

Henry's presence allowed her to indulge her curiosity about both the message and its sender. There was no one she'd rather have at her side this morning than him for this unusual call, especially after his declaration the previous evening.

I'm sure it's no surprise for you to hear how much I care about you, and I hope there is the chance for a future between us.

To know he wished to further their friendship into something more brought a light of joy to her heart...yet even that didn't remove the dread currently knotted in her stomach.

Amelia had been certain the resolution of her late husband's murder would allow her to move forward with her life, but somehow the visit to Mrs. Nettle felt like a step back.

Would this meeting which she didn't want—had refused once already—bring news from Lily, the daughter she'd lost to scarlet fever nearly four years ago, or Matthew, her late husband, murdered almost two years later?

Was it selfish to hope it didn't?

Remorse washed over her. She was finally finding some measure of peace and occasional happiness, despite the grief that would forever be a part of her. She prayed they were at peace in the afterlife...but what if they weren't?

"If you're sure you wish to come inside..." Henry frowned, his concern obvious, as he hesitantly reached to take her hand and give it a gentle squeeze between his. "Please know that you can change your mind. And we can leave the moment you become uncomfortable."

"Thank you." Amelia returned the gesture, pleased when he made no move to withdraw his hold on hers. His words and his touch did much to steady her.

She'd thought that once her late husband's unpunished murder no longer stood between them, and justice—even if not what she'd expected—had been served, she could look to the future instead of the past for the first time in a long while.

Yet the unsettling message from Mrs. Nettle cast a cloud over that hope. Communicating with the spirit world was not something Amelia felt comfortable with, not after the loss of both husband and daughter. While she missed them more than she could say, she remained wary of the idea of them reaching out from beyond the grave.

Mrs. Nettle hadn't suggested anything of that sort in the letter she'd sent to Amelia's editor or the message she'd sent last night to her home, but Amelia couldn't think of any other reason for the woman's determination to contact her.

"I...I remain confused as to why Mrs. Nettle insists on speaking with me rather than accepting the offer of another correspondent," Amelia murmured, hoping Henry would share his opinion.

"As do I." His watchful gaze took in the passing scenery. "I can't say I have any belief in those who claim to channel spirits, but I am curious to hear if she truly knows the location of a body. And why she chose to inform you about it rather than the police."

"It's especially concerning since you aren't aware of any missing young ladies at the moment, let alone murdered ones." Amelia latched onto the opportunity to focus on a potential investigation rather than her unease at the prospect of speaking to the woman.

Her position as an unofficial assistant to Henry had proved fortuitous in several cases over the past six months. Though it occasionally came with danger, it also brought purpose, something she craved in her quiet, directionless life.

"A lack of a victim is one reason I am doubtful she has anything helpful to share, but we shall soon see," Henry added as the hansom cab rolled to a halt.

Determined to focus on her curiosity and nothing more, Amelia patted her reticule, which held her notebook and pencil.

"I hope Mrs. Nettle tells us something interesting that might also provide the basis for an article."

Henry stepped out and offered his hand. "Have you decided to write one after all?"

"I don't yet know. I suppose it depends on what she has to say."

"Then forgive me if I hope it isn't too interesting."

Amelia smiled. Henry's dry wit was only one of the many reasons she admired the handsome inspector.

With a deep breath, she turned to observe the modest, red-brick townhouse before them. The neighborhood appeared to have seen better days, with some homes in need of repair. Crumbling bricks, crooked gutters, and weeds lining the wrought-iron fences were visible on several houses. However, Mrs. Nettle's home was quite tidy in comparison.

She took Henry's proffered arm, taking pleasure in the thought of them as a couple—not that she would share the term with anyone aloud, including him. The change in their relationship was too new, just a few hours old, and she didn't yet know what to expect. It was enough for now to know they both wanted to spend more time together. That Henry, too, wanted their friendship to grow into something more.

A glance at him from under the brim of her hat had her sighing in appreciation.

There could be no harm in admiring Henry's masculine profile and broad shoulders rather than focusing on the unsettling visit ahead. Worry brought nothing more than wrinkles, as Amelia's mother frequently told her.

Amelia found it quite pleasant to rely on Henry to knock and state their business to the maid who answered the door. While she valued her initially unwanted independence as a widow, she appreciated having someone with whom she could share such tasks.

As if sensing her regard, Henry paused in his observations of the home to hold her gaze, the hint of warmth in his eyes welcome. She had been alone for over a year and a half, and in a less-than-ideal marriage prior to that, and appreciated his admiration and regard.

With a concerted effort, she shifted her attention to where they waited while the maid hurried away down the hall.

The interior of the home matched the exterior—modest, but cared for. Brown and cream striped wallpaper lined the walls, the wooden floor polished to a dull gleam, and the scent of lemon lingered in the air. A narrow entry table stood in one corner with an empty blue and white porcelain vase upon it. Stairs on the left were covered with a worn paisley carpet runner and brass rods holding it in place. An unremarkable oil landscape painting with an ornate gold frame graced one wall.

Before she could ask Henry his impressions of the home, the maid returned.

"Mrs. Nettle will see you."

Amelia nodded, more than ready to have the meeting over and done. Henry's presence would no doubt come as a surprise, but Amelia had no regrets about accepting his offer to accompany her.

The maid led them down the hall, then stood aside as they entered a reception room where a woman, who appeared to be near Amelia's own age of six and twenty, stood before a wingback chair.

"Mrs. Greystone. What a pleasure to meet you." Her obvious enthusiasm was flattering, in all honesty, doing much to allay Amelia's nerves.

The woman's pale face with pleasant, even features lit with delight as Amelia walked closer. A small scar high on one cheekbone didn't detract from her hostess's poised appearance. Brown hair was drawn into a loose knot atop her head with several wiry stands escaping.

"Mrs. Nettle." Amelia nodded, half afraid the woman intended to offer her hands for a more physical greeting. To discourage the possibility, as she couldn't help but worry whether that might provide some sort of spiritual connection, Amelia turned toward Henry. "May I introduce you to Scotland Yard Inspector Henry Field."

"Ah, yes." Mrs. Nettle looked him over from head to toe, her blue eyes shining with curiosity. "I've read of your exploits in the news sheets, Inspector. Such a pleasure."

"Mrs. Nettle." Henry dipped his head politely, hat in hand.

"Please join me." Their host gestured to the settee opposite her. Her flowered cotton day dress with a dark blue underskirt flattered her trim figure as she lowered herself into a chair.

Though the day was a chilly one, no fire burned in the hearth. Whether that was due to economy or because the formal room wasn't often used was unclear.

Amelia perched on the edge of the settee, gripped by disquiet once again at the thought of speaking about spirits. "Needless to say, we were quite curious after receiving your message," she began formally. "The mention of a missing lady and the whereabouts of her body are the reasons Inspector Field joined me."

Though Henry was more than capable of leading the interview, this was not yet an official investigation—and perhaps Mrs. Nettle might speak more freely if some of the questions came from Amelia, since she'd sent her the letter.

The woman gave a girlish giggle and held a hand to her chest. "I must confess, I'm flattered to have gained the attention of both of you."

Amelia could practically feel the disapproval radiating from Henry but knew he'd keep it hidden. Though tempted to ask Mrs. Nettle if that had been her intention, she cleared her throat. "Could you tell us how you came to know about this missing person?"

Mrs. Nettle sighed dramatically and placed her hands on each arm of the chair, her back straight as if she bore a great burden. "My ability is rarely understood, you know...but I will do my best to explain it."

Amelia had the impression the medium enjoyed doing just that. Still, she retrieved her notebook from her reticule with a polite smile. "You don't mind if I take a few notes?"

Mrs. Nettle had already requested that Amelia interview her, so her ready agreement came as no surprise. Though Henry didn't have much time as he had other pressing cases to attend to—or the patience—to delve into the medium's supposed skills, it might be helpful to better understand her methods to discern what truths, if any, could be gained from speaking with her.

"I've had *the gift* since childhood," the medium began dramatically. "Very little of it is within my control. The spirits choose if and when they speak to me."

"Speak?" Amelia asked with a lifted brow. She already had more questions.

The medium offered a pitying smile, as if Amelia couldn't possibly understand. "Of a sort. On occasion they share words, but mostly images appear in my mind at their behest."

"Visions?" Henry suggested.

"Yes." Mrs. Nettle's eyes gleamed with excitement, as if pleased he understood. "You could say that. The images appear in brief flashes and make little sense at first. It's nearly impossible to understand what they're trying to tell me until I receive several."

"They?" Who precisely did she think spoke to her, Amelia wondered.

"Several spirits, though of course not all at once."

Amelia bit back her impatience. It might be quicker if she allowed the woman to tell them her version and Amelia asked questions afterward. Still, she wanted to know who these spirits were and why they were communicating with her.

"Often the visions come at night, or rather very early in the morning." Mrs. Nettle lifted one finger as she looked at Henry. "And no, they're not dreams."

A glance at Henry showed him frowning, leading Amelia to think that was precisely what he'd been about to ask. He would not have been alone.

"When they occur, I have learned to rise and jot down the things that appear in my mind. There's no purpose in attempting to interpret them at first," their hostess said quietly. "Sometimes I draw what I see, though I can't make any claim to artistic skills."

"And what about these...these images suggested a missing lady?" Henry asked, skepticism coloring his tone.

If Amelia were to guess, she'd think the tone was deliberate. Putting people on the defensive was a questioning technique he'd used before in her presence. Portraying doubt or disbelief often caused people to say things they didn't intend to.

Mrs. Nettle turned to look out the window for a moment, seeming to gather her thoughts. "First, I saw an older woman weeping. Then a body, lying on a dirt floor...in a dark place. Still and quiet." She grimaced briefly and gestured to her own head. "A terrible injury on her head. Blood in her hair."

Amelia jotted down the words, relieved to see Henry pull out his own small notebook and pencil from his pocket to do the same.

"What do you think happened to the young lady?" Amelia asked. "An accident, perhaps?"

"Oh, no." Mrs. Nettle shook her head, her expression grim as she looked between them. "Most definitely not. This was no accident. It was murder."

Chills ran along Amelia's skin as she shared a worried look with Henry.

It seemed he might have another murder case on his hands after all.

Chapter Three

Henry held Amelia's gaze momentarily, noting the concern in the depths of her brown eyes. Clearly she believed the medium's claim had merit.

Unfortunately, he couldn't state the same. While Mrs. Nettle appeared sincere, the source of these vague details she'd shared was what concerned Henry. Learning from 'spirits' of a murder wasn't a good beginning to an investigation.

He returned his attention to the medium. "What makes you believe the images involve murder?"

Mrs. Nettle heaved a shaky breath, pressing trembling fingers to her mouth for a brief moment as if the distress might overcome her. The movement appeared more dramatic than heartfelt, in his opinion.

Amelia shifted on the tufted cushion beside him, and he had to resist the urge to place a hand on her arm to offer reassurance, perhaps to himself and to her. In truth, it was delightful to have her at his side despite the unusual circumstances, and he looked forward to discussing their impressions once they departed.

He only hoped they weren't in complete disagreement.

Though he'd prefer to keep this woman as far away from murder as possible, with each week that passed, such a feat was beginning to feel impossible. Perhaps he needed to learn to welcome her involvement in some of his investigations to a certain degree—as long as she remained safe from harm, of course.

"I can make no assumption other than murder," the medium said at last. "There is a certain...heaviness in those scenes which is undeniable."

"I see." He didn't exactly, but he didn't really want to hear her explain what that meant. He needed evidence in order to pursue a case; feelings played no part in murder investigations. "Can you tell us anything about where you think this victim is?"

If there even was a victim...

Again Mrs. Nettle gazed across the room, a vacant look in her eyes. "An old wooden door with a padlock. A rusty cart of some sort before it. An...an overgrown place." She shook her head, her brow furrowed. "I can't say I've seen anything like it before."

Impatience trickled through Henry. That wasn't enough to even try to guess where the woman might be. She might not even be in London.

"You mentioned an older woman crying," Amelia said in a soothing voice as if she hoped to encourage the medium to tell them more. "Can you tell us about her?"

Henry dipped his head with silent approval. The identity of anyone involved could help find the victim.

"The image felt motherly to me—though I couldn't say for certain."

Felt? Again, that wasn't a word Henry used during investigations. He needed proof, or at the very least, a trail of clues to follow. While he relied on his own hunches on rare occasions, that was the full extent to which he was willing to use emotions to solve cases.

Amelia cleared her throat. "Do you have anything more? Perhaps a name or address? Something solid that could aid the police in finding the lady?"

Mrs. Nettle glared at Amelia, clearly not appreciating the direct question. "No, no. Nothing so definitive. That's not how my *gift* works." She drew a deep breath. "At times, I wonder whether I'm *cursed*."

"Seeing murder victims must be quite difficult for one's constitution," Amelia said politely. "What of the mother? Where was she?"

Henry reviewed his notes, ready to end the interview. With so few details, it would be impossible to pursue this further—if there even was a case.

"A kitchen. A very simple one with a scarred worktable. She wears an apron and uses it to wipe away her tears."

Descriptive, but hardly helpful. Clearly the time had come to thank the medium for her time and escort Amelia to the door before—

"Let us return to the poor victim," Amelia said as she studied her own notes. "Do you believe this location with the wooden door and rusty cart is in London?"

"Oh, yes. I nearly forgot that I saw a clock." She looked between them. "You know, it reminded me of the one at King's Cross station."

Henry's interest was piqued. Now they were getting somewhere. The items she described could very well be located at the railyard near the station, if his memory served him.

"That is helpful." Amelia gave the medium a nod of encouragement. "And do you know when the murder occurred?"

"Hmm. I think last evening just before I sent you the message, though I suppose it could've been the night before. The spirits didn't say."

Henry was beginning to think less and less of these spirits and the limited information they offered. *Why bother?*

"What more can you tell us?" Amelia asked.

Seeming weary from her efforts, the medium closed her eyes again. "There's a ruby ring. Pretty. A rather valuable one."

Henry frowned. That didn't fit with the rest of what she'd said.

"Is the young lady wearing it?" inquired Amelia gently.

"No, but it is somehow involved."

Henry clenched his jaw, his patience at its end.

"And the victim's clothing?" Amelia continued, pressing despite the limited answers their host was willing to provide.

A long moment passed before the medium opened her eyes. "A dark jacket. Trousers. Scuffed work boots."

"Trousers and—and work boots? I thought you said the victim was a woman?" Amelia beat Henry to the query.

"Well. Yes, I did." Mrs. Nettle frowned, her gaze darting about the room. "I thought so because the scene holds a certain feminine energy. But that might be wrong. As I said, the images aren't always *clear*."

The admission made Henry wonder what else she had wrong...but surely there weren't so many wooden doors with padlocks in the yard near King's Cross. He'd send a constable to conduct an initial search, and they could proceed from there.

He glanced at Amelia, more than ready to depart, though she surely had more questions to ask before she decided whether to write an article. To his surprise, she closed her notebook and met his gaze with an expectant look, obviously prepared to leave.

"Thank you for your time, Mrs. Nettle." Henry stood, and Amelia did the same. "We will certainly look into the matter."

"You'll advise me of what you find?" The woman rose with a worried expression, hands clasped before her, knuckles white. "That poor mother—"

"I can't make any promises, but I will do my best." That was as much as Henry could offer.

If they found no body he wouldn't bother to send word, as that might only encourage the medium to contact him or Amelia again.

And if a victim was found, an investigation would be conducted and any information discovered would remain confidential.

"Oh." Mrs. Nettle's shoulders sagged with disappointment. "I admit, I would rest easier if I knew the outcome."

As if sympathetic, Amelia nodded. "That's understandable, given the disturbing images you were shown. If Inspector Field permits it, I will be sure to send word of the results."

The woman's relief was visible. "I appreciate that."

Amelia nodded politely and turned to lead the way out.

"Mrs. Greystone?"

Amelia looked back, wariness evident in her expression.

"As I said in my first letter, my husband and I are great admirers of your articles. I...I would consider it an honor if you chose to feature my divination gift." Mrs. Nettle's cheeks grew pink with the admission.

"I will certainly reflect upon it," Amelia said, her smile tight.

The medium took a step forward, reaching a hand toward Amelia, only to allow it to fall to her side. "You must be wondering why I chose to write to you."

Amelia's hesitancy squeezed Henry's chest in a painful grip. "The question did cross my mind."

"My husband and I appreciate the fresh view you have, along with your vibrant writing style." Mrs. Nettle drew nearer, eyes darkening as she locked gazes with Amelia. "But there are other reasons. You see, the shadows of your past have whispered to me, and I felt compelled to reach out to you. There might be a message arriving for you soon."

Alarm filled Henry as he looked between the two women. This was what had worried him from the moment Amelia had shown him the medium's message. How could he protect Amelia from something neither of them could even see?

Amelia gave a single nod, her body stiff. "Thank you for your time, Mrs. Nettle." She strode quickly toward the door, leaving Henry to follow in her wake.

Chapter Four

AMELIA MURMURED A POLITE 'thank you' as Henry handed her into the hansom cab, her body stiff and thoughts racing, and they were quickly on their way back to her house.

She didn't dare look at him when she felt as if one word might shatter the fragile hold she had on her emotions.

The shadows of your past have whispered to me, and I felt compelled to reach out to you. There might be a message arriving for you soon.

What did all that mean? A message from who? Compelled for what purpose? How terrible that she wasn't certain she wanted to know. Now that she had finally gained a fragile hold on happiness, how much was she willing to risk to learn what this Mrs. Nettle had to say?

"Amelia?" Henry's quiet voice at her side pulled her from her swirling thoughts.

She swallowed, her gaze fluttering in his direction though she couldn't bring herself to meet his eyes, too afraid of what she might see there. "You...you must think me quite the coward."

"Never." He shifted on the seat, seeming to hesitate a moment before wrapping a comforting arm around her and drawing her close. "You are one of the bravest people I know."

His words brought tears to her eyes, even if she couldn't believe them. She'd been anything but brave.

Still, Amelia placed a hand on his chest, his solid presence bringing security, as did his show of affection and support. The faint scent of his cologne didn't hurt either. She rested in the moment, appreciating how right it felt to be in his arms.

How lucky she was to have him in her life; to call him a friend and now a suitor. She held tight to the joy the thought brought.

After a minute or two, she felt steady enough to ease back to meet his gaze. To her surprise, only admiration gleamed in his eyes—no judgment or doubt.

"Brave? I wish that were true," she managed with a smile.

"I assure you it is." Henry removed his arm but took hold of her hand, a gesture she appreciated since she still felt fragile.

With a sigh, Amelia leaned back against the seat as the cab bumped and swayed. "It is odd," she began, before halting, unsure how to articulate her frantic thoughts.

"What is?" he asked gently.

"I can't say I believe in channeling spirits, yet I am still reluctant to hear anything Mrs. Nettle might say about Lily or Matthew."

"That is understandable. It has surely been difficult living with your grief," Henry said quietly. "The idea of hearing from them through a stranger you're not sure you can trust would be unsettling for anyone, to say the least."

The tightness in her shoulders eased at the logic of his words and kindness in his tone. "Thank you for understanding."

"Of course. I would feel the same way in your position."

Amelia had difficulty believing that. After all, Henry had acted courageously time and again. Still, she nodded all the same. "And what did you think of Mrs. Nettle?"

He paused to consider the question. "I will have a constable check the railyard near King's Cross. Beyond that, it's difficult to say."

"She certainly has a flair for the dramatic. Some things she said sounded plausible, but others lacked clarity and are surely impossible to believe." Amelia glanced out the window, noting the clouds settling in. No doubt it would soon rain, the ground only just dry from yesterday's downpour.

"Agreed." Henry was quiet for a moment before adding, "I would be curious to see the notes and drawings she creates from her visions. Those might be more enlightening than what she chose to tell us."

"Perhaps she'd be willing to share them if you discover there's some truth to her claim."

He nodded, then held her gaze, his expression one of concern. "And do you intend to write an article about her...abilities?"

The question nearly made Amelia shudder. "I-I'm not certain I can."

"Then you shouldn't."

Relief washed over her at the simple response. Yet somehow, she didn't think it would be that simple.

Henry continued, "You said the editor at the periodical accepted your refusal previously. You shouldn't feel any obligation to do it."

Then why did she?

The answer to that was something she would have to ponder later. Just because she felt an obligation didn't mean she had to give in to it. For now, she preferred to focus on the case. "I wonder what Mr. Nettle thinks of her abilities."

"Excellent question. I must say, I sympathize with him. It wouldn't be easy to have a wife with the unique talent of communicating with the dead." Henry's dry tone made her smile.

"True, though it must be difficult for her as well, if what she says is true." Amelia had mixed feelings on the matter and didn't know what to believe.

Her companion snorted. "I understand she's assisted the police in a case or two, but I am not familiar with them. It might be worthwhile to speak with those who are."

"If there is a body at the railyard," she suggested.

"Indeed. That is where it starts and might very well end unless something—or someone—is found."

"How odd that she said the victim was a young lady, but that shifted as the conversation continued." Amelia found that concerning. It certainly cast doubt on the medium's abilities to foretell much of anything of use.

"It always pays to continue questioning a witness to see if the story changes when they're pressed for details."

Amelia patted Henry's arm. "I have learned much about investigations by listening to and observing you."

His brows lifted, surprise widening his brown eyes as the cab rattled down the London streets. "Oh? Why am I not certain if that is a good thing?"

"It is. Trust me. I like assisting you with cases," Amelia admitted. "They are puzzles, and one must sort through the information to find clues that point in a particular direction."

"Hmmm. I admit that I enjoy discussing them with you, given your cleverness, but I'd rather your involvement is limited to better protect you—body, mind, and soul."

"Thank you. I appreciate that." His words warmed her. "But this is another case where I would be involved regardless of whether or not you were. If anything, you could argue that you're joining my case." Amelia smiled. "Perhaps we should take that as a sign we are meant to work together." She glanced at him, hoping he would agree.

Unfortunately, as was so often the case, he hid his thoughts too well. "Perhaps."

At least he hadn't denied the idea. She took that as a positive sign.

Meanwhile, she needed to decide whether she could remain objective and distance herself from Mrs. Nettle's remarks enough to conduct an interview for a story. The thought was tempting; she genuinely found the concept of divination into the spirit world interesting, and was certain her readers would too. But hearing the medium say a message from the spirits might be arriving soon for her stirred naught but unease.

"Will you advise me if you find anything at the railyard?" Amelia asked suddenly.

"Of course." Henry glanced at her. "But even if we do, it doesn't mean you should write the article."

She had to smile at his insightfulness. "No wonder you make such an excellent detective when you so easily guess my thoughts."

He smiled in return. "I believe that has more to do with my feelings for you than any investigative skills."

Amelia's breath caught even as heat stole into her cheeks. She might not be prepared to put a name on her own feelings for him, but she cared deeply for Henry and knew he felt the same. "You are far too modest about your abilities. One day soon, you'll be forced to admit you are an excellent detective."

"We shall see."

Amelia nodded, pleased at his use of 'we'. They would be together to see that day.

All too soon, the hansom cab had come to a halt and Henry was seeing her to her door with the promise of being in touch when he learned more, before bidding her goodbye.

She sighed as she watched him through the narrow window beside the door, his figure most impressive as he stepped back into the cab. A delicate cough behind her made her aware of her butler's regard.

"And was the meeting successful?" Fernsby asked.

The stately butler and his wife had been with Amelia through many challenging times, as well as good ones, steadfast in their support through it all. She didn't know what she'd do without them—her maid and cook as well.

"It was interesting." Amelia turned away from the window to look at him. "The medium says someone was murdered and believes the body is at the railyard near King's Cross."

The butler's brows rose. "Would that not have been helpful information to include in the message she sent?"

"True." He had a valid point. "I had the impression she wanted an audience when she shared the details."

"Ah." Her butler nodded. "The lady has a penchant for drama and appreciates attention?"

"I tend to think so. And that is what worries me." As if divination wasn't worrisome enough. The additional antics further complicated matters, as far as Amelia was concerned.

"And what of her request for you to write an article about her abilities?" Fernsby's tone held no judgment, but he'd previously shown a hint of disapproval only as he thought it would upset her.

Her servants were much more than mere hired help; they were a family, of sorts. Her parents lived north of London and she was close with them; her Aunt Margaret now lived in the city, having moved there before Christmas, and Amelia enjoyed her company. But her staff were the ones who supported her through the daily ups and downs of life.

Mr. and Mrs. Fernsby, her lady's maid, Yvette, and the cook, Mrs. Appleton, had remained with her despite the danger that clung to the household since Matthew's death over a year and a half ago—so dangerous that Henry had stayed the night to watch over them after the murder of the ravenkeeper.

Once Henry had solved that case, she'd expected life to return to normal. Instead she'd been embroiled in the mudlark murders, followed by the one at Gravesend, and soon after, they'd discovered who had killed her husband. Their most recent case involved the rookery killer, which had finally put an end to any danger to her and the staff with the death of her husband's murderer.

Her servants' loyalty had been tested time and again, and she didn't know what she would do without them.

"I have yet to decide about the article," Amelia admitted as she pondered the possibility once again. "Once Inspector Field determines whether the medium was right about this body in the railyard, I will decide."

"Logical." The butler dipped his head. "After all, if Mrs. Nettle is wrong, it would be difficult to write about her abilities—unless you wish to expose her as a fraud."

Amelia smiled wanly. "I will leave such things to Fleet Street. I much prefer to remain focused on the unique and unusual, and I think my editor feels the same."

"A wise choice, madam."

Before Amelia could say anything further a cat, a recent addition to their household, trotted down the stairs, greeting her with a, "Meow."

"Hello to you, too, Master Leopold." Amelia smiled and bent to scratch his head. "What have you been up to in my absence?"

The feline had already managed to capture everyone's affection in the household, including Amelia's.

"He has been making the rounds between all of us to make certain we're seeing to our duties." Fernsby's smile as he watched the cat suggested he didn't mind in the least.

"Of course you have." Master Leopold wound against Amelia's skirts then trotted off toward the rear of the house.

The butler cleared his throat. "I do believe Mrs. Appleton has a light luncheon prepared for you if you'd like."

"Perfect. I am famished after this morning's activities." Yet the remainder of the day stretched out before her, far too empty. "Perhaps I will work in the laboratory this afternoon."

Her interest in chemistry had led her to set up a workspace in the attic for her hobby. Her father worked as an apothecary, which had long ago sparked her interest in the field. She'd quickly found she had a talent for it.

"Excellent. Has the fertilizer experiment produced an obvious winner?"

Amelia was testing several different methods to improve plant growth to help Mrs. Appleton with the garden. "Not as of yet. I do believe we will know more in another week or two."

"The staff has placed wagers on the outcome." He leaned closer as if imparting a secret. "Not the monetary sort, of course."

Amelia laughed, amused by the thought. "I look forward to hearing who wins."

Fernsby departed for the kitchen as Amelia walked into the dining room.

Seeing the solitary place setting on the table caused her to sigh. She already missed Henry and couldn't help but hope he'd call this evening to update her about whether he had indeed found a body at the railyard.

Chapter Five

HENRY RETURNED TO SCOTLAND Yard and sent word to the constable who patrolled King's Cross to take a close look at the railyard for an old wooden door with a padlock—and a body.

He had no idea if either would be there but hoped for Amelia's sake that the body wasn't. That would surely lessen any urge she had to speak with the medium again, and he didn't care to see his—*his* Amelia upset.

She truly was brave, just as he'd told her, far stronger than she realized. Not many ladies Henry had met over the years could've withstood the loss of not only a beloved daughter, but also a husband, and so young in life. Then there was the danger she'd faced while involved in each of his investigations—risking her very life.

But just because she was courageous didn't mean she should put herself through an interview that would make her uncomfortable. While Henry didn't believe in ghosts or divination, he did think some things were better left alone, and he worried Mrs. Nettle had somehow discovered details of Amelia's past and reached out because of it—with the plan to play on those vulnerabilities.

Henry intended to protect Amelia however possible and was pleased he'd been with her when she'd received the message from Mrs. Nettle. He didn't like the thought of Amelia dealing with the situation on her own.

He straightened his shoulders. As her friend and now formally her suitor, he would do all in his power to ensure her safety and wellbeing. Assuming she'd allow him to, of course. The lightness in his heart at the thought of deepening their relationship was something he had yet to become accustomed to, though he welcomed it. His feelings for the lovely widow had grown steadily in the last few months, and he was more than ready to move forward...he just hadn't expected their first outing after she'd agreed to allow him to court her to be a meeting with a lady who claimed to channel spirits regarding a dead body and a mysterious message from the grave.

"Field?"

Henry looked up from his desk to see Reynolds, the Director of Criminal Investigations and his superior, approach. "Yes, sir."

"What did the medium have to say?" Curiosity lit the older man's eyes from behind his gold-rimmed spectacles. He was well into his fifties with a round face and dark hair neatly parted in the middle, balanced by a thick moustache and muttonchops that left his chin bare.

"To look for a body at the railyard at King's Cross." The Director hadn't been that keen to allow Henry time to visit the medium with Amelia, as he held the supernatural in low regard. Still, Henry had managed to convince him otherwise.

Reynolds frowned. "Why wouldn't she have notified the police rather than Mrs. Greystone in that case?"

"I intend to ask the same question—if we find a body."

Henry liked to think he and the Director now better appreciated one another's skills after the events of the last week, since Henry had uncovered the officers involved in corruption within their department.

Discovering that a member of the force had been behind several recent murders continued to disturb Henry. That the officer's duplicity had been ongoing for a couple of years made it even worse. However, the rot had been removed from Scotland Yard, and additional measures would be put in place to prevent a recurrence. How long those remained effective before someone else gave in to temptation and it happened again...well, that remained to be seen. In Henry's experience, if someone chose a dishonest path, they would find a way to pursue it.

Meanwhile the guilty ones were behind bars awaiting trial. Director Reynolds had closely overseen the final details of the case after Henry had apprehended them. Henry had even more respect for his superior after watching him work and liked to think he felt the same.

"I will be interested to hear the results of the search. While we wait, I have another case for you." Reynolds handed him a file.

"Thank you." Henry couldn't help but look at the pile already on his desk. Each time he thought he was making headway, another case surfaced.

"I'm sure you'll have it sorted out in quick order." The Director smiled and returned to his office.

With a sigh, Henry opened it to see another theft had been reported. Murder cases took precedence, but he didn't have any of those at the moment. The rest were additional thefts, a betting ring, a false investment scheme, and a potential forgery case. Some required only instructions to a constable to pursue with oversight, but many required his direct involvement. He worked steadily for over an hour to update notes and write instructions on others.

The Yard was relatively quiet as the luncheon hour approached, though a few other inspectors worked at their desks and one or two constables came and went. Some Henry were friendly with, and others he wasn't.

One such officer, Inspector Perdy, wandered into the office. The mere sight of him was enough to send irritation coursing through Henry. He had no respect for the other inspector after having witnessed his ineptitude on several occasions, nor did he appreciate the man's constant digs about Henry's quick rise to the rank of inspector due to his last name.

Policing might be in Henry's family, but being a Field had offered him no favors. Not that Perdy agreed.

"Field." Perdy leaned against Henry's desk, managing to shift the carefully stacked papers Henry had organized as he worked.

"Perdy." Henry glared at him, not wanting to hear whatever new jest he'd come up with, even as he saved the papers from being crushed or pushed to the floor.

The other inspector cleared his throat, an uncomfortable look on his face as if he'd just swallowed a frog. "I've...well, I've been meaning to tell you..." He ran a hand along the back of his neck. "That is to say, I-I'm sorry to have assumed you were behind the theft in the evidence room and some of the other...things."

Henry's eyes widened, and he waited a moment for Perdy to add a subtle dig in another attempt to make Henry look like a fool. The other inspector had been relentless in making it clear that the only possible reason for Henry's quick rise in the police force was because of his last name. Both Henry's father and grandfather had retired as chief inspectors, both well regarded for their detecting skills. What no one knew was that Henry was adopted, something he'd learned in his youth quite by accident. That moment had shaken him, as he'd already planned on following in their footsteps. Doubt as to whether he could ever fully do so was a frequent cloud on his horizon.

To his surprise, Perdy didn't say anything further, leaving Henry nearly speechless.

"Oh. Thank you." Not for a moment did Henry believe he and Perdy were on their way to a better working relationship, let alone a friendship. He had no time for the other man's tendency to find the easiest solution to every case he was assigned, or his poor treatment of the less fortunate. But Henry accepted the unexpected olive branch and decided to hope for the best.

Perdy nodded, cheeks ruddy as he glanced around as if to see if anyone had overheard him.

Henry couldn't hold back a smile to see several officers listening, including Sergeant Fletcher, who had just arrived and frequently assisted Henry. The sergeant bore the same dislike of Perdy as Henry did. The newest inspector, Clarke—who happened to be Fletcher's uncle—had entered the Yard with him and was listening as well. Inspector Duncan stared in disbelief from across the room with his mouth agape.

Perdy frowned at the sight of them staring. "What are the lot of you looking at?"

"Didn't know you had it in you to admit any wrongdoing," Duncan murmured before returning his attention to the file before him. "More surprising than the second coming."

Laughter erupted at his observation.

Fletcher's mirth took a while to subside, even as he shared an incredulous look with Henry.

"Can't a man offer an apology without the entire office taking note?" Perdy demanded, eyes flashing at the others.

"Clearly not."

Henry turned to see Director Reynolds in his office doorway with a smile on his face. Apparently even he had overheard Perdy and felt compelled to comment, though the Director quickly disappeared.

"Well, I never." Perdy shook his head and stalked out of the office as more laughter sounded.

Henry sat back in his chair, hardly able to believe what had just happened. He never would have guessed Perdy might apologize when he'd made it clear the man thought Henry guilty of not only stealing a valuable item from the evidence room, but of several other misdeeds.

"Tell me that didn't just happen." Fletcher, a gruff former Navy man with years on the force and an impressive moustache, sauntered over to Henry, wiping a tear of laughter from his eye.

"I could do so and sound convincing," Henry claimed with a smile. "Goodness, that was out of character for the man."

Fletcher leaned close with a wary glance around. "Do you suppose the Director put him up to it?"

"Surely not," Henry quickly denied, unable to imagine it.

"Then who?" His friend shook his head. "You can't tell me he decided to do that of his own accord?"

"Difficult to say. I suppose we may never know."

Fletcher straightened. "Another of life's mysteries." He cocked a bushy brow. "Speaking of which, how was the meeting with the medium?"

Before Henry could respond, Constable Stephens rushed into the office. "Inspector Field, sir, I've been advised to tell you right away that a body was discovered at the King's Cross railyard."

Henry stilled, stomach knotting, as he processed the news. "A body? Is that right?"

"Yes, sir," Stephens continued, slightly breathless. "The constable said you'd want to know straightaway as you're the one who...who told him it was there." The wary look on Stephens' face caught Henry's notice. "Sir, may I ask how you knew?"

"You may, constable. But the answer will have to wait until after Fletcher and I have a look." Henry stood and reached for his hat, then moved to the open door of the Director's office. "We have a body at the railyard, sir."

"Do we, by Jove? Well then, there's not a moment to lose."

"Yes, sir." Henry turned and strode to the door, aware of Fletcher following in his wake while the young constable stood watching, eyes wide, clearly uncertain what to make of the scene.

"Only last week Stephens feared you might be capable of theft," Fletcher muttered as they stepped out onto the street. "Now he's going to think you're clairvoyant or some such nonsense."

"He'll learn the truth soon enough." Henry walked quickly, anxious to see what—and who—had been found at the railyard. "How disturbing that it sounds as if the medium was right."

"Hmmm. This is turning out to be a very odd day." Fletcher's moustache twitched as if to confirm his statement.

"It is indeed."

"What exactly did the magical divination lady tell you?" the sergeant asked.

Henry repeated the few details Mrs. Nettle had told them, leaving out the last bit she'd said in parting to Amelia. He had yet to decide the woman's intent, but already knew he didn't like it causing Amelia such distress.

"Interesting. Care to wager how closely that description matches the scene?"

Henry glanced at Fletcher, surprised by the suggestion. "I didn't think you were a betting man."

"I'm not. But things like seances and mediums give me the creeps. I'd rather find a way to make light of it." His friend shook his head. "If the scene is as she described, you can't tell me that some spirit happened to be floating about the railyard when the person died and then hurried over to the medium's house to tell her."

Henry found the description rather amusing. "I don't think that's how divination works."

"Then how?"

He leveled a questioning look at his friend. "I tend to believe there is a more logical answer for the events. One that doesn't involve spirits from beyond the grave. Let's focus on that."

"Humph. Right."

The silence grew long as they strode the two miles or so toward King's Cross. Henry didn't care to waste his money on a cab if he could avoid it. A delay wouldn't save the victim.

"And what if there isn't?" Fletcher asked at length after they'd crossed a busy street.

"Isn't what?" Henry's thoughts had already moved on to the potential investigation ahead.

"A logical explanation."

The question gave Henry pause. He wasn't prepared to change his beliefs based on one conversation with Mrs. Nettle about her alleged divination skills, even if she had been right about this. "We will have to consider other options once we know more. For now, we shall treat this case like any other: a flesh and blood person died due to a reason we will soon uncover, along with their identity. Whether murder is involved remains to be seen."

"Right." Fletcher straightened, tugging on the bottom of his uniform. "Business as usual. Even if that business might be murder, eh?"

Henry smiled. "Yes."

They had crossed another street as something else came to Henry's mind. He considered Fletcher one of his few friends and trusted him. The last several months had made Henry realize that his social life was mostly non-existent, and he'd been working to improve the few friendships he had, including the one with Fletcher.

Sharing his personal life with his friend should be natural. Unfortunately, Henry realized his palms had grown damp at just the thought of sharing the most recent update.

Exactly why, he couldn't say.

He cleared his throat. "I have a bit of news," he began, uncertain exactly how to phrase it.

"Oh?" Fletcher frowned, clearly puzzled by the admission.

"I..." Henry coughed. Why was this so difficult? "I called on Mrs. Greystone last evening and formally asked to court her." It sounded a mite old-fashioned, but he knew of no other way to say it.

"Congratulations." Fletcher's eyes danced with delight as he grinned. "That is something. As I said, she seems like a fine lady."

"Aren't you going to ask what her answer was?"

"Clearly she said yes, or you wouldn't have raised the subject."

"Right." Henry should have realized that. Where were his observation skills?

"And she would have to be crazed to refuse you, being the good man that you are, and she doesn't seem so."

Henry glanced at Fletcher, prepared to see amusement in his face. Instead, it almost looked as if admiration shone in his eyes. He smiled at the compliment. "Thank you."

"Wait a moment." Fletcher's eyes narrowed. "The two of you agreed to courting, and the first outing you take together is to see a medium regarding a potential murder victim?"

"Well, yes. Not ideal, I suppose..." The thought hadn't crossed Henry's mind.

"Definitely not. I hope you have a plan in place to make up for that. Perhaps dinner at a nice restaurant again? Or maybe the theater?"

The theater? Henry frowned, uncertain how he felt about that suggestion. He'd only attended a few plays in his time and hadn't found them particularly appealing. "I thought of taking her to a museum. She enjoys those."

"No offense, sir, but that doesn't sound very romantic."

The remark had Henry reconsidering the idea, still thinking it was a sound idea. But what would Amelia view as romantic? He very much wanted to know—and looked forward to learning exactly that and more about her.

Chapter Six

King's Cross was teaming with people when Henry and Fletcher arrived. The station, the largest in all England when completed nearly thirty years ago, now threatened to burst at the seams. Additional platforms had already been added but more were needed. The underground rail system had been considered a radical idea when first proposed. Unfortunately the railway hadn't lessened the congestion in London or the surrounding areas from what Henry could tell. However, that wasn't his concern at the moment.

He shifted his focus to the nearby railyard, pleased when Fletcher gestured toward a gate farther along the tall fence. They found it unlocked and were careful to close it behind them to keep the public from entering.

"Over there, sir." Fletcher tipped his head to where a constable stood talking to another man in railway uniform a short distance away.

"Inspector Field. Sergeant Fletcher." Constable Perkins, an officer Henry had met before, greeted them. "This is Samuel Jolly, the watchman."

Henry nodded then surveyed the grounds to get a feel for the place. "What do you have for us?"

The large railyard appeared to hold a combination of old and new equipment, and everything in between, but if there was any organization to where items rested, Henry couldn't spot it. Overgrown weeds and grass grew between crates, lengths of steel, and railcar parts, some rusty while others looked brand new. Puddles littered the ground from the recent rain. The mud could prove advantageous for footprints—if the victim truly had been murdered.

"The door you told us to search for is down the slope, and the body inside, just as you thought it might be," Constable Perkins advised, pointing toward the back of the fenced area even as he sent a wary look in Henry's direction, clearly wondering how the inspector had known where they should look. "I was careful not to touch anything."

"Did you?" Fletcher asked the watchman, saving Henry from doing so.

"No, though it took a bit of effort to get the blasted door open." Jolly, a man larger than Fletcher, shifted a shoulder uneasily, suggesting he'd used it to do so.

Given the man's size, the door must have been truly stubborn. "Lead the way," Henry directed the constable.

"Yes, sir."

Henry and Fletcher followed Perkins and Jolly to what looked to be a large crater in the ground, several feet deep. Henry paused to study the damp ground, noting a few shoe prints marking the grassy slope. "Let's go around. Those footprints could be helpful."

The watchman frowned as he looked down at his own boots, suggesting his concern that his prints were already there.

Henry sent a pointed look to Fletcher, who nodded, suggesting he'd take care to differentiate the watchman's boots from the other prints nearby.

Several oddly shaped mounds of earth were visible among the tall weeds a short distance away in the fenced yard.

"What are those?" Fletcher asked.

"Dirt left from digging tunnels that were abandoned," Jolly advised.

"Abandoned?" Henry asked.

"Oh, it's quite common," the man said with a shrug. "They started digging, only to realize they had to change course for one reason or another. Sometimes officials changed their minds about where the tunnel should be, they hit rock, or encountered other issues. Hard to say."

Such problems were to be expected given the scope of the endeavor, Henry supposed. It was truly a miracle they'd managed to complete it.

They walked around the side of the depression and descended the slope to where an old wooden door stood in the sidehill, hanging crooked on its hinges and with a large rusty padlock on it.

Just as Mrs. Nettle had said.

The thought had Henry shifting uneasily before he shrugged away the feeling as the watchman jerked open the door. The hinges creaked in protest before daylight spilled into the dark space.

A body lay just inside on the dirt floor, the beginning of a tunnel stretching out behind it.

"Can't imagine what he was doing in there other than to get out of the weather...or hiding something he stole," Jolly murmured with a scowl.

"Does that happen often?" Henry asked, his focus on the body.

"More than we'd like. It's a large yard, black as ink at night, with too many hiding places and not enough watchmen. Makes it difficult to guard."

Henry nodded, easily able to imagine the place at night. "If the two of you would remain outside while we take a closer look," he suggested, not wanting any evidence to be disturbed by four sets of feet.

"Yes, sir," the constable readily agreed.

Henry was careful where he stepped, keeping to the edges of the doorframe, confident Fletcher would take the same care.

Despite the open door, the small space was still dark. The tunnel was only about eight feet deep, the ceiling held in place by a few timbers. Dirt and rock lined the walls, a musty scent catching Henry's notice, along with the sharp metallic smell of blood.

"A rather small man," Fletcher said in a low voice as he considered the body. "And young. Unlikely to have been able to put up much of a fight."

The victim lay on his back, arms stretched out, head turned to the side, eyes and mouth wide open. A cap rested on the ground near his head. The man's boots, trousers, and jacket all showed signs of wear.

"Must have been killed outside," Henry observed. A single, short scuff mark on the grass near the door signaled that the killer had dragged the body inside. How far the victim had been pulled along remained to be seen. They'd need to take a closer look at the prints on the grassy slope to know for sure. Might've taken place just outside the door or closer to the entrance of the railyard.

A match flared to life, and Henry nodded in silent approval as Fletcher held the flame near the victim's pale face. Dried blood matted the dark, wavy hair, and cracked bits of skull were in the wound. Part of his head was caved in.

"Damn," Fletcher murmured. "That's a terrible way to end a life." He moved the match closer to reveal the youthful features. "Short though it was."

"Can't be much older than one and twenty, if that," Henry suggested as he bent low to study the head. The round, smooth face, narrow nose, and full lips appeared almost feminine.

Was that the reason the medium had been confused as to whether the body belonged to a man or a woman?

Henry blinked away the question, not wanting to think about Mrs. Nettle or her observations at the moment.

"Must've seen the blow coming, eh?" Fletcher murmured as he stared at the terrified expression.

"Looks like it." Terrible that his last moments had been filled with fear. "This must've happened a day or two ago, based on the dried blood and the discoloration of the skin." Purplish-red marks were visible on the face and neck.

"Not much of an odor, but then it's fairly cold in here." Fletcher waved out the match before it burnt his fingers but quickly lit another. "Get us some lanterns, Perkins."

"Yes, sir."

The muffled voices of the two men outside suggested they were determining how best to do that as Fletcher held the second match near the injury again. A glint of metal caught Henry's notice just behind the body.

"What's on the ground back there?" he asked Fletcher, who moved the small flame to reveal a large wrench nearly the size of a man's arm on the ground. "Heck of a murder weapon."

The sergeant gave a mock shudder. "Surprised anything is left of the head." Too quickly, Fletcher had to extinguish the match again. "Blast it."

"Have a look at the padlock while we're waiting for more light," Henry directed. "Was it recently forced open?"

The sergeant stood and moved outside to take a closer look. "Based on the rust and the lack of any new scratches, I'd say it's been in disrepair for some time."

Henry straightened, pleased to see the two men returning with lanterns in hand. "It seems as if either the victim or his killer had to know of this place."

"Unlikely to stumble upon the door or the tunnel by accident. One of them must've been snooping around the railyard at some point," Fletcher agreed, watching to make certain Jolly and Perkins took the longer path down to the door. "Thank you." The sergeant made quick work of lighting the lamps and returned to hand one to Henry and place the other near the victim. "So dark in here that it eats the light."

"A disturbing description, though apt." Henry returned his attention to the body, aware of the other two men standing by the door watching avidly.

Henry held the lantern near the victim's face. "Jolly, do you recognize him?"

The watchman leaned closer to study the face, though his gaze kept shifting to the bloody dent on the side of the head. "Can't say that I do, but I work nights mostly."

"Any guess how he entered the railyard, assuming he didn't come through the gate?" Henry assumed any guard on duty would check doors and gates frequently as he made his rounds.

"There's a broken place in the fence we've repaired a time or two, but someone seems to find their way through it every time we turn around."

"Will you show it to the constable?" Henry asked. He'd have a look for himself later.

"Sure can." Jolly seemed eager to be of assistance and the pair returned up the slope.

"Perkins, search the ground for clues as you go," Henry called out through the open door. "Anything that doesn't look like it belongs could be important."

"Will do, sir." With a nod, the two men started slowly toward the fence.

"At a glance, I'd say the head wound seems to be the only injury," Henry murmured to his sergeant as he knelt next to the body.

"Blood and matted hair on the wrench." Fletcher frowned. "Interesting choice to leave the murder weapon beside the body. The killer obviously didn't care if it was found."

"Perhaps the weapon was convenient, something he picked up as he trailed the victim through the railyard."

"It's got a bit of rust on it," the sergeant observed. "Certainly could've been lying nearby."

Henry moved a lantern slowly around the body but didn't spot anything of note on the hard-packed earthen floor. There was no sign of the ruby ring the medium had mentioned. In truth, that came as a relief. He wasn't comfortable with her knowing all the details when the information supposedly came from the spirit world.

A review of the jacket pockets didn't reveal anything. Henry unbuttoned the jacket to find a simple cotton shirt beneath. No blood stained the fabric that he could see. He examined the trouser pockets, hoping for a clue to both his identity and that of the murderer, though he knew it was too much to ask.

Much to his surprise, one held a small wad of pound notes.

"How do you suppose he came by those?" Fletcher asked curiously.

"Hmmm. Possibly from selling goods he stole from the railyard?" Henry surmised.

"Makes sense. How else might he have known to find this space? Given his worn attire and thin frame, life hasn't been easy."

"Why the railyard?" Henry asked as he considered the possibilities.

"Lives nearby?"

"Possibly. Seems like he'd need some knowledge of the place to know where to look and what to steal, if that's what happened." It was too soon to say, and Henry wouldn't make assumptions.

Fletcher lifted the lantern higher for a better look at the tunnel. "Why wouldn't they fill it in if they decided it wouldn't do?"

"Too expensive? Such things cost time and money. Easier to put a door with a lock on it, I suppose." A faint vibration and rumbling sound coming through the dirt walls suggested a train was arriving.

"Can't say I care for that sound," Fletcher said, watching the ceiling as if half expecting it to fall. "Just seems messy to leave it, a big gaping hole. I wonder how many of these are around London."

"And who knows about them," Henry added.

"An even better question. Might be worth talking to someone other than the watchman—his superior or higher."

"Most definitely," Henry agreed. "Unfortunate there's nothing that identifies the victim." He studied the youthful features again. Were they that of a man...or a woman? The trousers would certainly suggest a man, as did the boots. He'd leave the question for the surgeon to answer during the postmortem.

"Shall I take another look outside?" Fletcher offered.

"I'll join you." Henry glanced at the sole of the victim's boot which had more than a few holes. "This doesn't have any distinctive tread other than being a fairly small size." He bent closer. "He has a knife tucked into the top of his boot but clearly didn't draw it."

"Might've happened too quickly for him to do so. Let's hope whoever followed him down here wore a shoe more easily identifiable." Fletcher led the way out the door.

A second set of shoeprints was visible on the slope, but it was difficult to determine their size as whoever had left them had slid with each step.

They went up the slope, searching as they went, and found a few additional partial prints, but Henry doubted they would be helpful as none had a distinguishable tread. There were no signs of anyone being dragged down to the door.

"Looks as if he came in here," Perkins called out and led them to a damaged section of the railed fence. "The braces have been cut here and here." He pointed to them. "Easy enough if one knew where to look."

"We've repaired this more times than I can count," Jolly said with a disgusted look.

"How big is the railyard?" Henry asked.

The watchman gave them a brief tour, giving Henry a better idea of its layout. He also provided the name of his supervisor while Perkins departed to request a police wagon to haul the body to St. Thomas' for examination.

A brief conversation with Jolly's supervisor in his tiny office in a corner of the railyard proved unhelpful. The man was shocked by the discovery of the body, insisted he couldn't imagine how the young man had broken in, nor did he know why he would've done so. Yes, there had been some missing items of late, but that was unfortunately a regular occurrence, something they often battled.

Henry described the victim as best he could, but he didn't sound familiar to the supervisor. That was unfortunate. The longer it took to identify any victim, the longer it would take to solve their murder.

No matter, Henry told himself. The clues might come slower than he'd like, but they would come. Impatience simmered within him as they spoke with a couple of other rail employees who weren't any help either.

"Shall we see if Perkins has returned with the wagon?" he asked Fletcher. "I would like one more look at the body before we move him."

"Very well." The sergeant looked around the yard. "I'll see if they can bring it closer so we don't have to carry him so far." He sent Henry a rueful look. "Not that he looks to weigh much."

"True, but we don't want to haul him out within sight of the public." With luck, Perkins would have brought some canvas to cover the body at the very least.

"Right. I'll have a word with Jolly to see if he has a suggestion."

"Good idea. I will meet you near the body." Henry wanted to make sure he hadn't missed anything.

He took his time as he walked, imagining the place in the dark. Such things always seemed to happen then.

The surgeon would confirm the approximate time of death after his examination. Significant rain had fallen the night before last, which would have made the yard even more difficult to navigate. Few would've been out in the poor weather without good reason.

What of the killer? Why had he been there? Was he also familiar with the railyard for some reason? Had he known the young man—possibly had a grudge of some sort against him? Or had it been more random than that?

As always happened at the beginning of an investigation, Henry had more questions than answers.

His pace slowed as he approached the slope and studied the ground, trying to picture the scene based on the trail of sliding footprints the killer and his victim had left.

The pound notes in the victim's pocket suggested he'd been up to no good. Why else would he have so many, given his tired clothing? And yet the killer hadn't taken the money—so gain wasn't the cause of such a terrible crime.

So what was?

One of the surgeon's assistants was clever with a pencil. Henry would ask him to sketch a likeness of the victim's face to show around the area in an attempt to help identify him, unless someone came forward before then.

That brought to mind Mrs. Nettle and her mention of an older woman crying, but whether that detail proved true remained to be seen. Still, his stomach lurched. So far, her description had been unsettlingly accurate.

Henry moved around the edge of the hollow where they'd descended earlier and neared the door. The thick grass near the entrance revealed little, so he moved to the doorway and considered the angle of the body.

He'd be guessing, but he tended to think the victim had sought the abandoned tunnel, hoping to hide. It would've been dark and raining, making visibility nil. The young man had surely been nervous with so much money in his pocket. Perhaps he'd been familiar with the railyard, otherwise he would've hidden closer to the fence. The door and the partial tunnel would've been difficult to find in the dark unless one knew where to look.

The sight of the wrench prompted him to search the area outside the door and move back up the slope until he found an indentation in the ground in which the wrench would fit. Perhaps the killer had nearly tripped over it and grabbed the heavy thing at the last minute. How else could he have found it in the dark?

Why had he killed the victim? It wasn't theft. So what? Revenge? Anger?

Henry returned to the abandoned tunnel and stepped inside, pausing to allow his eyes to adjust to the dim glow of the lanterns, then studied the injury and the weapon again. There had only been one or two blows based on the indentation in the skull, but that was another piece of information the surgeon would confirm.

Muffled voices reached Henry. He straightened and moved to the door to see Fletcher, Perkins, and Jolly at the top of the slope with a wooden barrow.

"This is our best option to get the body to the wagon," Fletcher advised.

Henry nodded. Though not ideal, it was better than carrying the poor thing the entire way.

Fletcher and Henry picked up the victim and got him through the doorway, where Perkins and Jolly helped to get him up the slope with only a few muttered curses.

"For one so slight, he still feels heavy," Constable Perkins said as he helped to lift him into the barrow.

"They always do," Fletcher advised curtly. "They don't call it dead weight without reason."

In short order, they had the body loaded in the police wagon. Perkins accompanied it to St. Thomas' with a request for the surgeon to have one of his assistants to sketch the victim's face as soon as possible.

"Where to next, sir?" Fletcher asked with an expectant look.

Henry considered. Logic. Evidence. That's what he needed. "Let's have a look around the surrounding area and ask a few questions. Someone has to know the victim. Come tomorrow, we will have the sketch to aid us."

They needed to discover his identity, and the quicker the better.

Chapter Seven

AMELIA SMILED AT THE sound of voices in the foyer that evening, her heartbeat speeding, certain the caller would be Henry.

Now that a constable was no longer watching over them and checking with Fernsby at regular intervals, the house felt even quieter than normal. Thank goodness the need for police protection had passed, along with the danger which had followed Amelia these last six months.

Her afternoon had been pleasant, if uneventful, as she spent it pottering in her laboratory. Of course, nothing had prevented her from wondering what, if anything, Henry had discovered at the railyard.

Had Mrs. Nettle's prediction proven true?

In all honesty, she continued to have mixed feelings on the matter. Rather than allow herself to dwell on them, she'd tended the pots from her fertilizer experiment and examined Master Leopold's hair under the microscope, simply to amuse herself. Heaven knew there was enough of the stuff lying about regardless of the maid's efforts.

To her amazement, cat hair appeared much different to human hair, with a strange sort of ladder structure inside. Why she found such things so fascinating, she couldn't say.

Knowing she could share the odd detail with Henry and that he would more than likely find it interesting too made her realize just how much she enjoyed his company.

Amelia set aside the book she'd been reading in her chair by the fire and glanced at the time to see the hour was nearing seven o'clock. Hopefully that meant Henry was officially off duty and could stay for a lengthier visit, perhaps even for dinner. Anticipation filled her at the thought.

"Good evening, Amelia." Henry greeted her from the doorway, the sight of him familiar yet still taking her breath away, along with the sound of her name in the low rumble of his voice. "I trust the remainder of your day was more relaxing than the start." He lifted a brow as he awaited her reply.

How nice that he was so interested. She only wished she had some exciting bit of news to share, other than the personal discovery of what cat hair looked like under a microscope.

"It was, thank you." She looked at him expectantly. "I've been quite anxious to hear whether anything was found at the railyard."

He sighed as he drew closer. Both his hat and coat had been left with Fernsby. She took that as a good sign. "Yes, a body, unfortunately. It seems I have another murder investigation on my hands."

"Oh?" How terrible that her interest was piqued by his words, even as her stomach dipped. "May I pour us drinks, and you can tell me what you will do about it?"

He hesitated, glancing toward the fire and back to her. "If it's no imposition."

She smiled, appreciating how he didn't assume anything. "I should very much like to spend time with you." Heat filled her cheeks at the admission, even if she'd already said as much the previous evening.

He offered a wry look. "I am only sorry we so often speak of my work when together."

"I would be happy to tell you of my day, though I'm certain it wasn't nearly as interesting as yours." She moved to the sideboard and poured him a whiskey and herself a sherry, handing him his glass as they settled in wingback chairs before the fire.

He sipped, seeming to savor the taste, before sending her a questioning look. "A new whiskey?"

"One my father gifted me while he was here." Her parents had come for a visit and departed only a few days ago, having met Henry and given their approval, though Amelia hadn't directly asked for it. As a widow and an independent woman, she could make her own decisions...but she still appreciated their opinion.

"He has fine taste."

"He will be pleased to hear you think so."

It was no surprise when Master Leopold trotted into the room, head and tail high as he surveyed his domain with a meow before moving directly to Henry. The cat seemed to consider it his duty to inspect and approve any and all visitors, even familiar ones.

"Good evening, Master Leopold," Henry reached to scratch the cat behind his ears. "How was your day?"

The cat meowed politely in reply as he permitted the attention, then settled on the rug before the fire to lick a paw.

"He likes you," Amelia declared warmly. "He tends to ignore my aunt."

"I'm pleased you think so, as I am quite fond of him as well."

"I think he knows you're responsible for his rescue and his place in our home."

Henry had discovered the cat at a murder victim's residence in Gravesend and, with none of the family wanting to keep the animal, had asked Amelia if she would do so.

"Perhaps you're right." The sparkle in Henry's brown eyes suggested he liked the idea.

"Now then, do tell me what you found at King's Cross. Were Mrs. Nettle's details correct?" Her stomach tightened at the thought.

Henry shared more details than she'd expected, leaving her to wonder if that was because she knew what Mrs. Nettle had said, or because he trusted her to keep his confidence. Perhaps it was a little of both.

"My goodness. So you still don't know the young man's identity?"

"No, but a sketch has been prepared for us to take to the railyard tomorrow. If no one recognizes him there, we will ask around the neighborhood and see what we can discover."

Amelia nodded, then took another sip of her sherry, her thoughts on the unfortunate victim. "Having one's skull smashed in sounds like a terrible way to die."

"True." Henry gave her a rueful look. "Then again, there aren't many good ways to do so unless one simply passes away in their sleep. At least death would've been relatively quick."

"You're right, of course." She nearly shuddered at the thought of how Matthew had died. A single gunshot to the head might have been quick as well, but she often wondered how terrified he'd been in those last few minutes: whether he'd thought of her or Lily, and if he regretted the choice he'd made to deal in illegal antiquities which had brought him into contact with his killer.

Unless Mrs. Nettle was right, she would never know.

"Once we learn who he was and where he lived and worked, we should have additional clues to pursue," Henry murmured as he stared into the coals in the hearth, legs stretched out relaxed before him.

The impression of ease pleased her more than she could say. She wanted him to be comfortable in her home, since he certainly couldn't entertain her at his lodging house.

"Would you care to stay for dinner?" she asked after a few moments of silence. "I can promise before you demure that it's no imposition."

"I should like that very much."

Warmth flooded Amelia. "Good. The cook took your compliments to heart and seems determined to make certain her dishes are better than those of your landlady."

Henry chuckled. "Trust me when I say that Mrs. Appleton's efforts have already far exceeded anything my landlady has prepared. There is no comparison."

"I do believe she made something special for this evening in the hope you would join me." Amelia rose to pull the bell, motioning for Henry to remain seated, then moved to the landing to advise Fernsby when he entered the hall. The method was more effective than sitting in the drawing room to wait for the older man to walk up the stairs to see what she needed.

"I will admit, I took the liberty of setting a place for Inspector Field, just in case," Fernsby advised with a dip of his head upon hearing her request.

The butler's respect for Henry nearly exceeded her own. "Thank you, Fernsby." There were times when she felt the urge to hug him.

"My pleasure, madam."

"It seems we are one step behind my staff," Amelia said when she returned to her seat.

"That comes as no surprise, given their efficiency."

Amelia watched Henry for a moment before deciding she should speak her mind. "Dare I ask if what you found at the railyard changes your opinion of Mrs. Nettle?"

He sighed, shifting in his chair as he set aside the empty crystal glass. "You may, but I can't say I have an answer."

"I confess to feeling the same. That the details you found match what she said so closely is concerning."

Henry nodded. "I find myself searching for an explanation for it. One that doesn't involve anything of the otherworldly sort. In fact, I have to wonder if the medium or her husband could be involved in the crime."

"Do you think that possible?" Amelia asked.

"I intend to find out."

She had to smile at his disgruntled tone. That the involvement of the spirit world bothered him came as no surprise when his job was to find evidence in order to solve cases, not to rely on hearsay of any sort—including from the dearly departed. "You mentioned she worked with the police in the past. My editor said the same when he first asked me about interviewing her."

"I intend to find out who it was to see what they have to say. That could prove helpful." His skeptical tone belied the words, suggesting he was uncertain whether that was true.

"I don't quite know what to think." Amelia's thoughts returned to their visit to the woman's home. "At times, she seemed more interested in her performance than the information she was sharing."

"While such actions might be helpful before an audience, I can't imagine why she thought a member of the police force would appreciate it."

"Yet she had several of the details correct," Amelia pointed out uneasily.

"But her uncertainty on whether the victim was a male or female concerns me." Henry's frown surely matched her own. "Though I must admit that his features were somewhat feminine in appearance. Add that to his small frame, and..." Henry lifted his hands, palms up. "He could be mistaken for a woman."

"How interesting. It's odd that some of what she supposedly saw was clear while other parts weren't. No ring. The uncertainty of the victim's gender. But maybe that's how divination works." Amelia bit her lip, pondering whether to offer to speak with the medium again given how uncomfortable she'd been. The woman's last words had been nothing short of unsettling.

"No." Henry's firm tone had her looking at him in surprise.

"Excuse me?"

"No, there is no need for you to visit with Mrs. Nettle again. If you wish to send word that a body has been found and an investigation is underway, that would be more than sufficient—beyond what could be expected. But you do not need to speak with her again or take any action that makes you uncomfortable."

Pleasure spread through her that he knew her so well. "I only considered it because she might have more to add to what she told us. About the victim, I mean." And if there were a way for Amelia to aid the investigation, she would like to do so—anything to have purpose and help Henry.

"Then she should send me that information." Henry leaned forward to hold her gaze even as he reached out to touch her hand where it rested on the arm of her chair. "I don't care to see you upset, and you can't deny that speaking with her did just that."

"She...she certainly makes me uneasy." Amelia shook her head. "I'm not quite sure what it is about the idea of hearing from the spirit world that concerns me, but..." She couldn't finish the thought when even thinking about it caused her heart to rise to her throat.

Why did it make her so uncomfortable? What did she fear to hear—or not hear?

Henry rubbed the pad of his thumb along the back of her hand, the motion already soothing her angst. "That is only natural. I think many people share the same sentiment. While a few might miss their departed loved ones and desire one last conversation with them, I wouldn't."

"Truly?" Why? Amelia welcomed anything to help ease the guilt pressing on her for her reluctance to delve into the subject personally.

He released her hand and sat back, seeming to consider his response. "I loved my grandfather dearly, and while I would enjoy one more conversation with him, I wouldn't want to do so if I knew it was the last one. It would be too bittersweet, I think. I wouldn't enjoy it because it would be so difficult to say goodbye all over again."

Amelia slowly nodded. That was part of it. Yet for her there was more involved, some of which she didn't want to face; didn't care to drag herself through the emotional trauma of regrets overshadowing her the weeks and months after first Lily's and then Matthew's deaths.

"What is it?" Henry asked, his warm brown eyes holding on her without judgment or expectation—only concern.

She shook her head and managed a smile. "Perhaps the past is best left behind us."

"You may be right. And as I said, there is no need for you to speak to Mrs. Nettle again unless you want to for the purpose of writing an article. However, I am certain there are many other subjects you could research instead."

Amelia nodded but didn't mention that she had already scoured the news sheets for exactly that without success. She need only be patient, she told herself. Either an idea would come to her or her editor would suggest one. There was no hurry for either to occur, though she dearly wished for something to do to fill her days.

But before she could say anything more, Fernsby arrived to announce that dinner was served.

As expected, the meal of braised beefsteak with mushrooms and boiled new potatoes was delicious. Seeming to be of the same mind, they spoke of inconsequential matters while they enjoyed the meal. She savored each moment as much as every bite.

Already it felt as if the bond between her and Henry had deepened now that they had an understanding between them. While it was too soon to say whether it would lead to anything permanent, Amelia intended to enjoy it and hoped Henry felt the same.

She'd been courted before, of course, but this time the expectations of both Society and her own were nothing like what she'd experienced that first time. She was older, wiser, and being a widow afforded her a certain amount of freedom in this situation, as in other aspects of her life.

Fernsby cleared their plates and poured them each more wine, then stepped out of the room.

"Amelia," Henry began, his fingers steady on the stem of his wineglass and his eyes sincere, "I hope you already know this, but if there is ever a time when you would prefer to slow down our...our relationship, you need only tell me. If my visits are too frequent, please let me know. I would never want to ask you for anything you're not ready to give."

It was all she could do to keep from pressing a hand to her heart at his sweet words. "We both agreed that honesty would be an integral part of our relationship, and I think after all we have been through together, we respect one another enough to hold to that agreement. Such conversations might be uncomfortable or difficult, but they are vital."

He nodded. "I agree."

"I...I wouldn't want to ask you for more than you're willing to give either," she continued, heat rising in her cheeks. "I realize your work as an inspector is important to you, and that is your first priority."

Henry frowned, his lips tightening. "I'm no longer sure that is true."

She stilled in surprise, unable to imagine his meaning as the man continued.

"Coming to know you has helped me realize there is more to life than a career. I do enjoy my work and hope to continue it, but I will not deny that you are important to me as well."

Her heart bloomed in her chest, sending flutters stroking along her skin. "Thank you. I feel much the same and look forward to spending more time together."

"As do I." Henry lifted his glass. "To us."

She did the same. "To us."

Hope was a fragile thing, something she intended to treat with care. But it felt wonderful to hold onto in the moment.

Chapter Eight

THE FOLLOWING MORNING HENRY woke with a lightness in his heart he hadn't felt in a long time.

It wasn't that he'd been unhappy before. Rather, he had kept his emotions in check, experiencing few highs or lows in his personal life as it had been nearly non-existent. His focus had always remained on his work, putting one foot in front of the other and making his way steadily through each day.

But this morning was different—he *felt* different—all thanks to Amelia. Now thoughts of the future, in addition to the tasks he wanted to complete by the day's end, ran through his mind as he dressed for work.

He even managed to startle Mrs. Douglas, his landlady, when he offered a smile with his customary greeting upon entering the dining room. Perhaps it had been too broad a smile?

With a shrug, he quickly ate the bowl of tasteless porridge, knowing it would stick to his ribs, even as he wondered what Amelia enjoyed having for breakfast. Perhaps one day—one day not too far away—he would find out. The thought had him smiling yet again as he walked to Scotland Yard, the faint spring sunshine seeming to approve of his good mood.

The postmortem report wouldn't be available until at least later in the day, so he collected Fletcher and they returned to King's Cross station with the sketch in hand, hoping to identify the victim.

"You seem to be in fine spirits this morning, considering we have a murder case on our hands." Fletcher frowned as he studied him. "I assume the investigation is not the reason."

"Not hardly," Henry said with a chuckle. "I had a pleasant dinner with Mrs. Greystone last evening."

"Oh? Did you take an old married man's advice about being more romantic?" Fletcher lifted a brow, amusement twinkling in his eyes.

"Not as of yet, but thank you for your concern." The question reminded him that he'd failed to confirm when he and Amelia might see one another again. He couldn't continually dine at her house, even if he did appreciate the privacy that doing so offered. There might be talk.

Courting a lady was more complicated than he remembered. It had been several years since Henry had done so, and that had been brief with both deciding not to pursue the relationship shortly after their first walk together. Since then, Henry had allowed his career to fill his days and many of his nights. Meeting Amelia had made him realize there was more to life and hope that happiness might be within reach. He certainly felt so when with her.

"I'm happy to share what I can, sir." Fletcher lifted his chin with no small measure of pride. "Been happily married for well over a decade, you know."

Henry looked both ways before they crossed the hectic street, feeling more uncomfortable by the minute. While he considered Fletcher a friend and wanted that to continue, perhaps even deepen their trust, this topic felt decidedly personal. "Care to share your secrets for a happy marriage?" he asked as lightly as he could manage. While he'd never expected to seek romantic advice from his sergeant, he was curious how the usually gruff man would answer.

"Well, there's a question. Hmmm." A long moment of silence ensued before the sergeant cleared his throat, making Henry think he was surprised by the inquiry. "I suppose we don't have many outings these days. It's more about the small moments in our day." His face took on a ruddy hue. "A kiss in the morning when we wake. Another upon my return home. Listening, really listening, when she has something to say."

The frank answer had Henry looking away; it was far more intimate than he'd anticipated. Still, he appreciated Fletcher sharing the details. "It's important to make each day matter." His parents did much the same, though they had an active social life.

"Indeed." Fletcher didn't meet his gaze when Henry finally glanced in his direction.

The time had come to change the subject before either of them became even more uncomfortable. Luckily King's Cross station came into view. "Let us see if someone can provide us with a name for the victim."

The young man's potential familiarity with the railyard hinted he could have had some association with it. At least, that was Henry's hope.

It was the third employee they spoke with at the bustling station who nodded. “Ah yes, I remember him. Used to work here as a clerk, though I can’t tell you his name,” the man said. “Check with the office. Mr. Weston should be able to help you.”

He pointed them in the right direction, and in short order, they were shown into Mr. Weston’s office. The orderly piles of paper on his desk and his no-nonsense manner suggested efficiency was the man’s focus.

“Why, yes.” He frowned at the sketch. “Clarence Digby, former clerk.” Mr. Weston glanced between them. “Is he in some sort of trouble?”

“You might say that,” Henry began, pleased to not only have a name but someone who might be able to tell them more. “I’m sorry to say he was murdered, we believe a couple of days ago.” He paused to allow the news to sink in.

Mr. Weston’s lips pursed as he shook his head. “I’m sorry to hear that, though I can’t say that it comes as a surprise. Mr. Digby seemed to seek the easiest path in life rather than an honorable one.”

“How do you mean, sir?” Henry asked as he pulled his notebook from his pocket.

“He was dismissed from his position about two weeks ago for stealing items from the railyard to sell for his own profit.”

“Oh?” That explained his apparent familiarity with the place, even in the dark of night.

“Of course he denied it, but there could be no other explanation for the missing items and a particular key found on his person.” Mr. Weston shook his head again, his brow furrowed. “Perhaps we should’ve involved the police and pressed charges.”

Henry allowed the comment to pass. "What more can you tell us about him? We would like to notify his next of kin."

"Allow me to see." The man rose and stepped to the filing cabinet behind him to pull open an orderly drawer and retrieve a file. He returned to the desk and sorted through the papers. "Digby, Clarence, twenty years of age. Only one reference, but he was young. Originally from Kent."

"If you could provide us with his address and that of any family, we would appreciate it." Henry would've liked to read the information for himself, but somehow didn't think the efficient Mr. Weston would allow that.

The man pulled a blank sheet of paper from a drawer and jotted down the information, only to pause to look between them. "Oh, dear—Mr. Digby was not the one found at the railyard yesterday, was he?"

"I'm afraid he was," Henry confirmed.

The man looked horrified. "May I inquire as to what happened?"

"Had his head smashed in," Fletcher supplied before Henry could respond.

Henry sent the sergeant a questioning look at the blunt words, wishing he had put it more delicately. Fletcher shrugged in return.

"How...how terrible." Mr. Weston sat back in his chair, the task before him forgotten.

"Yes," Henry agreed shortly. "He was found in one of the abandoned tunnels."

"I should've put the two together when you said he was murdered." Mr. Weston drew a deep breath. "I can't say that I've ever known anyone who met with a violent end."

Henry gave him a moment to regain his bearings. While people were aware of crime, appearing on every news sheet page, it was easy to ignore until it touched them in some way. With luck, this was the closest Mr. Weston would ever be to murder.

"Do you have any idea who might have killed him? Perhaps a fellow employee who was angry with him?" Henry asked, glancing down at his notebook and seeing the notation of the twelve pound notes.

"No," Mr. Weston said after giving the questions some thought. "Though Mr. Digby wasn't particularly well-liked from what I saw. He kept to himself and seemed to think he was better than others, something he didn't bother to hide."

"If we could speak with his supervisor and those who worked closely with him, we would appreciate it." Henry glanced pointedly at the half-finished information the man had been writing down.

"Yes, of course." The man gave a slight shudder and completed the details. "There you are. If there's anything else I can help with, please let me know."

"We will." Henry took the offered paper and glanced over it before nodding. "Thank you. We would ask that you please keep the details of the murder confidential while we conduct our investigation."

"Certainly." Mr. Weston slowly closed the file. "Shocking news, just shocking. His mother will be terribly upset."

Henry looked at the paper again. "The one in Kent?"

"Yes, she came to visit a month or so ago and stopped by the railyard to see where he worked. Mr. Digby introduced her to several of us. She is...she was so proud of him."

Mrs. Nettle's mention of an older woman weeping flickered in his mind, but Henry pushed it firmly away. It was hardly unusual for a murder victim to have a mother who mourned them. Yet somehow he couldn't dismiss the detail from his mind.

Mr. Weston introduced them to Clarence Digby's supervisor, a short man who glared at Henry and Fletcher as if annoyed by their mere height. His responses were clipped as he answered their careful questions.

Yes, he'd known Clarence. No, he had no idea who might have killed him. Yes, he'd been the one who'd caught Clarence stealing, and yes he'd dismissed him on the spot.

"Caught him stealing?" Henry asked. That didn't match what Mr. Weston had told them.

"Well, not exactly," sniffed the supervisor, "but there could be no other explanation."

"I see. And where were you the evening before last?" Henry waited for an answer with his notebook in hand.

The man gasped in outrage, his body suddenly stiff. "You are surely not accusing *me* of murder?"

"Not at all. Accounting for your whereabouts will allow me to formally eliminate you from the list of potential suspects," Henry reassured him, then waited expectantly for an answer.

After several huffs and puffs, the man provided the address of his lodging house and the name of his landlady, who could verify his whereabouts, before striding off muttering about being busy.

Next they spoke with two fellow clerks, both of whom were young and clearly sweating at being questioned by the police. Henry took down their details as well, so their whereabouts could be verified. They hadn't been on friendly terms with the man either.

Henry and Fletcher departed King's Cross with considerably more information than they'd had upon their arrival, but without any actual clues, let alone a single suspect.

"Where to next?" Fletcher asked.

"His lodging house. Perhaps someone there can offer more."

The slow, methodical work was something to which Henry was accustomed, but it wasn't enough to keep his thoughts from returning to Amelia time and again. He hoped she hadn't felt compelled to call on Mrs. Nettle. The medium seemed determined to upset her.

"Why is it that I don't think your thoughts are solely on the investigation?" Fletcher asked as they walked.

Henry only smiled, unable to deny it. The sergeant would soon grow accustomed to the change.

The run-down lodging house just off York Way wasn't far from King's Cross, close enough to hear the train's approach.

"Mr. Digby?" An older woman with a faded apron, who'd answered the door and confirmed she was the landlady, shook her head. "That's mighty awful news, but he left here some ten days ago." She frowned. "He cleared out his things and left early one morning, and without paying what he owed me."

"I'm sorry to hear that. You might consider making a claim through the courts," Henry advised, thinking of the pound notes they'd found on Digby. "Did you notice anything different about him of late? Did he seem worried?"

"Oh, he was always concerned over money, counting every penny with care. He sent quite a bit to his mother every week, he mentioned that once. Just before he left, he seemed especially worried. Almost frantic. I asked if he'd lost his job, but he denied it."

Henry didn't bother to tell her that she'd been right. "Was he friendly with any of the other boarders?"

She considered the question briefly. "Well...no. Not really. He kept to himself. I always had the impression he didn't expect to stay here long, though he never said as much."

"If you think of anything else that could be helpful to our investigation, please let us know." Henry thanked her for her time, and they took their leave.

"That wasn't particularly helpful," Fletcher said with a sigh. "It would be nice for once if it was simple to find a killer within four and twenty hours of finding a body."

"Then everyone would be solving murders, and our skills wouldn't be needed." Yet Henry couldn't deny that he felt the same. "I want a word with Inspector Robertson at F Division at the Covent Garden station, then we need to return to Scotland Yard and send a telegram to the town in Kent where Clarence Digby was from to advise his family of his passing."

Covent Garden station wasn't far from Scotland Yard, and their steps wended that way. Henry's mind tried to take in all the moving parts of the investigation. Kent. King's Cross. A mystical message from beyond the grave. Amelia. The twelve pounds. A young man with no friends. How did it all tie together?

"How is Robertson involved?" Fletcher asked, breaking into his thoughts.

"He worked with Mrs. Nettle on a case several months ago." Henry had mixed feelings about speaking with him, not wanting to give too much importance to what the medium had said. But he could hardly fail to follow up a lead.

"The divination lady?" Fletcher asked with a frown.

"Yes. According to one report she was pivotal in solving a murder case, and Robertson was the detective assigned to it."

"Huh." Fletcher shifted his shoulder. "I have difficulty believing any inspector would willingly admit to relying on the supernatural to solve a case."

"We will see what he has to say. However, we must keep an open mind if it proves true." Henry was trying to, but found it more difficult than he'd expected. He couldn't deny that Mrs. Nettle had been correct about the location of the body. "We need to verify the whereabouts of the medium and her husband. After all, without her, who knows how long it would've been before we discovered Digby?"

"Humph. I still can't say I like the idea of spirits speaking to anyone, especially me."

Nor did Henry, which brought to mind his conversation with Amelia the previous evening. "Would you want to speak with any friends or relatives who have passed, if given the chance?"

"No." Fletcher didn't hesitate, his feelings on the matter clear. "Those who are gone before us are exactly that. Gone. The timing of death can be unfortunate and even tragic, but it's final."

Henry nodded, appreciating his friend's frank opinion. "What if that loved one failed to tell you something important? Some detail you desperately need to know?"

"Like where a treasure was buried?" Fletcher asked with half a smile.

"Something like that." *Or why they'd chosen to dance with danger and sell illegal antiquities.*

"I don't think a conversation with the deceased would be anything like we would expect. Certainly not like we're speaking now."

The silence grew long as they wound their way through passersby along the street. Clouds had settled in, and the temperature had dropped.

"Would you?" Fletcher asked at last.

Henry shook his head. "I tend to agree with you, though I can understand the desire to try, if one feels there was unfinished business to resolve."

"Have you ever attended a séance?"

"No." Henry glanced at the sergeant in surprise at the unexpected question. "Have you?"

"No, but the missus has and she swears it was real."

Perhaps if Henry saw evidence for himself, he would reconsider his opinion of such things. Until then, he needed facts—cold, hard evidence.

With that in mind, they entered the Division F office.

Chapter Nine

Henry nodded at a few familiar faces as he and Fletcher entered the Covent Garden police station. With luck, Robertson would be in. If not, they'd leave a message to request he come by Scotland Yard.

"Robertson?" The sergeant at the front desk frowned. "I know I saw him earlier. Go on in and look for yourself."

This division was approximately the same size as Scotland Yard and appeared just as busy. Numerous officers, some in uniform, an equal number in plain clothes, went about their business with a focus to which Henry was accustomed. Criminal activity never seemed to slow.

"Over there," a constable pointed when Fletcher inquired.

Henry looked to see Robertson stepping out of an interview room along the near wall that held several men, one of whom shouted obscenities. The other inspector's attention caught on Henry and he nodded in greeting, waving them over.

"Field, Fletcher, what brings the two of you by?" Robertson asked as he shook their hands.

"Hoping you have a few minutes to tell us of your experience with Mrs. Nettle, the medium," Henry revealed with a wry smile.

"I'd be pleased to." The other inspector glanced around as if in search of a place they could speak, smoothing his narrow moustache as he did so. "There should be an empty interview room in the back that we can use for a few minutes."

They followed the stocky inspector to a small room with four chairs and a table. Henry appreciated the chance for privacy and to sit, no matter how briefly, and knew Fletcher did too.

"What would you like to know?" Robertson lowered himself into a chair, looking between them with interest.

"With what case did she aid you?" Henry asked.

"It was a missing person investigation that had gone on for well over a week with no sign of the man anywhere. No clues to speak of. It was as if he had disappeared into thin air. Mrs. Nettle sent a message saying she knew where he was—his body, anyway." Robertson shook his head. "Our missing person case quickly turned into a murder investigation." A look of amazement came over his face. "I could hardly believe it, the information she shared was so accurate."

"How so?" Henry wanted details.

"She told us the victim was under the floorboards in an old building that had collapsed a year or so ago, just off Rose Street. She said we'd find the knife that had killed him in a rubbish pile a short distance away."

"And did you?" Fletcher asked, his gaze fixed on the other inspector. "Find both, that is."

"Yes, and the knife proved to be the murder weapon."

"Interesting," Henry murmured as Fletcher shifted in the chair beside him.

"It took some work, but we soon found the killer. I'm fairly certain we never would've located the body without Mrs. Nettle's information. Why do you ask?" Robertson looked between them, eyes bright with curiosity. "Did she contact you? Another body?"

Henry shared the basics, leaving out Amelia's involvement. "The victim was at the railyard in the location, just as she described."

"Unsettling, isn't it? I can't explain how her ability works, nor am I sure she can," Robertson said heavily. "I suppose there are some things in this world that are beyond our understanding."

Henry appreciated the other inspector's opinion but wasn't sure he could simply accept the situation at face value. He couldn't help but wonder if there was a more logical explanation. "Was she a suspect at any point?"

"Of course, but we quickly eliminated her as she had an alibi."

Henry nodded, already intending to verify Mrs. Nettle's whereabouts once he received the postmortem report and confirmed the approximate time of death, yet he wasn't certain even that would put an end to his questions about her.

Robertson's focus shifted across the room as if sorting through his thoughts. "You know, when Fleet Street got hold of the story, Mrs. Nettle dealt with it in a good fashion and didn't blabber. Not a complaint out of her, even when reporters painted her in a less than flattering light."

"They are rarely kind to any who come to their attention." Henry had his own poor experience with a few reporters who preferred to share only a portion of the truth in their stories, hoping to sell more papers. "The police force and Fleet Street are often at odds."

"Indeed. They finally gave her due credit when the details came out, though I suppose they only really relented because the truth was more interesting than their lies."

"Has she provided information on any of your cases since then?" Henry asked curiously.

"No, though I heard she helped another officer at some other division." Robertson frowned. "I can't remember the circumstances, but you could ask around. Someone must know."

"Did she send the message about your victim to you directly?" It continued to concern Henry that the medium had chosen to reach out to Amelia rather than the police. While Mrs. Nettle had admitted to being an avid reader of Amelia's articles, it still didn't make sense.

"To the station. I was the only one working on a missing person case at the time." The other inspector shrugged. "I suppose she picked the division closest to where she thought the body was."

"Interesting." So why hadn't she done so in Digby's case?

"I found her to be helpful and would be pleased to work with her again." The other inspector grinned. "Didn't think I'd ever say that about working with someone connected to the spirit world, but as I said, we wouldn't have solved the case without the details she provided. She cracked the case."

"Thank you." Henry stood, as did Fletcher. "What you've shared is helpful."

"But it hasn't convinced you," Robertson suggested, with a knowing smile.

"It's given us more to consider, at any rate." That was as much as Henry was willing to say. "Thanks again."

Henry waited until they were out of the police station before glancing at Fletcher. "Well?"

"He seems convinced the medium is real." Fletcher shook his head. "I'm not sure how that aids us."

"I find it somewhat reassuring, I suppose." Despite Robertson's comments, Henry would've preferred that Mrs. Nettle not be involved.

"Do you intend to speak with her again?"

"Not for the time being, though I'll verify her whereabouts. We shall continue with the investigation as we would any other, especially as she didn't offer any suggestions as to who killed the victim. Nor did she mention the murder weapon."

"Now if she'd provided a suspect or two, that would be something I'd like to hear about." The sergeant's eyes sparkled with amusement. "A medium who finds those guilty of crimes. I would wager Director Reynolds would hire her on the spot."

Henry chuckled. "Then you and I would most definitely be looking for a new line of work."

Fletcher grinned as he matched his stride to Henry's, the brisk air chilly, unwarmed by the sun. "Back to Scotland Yard now?"

"I'm going to stop by St. Thomas' first to see if the surgeon had a chance to examine the body, then I'll send a telegram requesting that Digby's mother's local force notify her." Though Henry preferred to advise family members in advance that a postmortem would be performed, he hadn't wanted to delay it when they hadn't known the victim's identity. "Can you verify the whereabouts of his colleagues? And the watchman as well? Jolly is a suspect until we can rule him out."

"Of course. Meet you at the Yard afterward to head out for a pie?"

"Yes. Hopefully we'll both have news to share."

They went their separate ways, and Henry quickly arrived at St. Thomas'. To his relief, Arthur Taylor was working on a report at his desk rather than over a body in the examination room.

Henry tapped on the open door and Arthur looked up with a smile.

"Morning, Henry. Come in." The surgeon gestured toward the empty chair in the small space.

"I hope the day finds you well, Arthur." Henry sat and glanced at the numerous papers and files on the man's desk. "Looks to be a busy one, eh?"

"I prefer to view my desk as a sign of being needed rather than overworked," Arthur jested as he followed Henry's gaze.

Henry grinned. "Clever. I might have to adopt that view as well."

Arthur had become more than just a colleague in recent months. Henry appreciated their friendship and had been doing his best to nurture it after realizing how solitary his life had become, even if most of their interactions started over a corpse.

The surgeon leaned back in his chair and studied Henry. "This should be an interesting case. Quite the injury to the victim's head, eh?"

"Terrible. We learned his name this morning. Clarence Digby."

Arthur wrote down the information, then looked at Henry with a lifted brow. "Clarence, eh?"

"Yes. He worked as a rail clerk until he was dismissed for stealing. Makes sense as he was found in the railyard."

"I see." The surgeon tapped the paper on his desk with one finger. "We have one minor problem. Or perhaps it's a major one."

"What might that be? What's wrong with him?"

Arthur smiled. "Nothing. The victim is a woman."

The air rushed from Henry's lungs as he processed the news. "A woman," he repeated steadily. "I thought his features had a feminine look to them, but still, I wouldn't have guessed." Chill bumps ran along his skin at the memory of the medium's confusion as to whether the victim was a man or a woman. He didn't know if that made Mrs. Nettle more credible or not. And in all honesty, he would've preferred she'd been wrong about some of the details. Perhaps he was letting his doubt about anyone who claimed to connect with spirits shade his objectivity.

"She had her chest bound and wore her hair short." Arthur shook his head. "If those with whom she worked didn't realize he was a she, it's understandable you didn't notice. She was well-practiced. It makes you wonder how long she'd been disguising herself."

"And why." Henry ran through the possibilities, still annoyed he hadn't seen through the disguise. "Perhaps she determined she could get a better position as a male. I don't think many rail clerks are female."

"True. And if she was in London alone, without family, she might have felt safer dressed as a male. It's not unheard of."

"Right." Henry heaved a sigh. "Still, it would be a difficult secret to keep for long. Several of those who knew him—her—said he kept to himself. *Herself.* That would explain why."

"Your note said a large wrench appeared to be the murder weapon?"

"Yes, from the railyard where we found the body."

"Ah." Arthur nodded. "That explains the size of the dent and the damage it did." He lifted a brow. "You're certain of the weapon? I didn't take the time to analyze the skull fracture thoroughly."

"Hair and brain matter were on the wrench, and it was beside the body, so I am as sure as I can be. Of course, anything else you could tell me would be welcome."

Arthur sorted through a few papers on his desk and pulled one out to read. "Based on the angle of the impact, I would estimate the person wielding the weapon to be at least several inches taller than the victim. Perhaps more. It's difficult to say for certain."

"The wrench is quite heavy and large." Henry held his hands out to show the length. "And a few shoe prints at the scene looked to be a man's. Though Digby is small."

"A logical conclusion until one learns the victim wore men's clothing. She had a knife hidden in her boot, but she didn't draw it."

Henry nodded. "I noticed that. The blow must've come as a surprise. The crime scene suggested she was struck just outside the door of an abandoned railway tunnel, then pulled inside and the door shut."

"Definitely sounds like a man then." Arthur frowned. "Or at the very least, a strong woman. How was the body found?"

Henry glanced toward the open door and lowered his voice, preferring not to be overheard. "A...well, a medium directed us to the location. Without her assistance, I'm not certain how long it would've taken before we discovered the victim. If at all."

"A medium? How intriguing." Arthur's eyes widened with curiosity.

"It's an odd set of circumstances, to say the least. In truth, I am hard pressed to believe the spirits conveyed the location of the body to her. It would be more logical to think she is somehow involved in the murder."

Arthur's expression became maddeningly unreadable. "Is this the same medium, by any chance, that helped the police with a case a few months ago?"

"You're familiar with it?"

"I read about it in the news sheet. Quite...interesting."

Henry nearly smiled at the term since he'd used it several times since the start of the investigation. "Did you conduct the postmortem?"

"No." The surgeon gave Henry a considering look. "Do you believe in ghosts or the medium's claim of being connected to the spiritual world?"

"It's difficult to know what to believe." Henry waited for his friend to share his opinion to no avail. Apparently, a bit of prodding was needed. "Do you?"

A long pause ensued, one Henry chose not to fill.

"I don't know," Arthur said at last in a quiet voice. "Between you and me, there have been a few occasions when an odd...sensation, shall we say, has come over me during an examination."

Henry stared at him, uncertain as to his meaning. "What sort of odd sensation?"

Arthur shrugged his shoulders. "The kind you don't tell anyone about in case they decide you belong in an asylum."

"You are one of the sanest people I know, and hearing about a feeling that came over you wouldn't change my opinion," Henry told him, curious to hear more.

"Good to know." Arthur slowly folded his arms over his chest, clearly feeling defensive about the admission despite Henry's friendly reassurance. "It is difficult to explain."

It sounded even more fascinating. "Try."

"It almost felt as if someone was looking over my shoulder, but no one was nearby. Yet there was more to it than that. As if my slicing open the flesh caused a ripple in the air. That whoever watched *reacted* to the cutting of their body. The air stirred, and I thought...I thought I saw a movement out of the corner of my eye, but nothing was there." He shook his head then rubbed a hand over his eyes. "Probably just my imagination and too many hours staring at the dead."

"And this has happened more than once?" Henry couldn't deny having experienced odd feelings when examining a crime scene once or twice. A heavy feel to the place. He'd put it down to his imagination as well. Strange, to think he might not be the only one.

"Yes." Arthur offered a rueful smile. "Ignore me if you prefer. But there are times when I wonder if a soul...lingers, in some situations. Perhaps because of unfinished business. Who knows? Perhaps Mrs. Nettle has a connection to those unable to move on to the next world, whatever that might be."

"Hmm. You have certainly given me much to think about." That was all Henry was willing to admit for now. He needed to reconcile his own questions on the subject first.

"It doesn't hurt to keep an open mind about such things. At the very least, some people believe in it, and so often what one believes..." Arthur shrugged.

"They find confirmation of," Henry supplied.

"Something like that."

Henry didn't know what he believed, but in many ways, that didn't matter. He had to follow the clues and evidence he uncovered. Any talk of ghosts, spirits, or the supernatural wasn't proof of anything—nor would it do any good for victims like Miss Digby.

And he certainly didn't care for the distress the medium had already caused Amelia.

Chapter Ten

There was no help for it; it had to be done. Or so Amelia told herself as she prepared to call on Mrs. Nettle.

Henry's reminder that she didn't have to circled in her thoughts; something she appreciated, as there was every chance she'd change her mind before she rang Mrs. Nettle's bell. But she detested the way her unease about speaking with the medium again lingered in her mind. She had no wish for anything to have that much power over her.

The message she'd started to pen to advise the woman that a body had, indeed, been found as she'd foreseen sat half done on Amelia's desk in the drawing room. Something about sending it rather than telling the medium in person felt cowardly, nor did she believe sending it would settle her restlessness over the matter.

Besides, she truly wanted to help Henry with the case, and there were limited ways she could do so. Speaking with the medium alone might prompt the woman to share something more about her visions—and if Mrs. Nettle mentioned Amelia's loved ones, she would simply tell her the topic wasn't to be discussed, and that was that.

If only such reassurance quieted the tiny voice inside her that longed for one more connection with the two people who had previously filled her entire world.

"The hansom cab has arrived, madam," Fernsby said from the drawing room doorway, sweeping away the voice for the time being.

"Perfect." Amelia pulled on her gloves and retrieved her reticule, her cloak already on, then paused to pet Master Leopold. "I shall return directly, good sir."

The cat continued to slumber, paying her absolutely no mind.

"He's clearly bothered by my upcoming departure," Amelia murmured as she shared an amused look with Fernsby.

"I like to think the young Master hides his upset until we depart," the butler advised with a twinkle in his eyes as he led the way down the stairs. "It wouldn't do for us to know how much we meant to him."

Amelia laughed, easily able to believe the cat was doing just that. "I'm certain you're right." She nodded her thanks as Fernsby held the front door for her. "I hope to return within an hour. Perhaps two, at the most."

"Take care, madam."

She took his words to heart and was soon settled in the cab on her way to Mrs. Nettle's home, already missing Henry's presence. She would hold tight to the memory of them sharing another enjoyable evening together; that would surely bolster her spirits for the upcoming conversation, which she suspected might be as uncomfortable as the first one.

How often could she invite Henry to dine with her before it became untoward, she wondered. Time with him was precious and something she wanted more of. Time alone with him, even more so. She would have to give the matter significant thought.

The drive was relatively short, and she reminded herself that the sooner the meeting was over, the better. That didn't keep nerves from tightening her stomach as she bid the driver to wait, then rang the bell.

The same maid answered the door. "Good day, Mrs. Greystone."

"And to you. I would like to speak with Mrs. Nettle, if she has a moment."

"Allow me to inquire, please."

Amelia waited briefly in the hall before being shown to the same reception room.

"Mrs. Greystone." The medium smiled in welcome. "How kind of you to call." She nodded at her maid. "Thank you, Ida."

"Of course, madam," the maid dipped her head and departed.

Mrs. Nettle gestured to a chair. "Please join me."

Amelia sat, doing her best to relax, or at least appear as though she was. "I wanted to advise you that a...a body was found at the railyard as you...predicted." Was that the proper term for it?

A gleam of satisfaction shone in the medium's eyes as she nodded, sinking onto the settee. While Amelia supposed that was natural when she'd just learned she'd been correct, it also seemed out of place given that someone had been murdered.

As if reading Amelia's thoughts, the gleam was gone in an instant. Perhaps it had never been there. "I'm sorry to hear that.

Was it...murder?" Mrs. Nettle asked, a wary look tightening her face.

Amelia's jaw tightened. "It was."

"Terrible news, though I hope the information I provided was helpful."

"Inspector Field mentioned it was."

"Good." Mrs. Nettle stared into the hearth, though once again no fire burned there, leaving the room rather chilly. "It is odd. Isn't it?"

Amelia waited a moment, but no explanation was forthcoming, making her wonder if she'd misheard. "I beg your pardon?"

The woman shook her head and offered a small smile, the shadows beneath her eyes evident. "My ability. My visions. It is a strange gift to have. I confess that at times, I struggle with it."

A wave of sympathy caught Amelia by surprise, though the emotion was likely because the medium was being less dramatic and more personable than the previous day. "I'm sure it's not easy."

"It's not." Her hostess glanced at the doorway and lowered her voice. "My husband thinks I should act with more confidence, but that feels impossible." Mrs. Nettle shifted to face Amelia more fully, the earnestness in her expression undeniable. "So few understand my ability. But how can I expect anything different when I don't always understand it myself?"

Amelia nodded, uncertain what if anything to say. Had the medium's attempt to act confidently resulted in the dramatic antics of the previous day? If so, Amelia would advise the woman against it.

"Mr. Nettle's support means the world to me, of course." She paused, biting her lip. "It's just that—"

"Good afternoon."

Amelia looked to see a man in the doorway, a polite smile on his face.

"I understand we have a visitor, my dear." The man continued into the room, looking between them with a direct and curious expression.

"Edward." Mrs. Nettle pushed to her feet, her smile appearing strained. "My dear, I—I didn't realize you would return so soon."

"I told you I planned to leave work early this afternoon," he said smoothly as he joined his wife, then turned to face Amelia. "You have forgotten. Or perhaps you weren't listening. Aren't you going to introduce me?"

Amelia watched the man even more closely, assuming this must be the medium's husband.

"Of course." Mrs. Nettle smoothed her hands along her skirts. "Edward, this is Mrs. Greystone, the correspondent from *London Life*. Mrs. Greystone, this is my husband, Edward Nettle."

Mr. Nettle appeared to be in his late thirties and wore a modest black woolen suit with a crimson tie and white shirt. His pale hair was collar-length and parted in the middle. Long sideburns narrowed his clean-shaven face, his hazel eyes wide with interest as they settled on Amelia.

"What a wonderful surprise," he said, only to frown as he studied Amelia. "But I thought she declined our request for an interview."

The man's rudeness was intolerable! Amelia didn't appreciate the way he spoke about her as if she weren't there.

Yet before she could respond, Mrs. Nettle quickly spoke. "Mrs. Greystone called to advise me that a body was found at the railyard, as I predicted, not about the article."

While Amelia told herself not to be quick to judge, she couldn't say she liked Mr. Nettle. Something about him already rubbed her the wrong way, including the way he seemed to make his wife nervous.

"How nice to meet you, Mr. Nettle." Amelia forced herself to smile politely. "As your wife said, I am not here regarding an article, but I still find it quite interesting to learn more about her ability."

"Oh?" He turned to the medium with a lifted brow. "And why would she share details about her gift without reason?"

Although looking at his wife, he directed the question at Amelia. It was not only disconcerting but belittling to both of them, as far as Amelia was concerned. She chose to ignore him and the question. Unpleasant man.

"Mrs. Nettle," she began briskly. "I wanted to ask if there was anything more you could tell me that might aid Inspector Field's investigation." Amelia offered an encouraging smile to the flustered woman.

"Oh. Well." She glanced at her husband before looking back at Amelia, her smile wan. "I can't think of anything."

"You mean you didn't *see* anything else," her husband suggested promptly.

"Yes. Yes, that's right." Mrs. Nettle quickly nodded, her cheeks flushing. "Thank you, dear."

Mr. Nettle offered a condescending smile to his wife as he placed a comforting arm around her. "I'm just happy to be able to lend you assistance, meager though it may be."

"I-I don't know what I'd do without you." Mrs. Nettle smiled at him, yet her hands trembled before she clasped them before her.

Amelia's annoyance at the man increased. The situation was uncomfortable, but she wanted to gain a better understanding of the odd relationship the couple seemed to have.

And more importantly, why Mrs. Nettle acted nervously around her husband.

"Now then," Mr. Nettle said as he assisted his wife to sit and then settled beside her, "what of Mary's prediction about the person at the railyard?"

Amelia hesitated, reluctant to tell him anything. "A body was indeed found, and an investigation is underway."

"Was it a man or a woman?" Mrs. Nettle asked, her brow puckered. "I received several conflicting messages regarding that."

"A man, I believe." Amelia didn't think Henry would mind her telling them that much. What harm would that detail do?

"You knew it was a man, remember?" her husband suggested. "You confirmed that before I left for work yesterday."

"Yes, of course." She smiled at Amelia, but it didn't reach her eyes. "I remember now."

Somehow, Amelia didn't think she did. Her husband's blatant control of his wife bothered Amelia almost as much as his condescending manner.

"How...how did he die?" Mrs. Nettle asked timidly.

"I'm sorry, but as it's an ongoing investigation, we're not at liberty to say." Stating that pleased Amelia from the inside out. 'We', her and Henry, even if her own role was unofficial at best. However, she liked to think she knew most of the rules Henry followed from the cases she'd been involved in and did her best to follow them.

"I hope it wasn't terribly brutal." Mrs. Nettle pressed a hand to her chest as if the worry weighed on her.

That only made Amelia think she knew it had been. What else might she know? "Are you certain there's nothing more you can tell us? The smallest details could prove helpful," Amelia pressed, her gaze holding on the medium. If only she'd had a chance to ask before her husband had arrived!

"I wish I knew more." The woman stared across the room, her thoughts clearly elsewhere. What was she thinking?

"Perhaps you'd like to learn about how Mrs. Nettle's gift works," her husband suggested to Amelia. "You must be curious about such things, given your own losses."

A shiver ran down Amelia's spine even as her stomach knotted. "My personal life is not anything I care to discuss," she said firmly, determined to make that clear. It was her line in the sand. The only reason she'd had the bravery to come here at all.

Mr. Nettle smiled. "I'm sure I understand why it makes you uncomfortable. Grief so often causes that reaction."

Though it was on the tip of Amelia's tongue to defend herself and explain why, she held back, certain that was what he wanted—for her to talk about the loved ones she'd lost.

"What do you do, Mr. Nettle?" Amelia asked, to guide the conversation elsewhere.

"I'm a manager at an investment firm. It's not far from here, so I often come by the house to check on Mary."

"I see." Did his wife require him to check on her? Did she like such surveillance?

"Her gift is unsettling at times and often leaves her...highly-strung." He glanced at his wife, taking her hand between his. "I offer whatever comfort I can."

"You certainly do." Mrs. Nettle nodded but didn't look at him.

"So often her visions come in the early morning hours. When that happens, she rises to jot down notes about what the spirits show her. Needless to say, she rarely sleeps well, which leaves her rather delicate."

Amelia was familiar with that issue as sleep had eluded her off and on over the years, grief making true rest nearly impossible for a time. "That must make for long nights for both of you."

"I often retire early." Mrs. Nettle appeared uncomfortable to have admitted as much, and sent a worried look toward her husband.

Amelia didn't care to know further details about their sleeping arrangements. "Are you usually able to interpret what you're being told?" she asked, unable to keep herself from asking, as her curiosity blossomed.

"Often, yes. Some visions are stronger than others. Some only appear when I am asleep or nearly so, most often in the early morning hours."

Amelia hesitated. Perhaps it would be wise to proceed with the article. Then she could ask more questions and better aid Henry. If possible, she'd prefer to return when Mr. Nettle wasn't there. She felt certain Mrs. Nettle would share more, if not for his looming presence.

"I am still considering the possibility of doing an article," Amelia began slowly. After all, a body had been found where the medium had said it would be, giving her more credibility.

"Oh?" Interest widened Mrs. Nettle's eyes. "I—"

"We can't tell you how delightful that would be," her husband interrupted.

It took all of Amelia's wherewithal not to glare at the man. Instead, she was careful to keep her attention on the medium. "I'm not certain of the exact nature of the report, but my intent would be to shed light on both the concept of divination and your unique skills."

"We would require Mary's gift to be featured in a positive manner, of course." The odious man patted his wife's hand, which he still gripped. "After all, there are times when she receives monetary gifts in exchange for her predictions."

Amelia stiffened. "If you hope an article will serve as some sort of advertisement for your ability, I will have to decline—"

"No, no, you misunderstand." Mr. Nettle shook his head, an amused look on his face. "Nothing of the sort. All we're suggesting—"

"You mean all *you're* suggesting?" Amelia corrected with an arched brow before he could continue. His wife might be willing to bow to his overstepping behavior, but she certainly would not.

Again, he smiled, but it didn't hold much friendliness. "I believe you will find we are of the same mind when it comes to Mary's gift."

Amelia returned the same chilly smile. "Then you won't mind if I hear it from her."

A flash of anger briefly darkened the man's eyes, but he said nothing further.

"What Edward and I would like t-to make clear is that if you find yourself unable to believe in my ability, it would be best if no article is written. I don't care to have my good name besmirched in...in any manner." The steel in Mrs. Nettle's voice was both surprising and pleasing, as far as Amelia was concerned. So she could speak her mind, if pushed.

"Do you think that might happen?" Amelia asked. If a body hadn't been found at the railyard, they wouldn't be having this conversation, as she would've kept with her initial refusal.

Mrs. Nettle lifted her chin. "No, I don't. In fact, I would hazard a guess that you, in particular, will find what I have to say and what I see enlightening."

The statement gave Amelia pause.

That was exactly what worried her.

Chapter Eleven

"A *WOMAN*, YOU SAY?" Fletcher shook his head in disbelief as they ate a late luncheon at one of their favorite pubs. "No. Surely not! How did we miss that?"

"My thoughts exactly." Henry grimaced, his pride still stinging from the oversight. Thinking the victim's features had appeared feminine didn't change that. Had he chosen to overlook the obvious because he hadn't wanted the medium to be correct about any of the details, but certainly not all of them? The thought bothered him more than he could say.

"Then again, if none of his—her co-workers or her superiors noticed, why would we?" The sergeant wiped his moustache after taking a sip of his ale. "*Miss* Digby's mother must've been aware of the ruse as Mr. Weston from the railyard mentioned meeting her."

The luncheon hour had come and gone, but they weren't the only ones eating. The low murmur of voices helped to keep their own conversation relatively private.

"I can only guess that pretending to be a man made it easier to find a better-paying position, not to mention keep her safer." The more Henry thought about it, the more sense it made. He certainly wouldn't want someone like Amelia living in a lodging house with strangers.

The steaming meat pie and an ale were more than welcome, given the damp chill of the April afternoon. Discussing cases over a meal allowed them to share any information they'd learned as well as consider various theories: in this case, the unexpected twist was that of the victim being a woman rather than a man.

Fletcher nodded. "Not an easy thing to do for any length of time. Perhaps her mother will explain after being informed of her daughter's death."

"That would be helpful." Henry had sent a telegram to the local police to advise them of the situation and ask them to give the news to Mrs. Digby. "So. We have a victim, a name, a weapon, but nothing on the killer," he summarized.

"Other than he can swing a hefty wrench with enough force to crush a person's skull," Fletcher added before taking another bite.

Luckily the sergeant's appetite was rarely dimmed by grisly conversations, and neither was Henry's.

"That's not even a start." Henry frowned as he studied the other patrons while he ate, musing about the puzzle that faced them.

Fletcher didn't respond, only taking another sip of his drink.

"We have a guess as to why the victim was at the railyard, but how did the killer come to be there?" Henry asked quietly.

While he wasn't comfortable following hunches or making assumptions, it often helped to discuss the various possibilities about the movements and motivations of the parties involved.

Theories, that's what they needed. Theories they could then eliminate with cold, hard facts.

"He could've simply followed Digby," Fletcher suggested. "Perhaps he caught sight of him—or rather, her—on the street, or somehow knew she'd recently sold some things and was plump with cash."

"Then why didn't he take it? A quick search would've revealed the notes in Miss Digby's pocket." Henry took another bite, thoughts churning as he searched for a plausible reason.

"Perhaps the killer was interrupted before he had a chance to do so. The watchman was surely making his rounds, even if he didn't see anything." Fletcher shrugged. "Then again, it's a good-sized railyard for one man to watch with far too many hiding places, especially in the pitch black of night."

"Indeed." Henry took another bite as he considered other ideas. "The killer could've known Digby."

"Right. Might've had a problem with her stealing from the railyard. Took it personal, for some reason."

That didn't ring true to Henry. "They could've argued about something, something important, and the murderer struck Miss Digby in a fit of rage."

Fletcher nodded. "Perhaps he was angry to discover *he* was actually a *she*."

"An interesting idea." Yet it raised more questions than answers, as far as Henry was concerned. "The killer might be associated with the railway station in some manner. Or he could've seen Miss Digby on the street, followed her through the broken fence, and into the railyard."

"Because he guessed she was female?"

"Maybe." Yet that seemed unlikely when none of Miss Digby's fellow employees had realized—or why a suspected man's femininity would warrant such a vicious response.

"The shoe prints we found at the scene suggest the killer wasn't the average man who lives or works in the neighborhood."

"True," Henry agreed. "It looked to be more of a dress shoe than a boot, like most wear in that area."

"Which makes it all the more curious that he was out at night in poor weather on rough streets." Fletcher's eyes narrowed. "I am at a loss to think of any other possible connections between them."

Henry played with a few possibilities out loud. "It could be someone from Miss Digby's past. Perhaps a person from her home who now lives in London. Perhaps she doesn't always dress as a man—a spurned lover? We could look into those she worked with more, but if she chose to steal and sell a few things while employed at a decent position, what—and who—might she have been involved with after being fired?"

"She was up to no good, based on the pound notes in her pocket." Fletcher lifted a brow. "The killer could be from a previous deal gone wrong."

"Then why not take the money in Miss Digby's pocket?" Henry couldn't get past that detail. "Even if the murder had nothing to do with the money, surely the murderer found it—so why not take it?"

"The case is a puzzle, though I suppose they all start that way." The sergeant scowled. "I just can't see where we go from here."

Nor could Henry as of yet. "Maybe the policeman from her village will tell us something helpful."

"Or they'll confirm she was trouble even before she came to London."

Henry frowned. "She still didn't deserve to die in such a brutal manner."

"No one does. Regardless, we still have a case to solve." Fletcher drained the rest of his ale. "I suppose we'd best get on with it."

"Let's see if a reply awaits us at the Yard then decide our next steps." Henry wanted something to point him in the proper direction, but that was probably too much to hope for.

A telegram had arrived, but was of little help. The local policeman was familiar with a Miss Clarissa Digby, and said she'd received a warning for petty theft a few months before she'd left for London. Her widowed mother was in ill health and devastated to learn of her death. Clarissa had been her only child and had been sending money home for her care.

"Our victim might have had her heart in the right place, even if she was going about it the wrong way," Fletcher said with a shake of his head as he read the telegram.

"Unfortunate circumstances." Regardless of them, they needed to find the killer. "Let's return to King's Cross with the sketch and see if we can find anyone who knew her. She might have sold whatever she stole near there since she had the money on her person." Henry knew it was a shot in the dark, but he also knew they had to keep asking questions until they found someone who could answer them.

They walked as a steady drizzle fell. The weather never seemed to bother Fletcher; at least, he rarely complained. No doubt that time in Her Majesty's Royal Navy had toughened him. As far as Henry was concerned, the weather was something that couldn't be changed, so there was no point in spending much time thinking about it. That didn't mean he appreciated his damp coat, the water dripping from the brim of his hat to obscure his vision, or the rain drizzling down his trousers to eventually dampen his socks.

"Where would you find someone willing to buy stolen items in a neighborhood like this?" Henry asked quietly as they paused under an overhang to survey the street.

"Some pawnbrokers might look the other way," Fletcher suggested. "Or a pub makes a good meeting place if she sold it to an individual."

Henry nodded. "It's worth showing a few people our sketch to see if we gain a reaction."

Two hours later they'd been to several pawnshops, some less reputable than others, a couple of pubs, and spoken to a few people they'd stopped on the street who worked in the area. No one recognized Miss Digby.

"We need a thief to tell us where to look for a thief," Henry mused.

Fletcher snorted as he gestured to his uniform. "Not sure where you're going to find one who will talk to us."

An idea struck. "I know someone who might be able to help us." He met Fletcher's gaze with a smile. "Marcus."

Fletcher grinned in return. "The lad has proven his worth time and again."

Henry had met the boy in Whitechapel while working on another case and had a good feeling about him from the start. Marcus had watched a lodging house for him and provided information that had been pivotal in the rookery killer case.

"This isn't his neighborhood, though." The sergeant lifted a brow. "Do you think he could still help?"

"Well, it might take him time to gain his bearings, but he has a feel for people, and there's a chance he could learn something to aid us." Henry shrugged. "Anything at this point would be helpful. I'll ask and see if he's interested."

As smart as the lad was, Henry would like to see him in school, but Marcus had only laughed and shaken his head when he'd suggested it the previous week. That didn't mean Henry was going to give up on him.

"Did you discover anything about his mother or father?" Fletcher asked. "Or whether he has any family living?"

"He mentioned them in passing, but I have to wonder if he did so to ease my concern. I will continue asking and hope he eventually tells me the truth."

Children in areas like Whitechapel lived a difficult life, Henry knew, but for many it was all they'd ever known. Accepting change of any sort, including a helping hand, didn't come easily. Henry had seen that firsthand when a local church offered the mudlarks the opportunity to attend school. Some had been eager to go, but others were wary and had refused.

"First we have to find him," Henry said heavily. "If you'd prefer to return to the Yard—"

"Not a chance that I'd allow you to venture there alone," Fletcher interrupted sternly. "We should have just enough time before the day's end to make it there and have a look around for him." He glanced at his pocket watch, then up at the sky. "At least the rain's eased."

Eased but not ended. For that reason, Henry caught a hansom cab, which dropped them off a few streets from Whitechapel.

Marcus had a knack for finding Henry, and he could only hope that proved true today. They made their way to Dorset Street, keeping a sharp eye out for the lad without success.

"I wish I knew somewhere to leave him a message," Henry murmured as they paused on a street corner to look around.

"That would be helpful." Fletcher shook his head. "Perhaps we'll have to try again come morning."

Henry didn't like to waste more time, but he wanted to keep in touch with the lad and make certain he was all right. Giving him a few errands and other small tasks allowed him to earn a coin or two. The amount wasn't much to Henry, but he hoped it made a difference as to whether Marcus went to bed with a full stomach.

They were returning the way they had come when movement across the street caught Henry's attention. Marcus—the boy darted around a cart and caught up with them.

"Wotcha! Wot brings you two fine gentlemen to my Whitechapel?" the lad asked with a grin.

"You." Henry returned the smile, pleased to see he looked well. "I need some help and thought you might be interested."

"Oh?" Marcus tucked his thumbs in the pockets of his oversized, tattered jacket and rocked back on his heels. "I might be."

Henry explained the situation and what they needed.

"King's Cross, you say?" Marcus frowned as he looked down the street. "I've only been there a time or two, but it's not far." He returned his attention to Henry and gave a single nod. "I'll give it a go."

"Excellent." Yet Henry couldn't hold back his worry even as he handed him a coin. Not for a minute could he forget they were trying to find a murderer. "Don't do anything that puts you in danger."

"Never met danger." Marcus offered a cheeky grin.

"Where can I leave a message for you if I need to?" Henry asked, forcing down a smile.

Marcus considered the question for a moment. "Jack at the Royal Arms might be willin' to pass messages for us. It's a pub, next street over."

Henry took note of the name. "Leave word with him if you hear anything, and I'll do the same." He held Marcus' gaze. "If you learned to read and write, you wouldn't have to tell Jack or anyone else what you need."

Marcus chortled. "Wot, me? Learn to read and write? Not likely. See ya." Before Henry could argue, the boy took off down the street and quickly disappeared into the crowd.

"Let him think on the offer for a time," Fletcher advised. "Chances are he'll come around when he realizes you're serious about helping him."

"I hope so." And yet Henry couldn't ignore the other people along the street of various ages, all of whom needed a hand. He couldn't aid everyone, but hoped assisting one or two made a difference.

Not for the first time, he thought of Amelia and how often she helped others, from the ravenkeeper's daughter to the mudlarks to Master Leopold, not to mention Henry himself. He was blessed to know her and hoped she felt the same way about him.

Chapter Twelve

AMELIA SENT A SHORT message to Henry's lodging house upon her return home from Mrs. Nettle's; she hadn't learned anything from the medium, but that was also important to tell him. Though tempted to ask him to come by when he had time, she held back. He was surely busy, and they had just seen each other the previous evening.

That didn't keep her from feeling rather lonely as the remainder of the day crawled by. Though she attempted to keep herself occupied with writing letters and reading, her mind frequently wandered.

A knock on the door as she was finishing dinner that evening lifted her hope that perhaps he'd read her mind.

Fernsby stepped out of the dining room to open it. "Good evening, Inspector Field."

Amelia rose from the table and moved into the hall, delighted that Henry had come by.

Thrilled, in fact.

"A rainy one at any rate." Henry smiled as he met Amelia's gaze. "I hope I'm not calling too late, but I just received your message."

"Not at all." She gestured toward the dining room. "I've just finished dinner, but there's plenty if you haven't yet eaten."

"I have, thank you."

Disappointment dimmed her happiness. Surely that meant his visit would be brief.

Henry's gaze shifted between herself and the butler with a hopeful look. "Though I wonder if I might ask what was for dessert?"

Fernsby smiled. "Lemon sponge cake with a spiced drizzle."

"Would you care for some?" Amelia asked, appreciating Henry's levity and certain Fernsby did as well.

"Oh, I wouldn't want to impose," Henry grinned with a boyish expression that had both Amelia and Fernsby laughing.

"If you would fetch a generous slice of cake, Fernsby, I am certain the Inspector would appreciate it."

"Of course, madam. Allow me to take your coat, sir," Fernsby said. "I shall place it by the stove in the kitchen with the hope of it drying while you enjoy some dessert."

"How kind. Thank you." Henry gave a mock shiver. "I confess that I have been damp most of the day."

"You must be chilled to the bone." Amelia walked closer, her sympathy caught. "Why don't we enjoy the cake by the fire in the drawing room so you can warm yourself?"

"I would like that very much."

"I will be back directly," Fernsby advised and, with Henry's jacket in hand, moved toward the rear of the house.

"I didn't expect you to come by, but I'm pleased you did," Amelia said as she led the way upstairs.

"I had a few other stops to make which were completed sooner than I expected, so I thought I would call to see how the meeting with Mrs. Nettle went." He lifted a brow. "The meeting I thought we agreed wasn't necessary."

Amelia appreciated the concern in his tone but waited until they reached the drawing room before responding. "I decided it was better to speak with her in person with the hope that doing so would allow me to learn more about the victim—and help to put the medium's request for an interview behind me." She gestured toward the sideboard where the crystal decanters stood. "A whiskey to help warm you?"

"Thank you, yes," Henry said, then moved to stand before the fire. "And did it allow you to put it behind you?"

Amelia poured a short measure and handed it to him before taking her usual seat. "Not particularly." She sighed, wishing her face did not reveal the tension she felt. "I am still considering whether to write the article, so asked a few more questions. I also met her husband."

"Oh?" Henry sat in the chair next to hers. "How did you find him?"

She'd been mulling over the meeting since her return and still wasn't sure. Merely stating 'unpleasant' was perhaps unfair. "He's rather controlling, which I did not care for. I think Mrs. Nettle might have said more if he hadn't interrupted our conversation. She did say her husband thought she should act more confidently. I wondered if that was the reason for the penchant toward the dramatic that we noted during our first meeting with her. She was much altered today."

"If so, I would like to advise her that it makes her less believable, not more so," Henry said dryly, then took a sip.

"My thought exactly. He also said that if I were to write the article that I should take care not to show Mrs. Nettle's ability in a poor light, and that she often received financial reward." Amelia shook her head. "His comment made me think he hoped the story might be some sort of publicity for her services."

"And you didn't care for that either, I would imagine."

"No, I did not. I made that clear." She waved a hand vaguely. "Of course, they both denied it, but still."

"It makes you wonder." Henry nodded, clearly in agreement.

"It does." If only she knew what the best course of action was. "I'm still not sure if I should proceed."

Henry pondered her question for a moment, his brow furrowed. "What reasons do you have for wanting to write it when the subject matter makes you uncomfortable?"

Amelia hesitated, wondering how honest she should be. "I...I would very much like to be helpful to your investigation, and I still think speaking more with Mrs. Nettle might provide additional clues to aid you—"

"I won't deny that we could use more in the case," Henry interrupted gently, "but I'm not convinced she will be of further help."

"That crossed my mind as well." Amelia stared into the fire, knowing there was more to it, but still undecided how much to share. Would Henry even wish to hear that she was thinking of her late husband? "I do think it is an intriguing subject and would be of interest to many readers."

"But surely not at the expense of your peace of mind," Henry added, leaning close to place a hand on her arm. "If today's second meeting made you uneasy yet again, I can't see how additional conversations would be any different."

Amelia rested her hand on top of his, appreciating the physical support as much as the verbal. "I'm sure you're right." She bit her lip, wishing she felt differently. "Yet I will admit, I don't seem to be able to let it go."

"Because of your potential personal connection to her gift?"

To her intense relief, his tone held no judgment. Instead, he sounded matter-of-fact, as if her feelings were to be expected. "I suppose that's it." With a sigh, Amelia continued, "What if...what if Matthew and Lily are the reasons I met Mrs. Nettle?"

Henry held her gaze. "How so?"

Amelia looked away, feeling ridiculous even to suggest it. "What if somehow...someway...they are trying to reach out to me through her?" She risked a look at Henry, certain he would think her half-crazed.

Before he could answer Fernsby entered the room with a tray holding an open bottle of dessert wine, two glasses, and two very generous slices of lemon sponge cake. "Here we are."

The efficient butler set the tray on the low table and served, giving Amelia time to regret her words. She was being ridiculous and shouldn't have shared her feelings with anyone, let alone Henry. She was a woman of science, and there was no proof spirits could communicate with the living. Henry had already expressed his doubts about the supernatural and Mrs. Nettle, regardless of the fact that they'd found a body exactly where the medium had said. His opinion added to her own wariness and caused Amelia to view Mrs. Nettle in a suspicious light.

She took the glass of wine Fernsby offered and sipped, hoping it would help steady her for what would surely be an uncomfortable conversation. Hopefully Henry wouldn't think less of her for what she'd said. Their relationship was too new to test it in such a manner.

"Thank you, Fernsby, and please thank Mrs. Appleton for me as well," Henry said, his gaze fixed on the slice of cake.

"Of course. Will there be anything else, madam?"

"This is perfect," Amelia replied, her voice carefully steady. "Thank you, Fernsby." She waited until the butler departed before looking at Henry. "Please forget I said that," she told him, embarrassment heating her cheeks.

Henry ignored the cake and the wine and instead reached for Amelia's hand as he stood.

Her heart leapt to her throat as she set down her glass and rose as well. *Oh, no.* Did he intend to leave? Had she chased him away before they'd had a chance to better know one another? "I'm so sorry—"

"Amelia."

She forced herself to look him in the eye, her heart racing.

"There is no need to apologize for sharing your thoughts and feelings with me. *Ever.*"

A flutter of emotion filled her, lifting her spirits the way the wine hadn't. "I appreciate you saying that."

Henry drew her closer, the proximity sending her stomach dancing. "I value your thoughts and opinions. You have every right to feel the way you do about your loved ones reaching out." He offered a wry look. "I was reminded several times today that there are many things in this world we don't understand, and the afterlife is most definitely one of them."

"Yet despite that, I doubt that changed your opinion about spiritualism," she said with a smile even as she rested a hand on his chest, appreciating the intimate contact.

He returned her smile warmly. "Not yet, though this case is far from over. But even if our opinions were to differ on this or any other issue, it wouldn't change my feelings for you." His focus held on her for a long moment until his gaze dropped to her lips. Before Amelia could think, could breathe, he gently kissed her.

Desire stirred, but before it could take a firm hold he drew back, the tenderness and admiration on his face squeezing her heart.

Amelia blinked, trying to clear the haze now filling her mind so she could offer an intelligent reply. "Nor...nor would it change how I feel about you, Henry."

He nodded and released her, gently caressing her cheek, the intensity in his gaze sending her pulse hammering. "I am pleased we are of the same mind."

Same *heart*, she almost corrected, but held back. That might be how she felt, yet she couldn't assume his feelings were growing at the same rapid pace as hers. She'd already nearly overstepped this evening and didn't want to risk doing so again.

His gaze shifted to the plate of cake, lifting the tension of the moment.

"Please do not delay enjoying your dessert on my account," Amelia said with a laugh as they each took their seats.

"I didn't realize I had such an affinity for dessert until enjoying several of Mrs. Appleton's concoctions." Henry took a bite, clearly savoring the taste. "She, at least, has a mystical talent."

"Indeed she does."

He took another forkful before looking at her. "Now then. To return to our discussion, I can tell you that I spoke with the Nettles' maid and a male servant earlier today, and both verified the couple was home the night of the murder."

Amelia nodded, feeling a small measure of relief. "So you've removed them from the list of potential suspects?"

To her surprise, Henry hesitated before answering. "For now, though I can't dismiss my unease that Mrs. Nettle knew the location of the body." He shook his head. "At any rate, please know I will support whatever decision you make about the article, but don't proceed with the interview purely for the sake of the case. I'd much prefer you consider your own feelings. That should be your priority. It should always be."

"Thank you. I appreciate you saying so." Amelia retrieved her wine glass as she pondered the situation further, gaze momentarily focused on the golden liquid. "I believe I will sleep on it and decide tomorrow."

"A wise choice." Henry nodded. "I wonder what her husband does, that he was home in the afternoon during your visit."

"I asked, as I had the same question. He is a manager at an investment firm not far from their home."

His eyes narrowed at the information. "Still seems odd."

"Much like Mr. Nettle." The words slipped out before Amelia could stop them.

Henry chuckled. "You clearly didn't care for him, did you?"

"I didn't care for the way he treated his wife—or me, for that matter." She shook her head. "They make an odd pair."

"In that case, I rather hope you decide against writing an article." Henry finished every crumb of the cake then reached for his wine, seeming in no hurry to depart. "That was delicious."

"May I ask what you discovered about the railyard victim today? What do you know of him?" If she did decide to proceed, the more she knew about the investigation, the better.

"I'm pleased you asked, as the case has taken an interesting turn. The victim has a name. Clarissa Digby."

Amelia stilled in surprise. "Clarissa—a woman?" The medium's confusion about whether the person was male or female returned to her mind.

"Yes. She worked as a rail clerk, disguising herself as a man so well that none of her coworkers realized the truth, as far as we know. She was dismissed two weeks ago for theft."

"Ah. A poor choice on her part," Amelia suggested, mind still reeling at the new information.

"Definitely, though it seems to have been a pattern started before she came to London. Perhaps her family's financial situation was dire, but still. She was the only child of a widowed woman in ill health."

"A terrible loss for her mother."

"Yes. One made worse since she died in such a violent manner."

Amelia nodded. Her late husband had been murdered, but was a gunshot preferable to having one's skull crushed by a heavy object? Was there a hierarchy of ways to be murdered?

Henry sighed, his brow furrowing. "Now I am the one who should apologize. I didn't mean to remind you—"

She held up a hand to stop him. "There is no need to say anything of the sort. Nor do you need to shield me from such things. I will tell you if something you say about one of your cases upsets me." In truth, she couldn't imagine doing that. She already knew how harsh life could be. Had lived it.

"I'm pleased to hear that." His smile was gentle as he held her gaze.

They spoke of inconsequential things for a time and Amelia relaxed, enjoying Henry's company more than she could say. The thought of more evenings like this pleased her. In all honesty, it was the ones without him that didn't.

And she wasn't quite sure what to think about that.

Chapter Thirteen

THE FOLLOWING MORNING, HENRY and Fletcher returned to King's Cross station. It was surely too soon to hope for a message from Marcus, and there was always a chance the boy wouldn't learn anything helpful.

After pondering the case during the walk home from Amelia's the previous evening, Henry concluded the railyard itself had to be the key. Both the victim and the murderer had been in the area the night of the murder.

A rainy, miserable night.

There had to be a reason they'd both been out. Miss Digby had surely been selling ill-gotten items nearby, but what of her killer? Did he reside or work in the area?

Assuming Miss Digby had found a person in the vicinity to sell whatever she'd recently stolen, someone must have seen her. Her youthful appearance and slight build might have caught the attention of a passerby on the street. Though the odds weren't great they'd find that person, it was still worth trying.

But first, Henry wanted to know how no one who worked with Miss Digby had realized she was a woman.

"I believe another conversation with Mr. Weston, Miss Digby's superior, is in order," Henry advised Fletcher as they neared the railway station. "I'll be interested to see his reaction to the news about Digby being a miss and not a mister."

"As will I." Amusement gleamed in the sergeant's eyes.

"Afterward, we'll each take a copy of the sketch and see if anyone in the area recognizes her, starting from the railyard and working our way out."

"A logical plan." Fletcher's tone reflected a definite lack of enthusiasm, his previous amusement vanished.

Henry glanced at the sergeant with a knowing smile. "Logical but tiring?" he suggested.

"Only because we rarely discover much with that kind of questioning," Fletcher admitted with an easy shrug. "But what else can we do without a clue or two to aid us?"

"Perhaps Mr. Weston will surprise us."

A grunt was Fletcher's only response. The sergeant's lack of optimism didn't bother Henry, especially not after spending another enjoyable evening with Amelia which had considerably lightened his mood—even if worry over her safety persisted.

Mr. Weston stood with a nod as they entered his office. "You've saved me from sending you a message." He gestured to the chairs before his desk.

"Oh?" Henry shared a curious look with Fletcher.

"I have just been advised that we've received several complaints of stolen items from the baggage compartments." Mr. Weston appeared less than pleased by the news. "One employee claims to have seen Mr. Digby exiting the area. He called out to stop him, but Mr. Digby hurried away. Makes me think he was guilty."

"What items were taken?" Henry asked, pulling out his notebook. Any information could prove helpful—more motives for murder, perhaps?

"Several rather valuable pieces of jewelry, among other things."

"Is it possible to request a description or sketch of the items? Especially any distinctive ones," Henry requested. 'Jewelry' wasn't much to go on. "That would not only increase the chance of locating them so they can be returned to their rightful owners, but could aid us in solving the crime."

"I will ask." Mr. Weston shook his head ruefully. "Gives the railway a bad reputation. It's a shame that we have to ask customers to provide those details."

"Perhaps it is an inconvenience, but still necessary if they want even a chance of having their property returned." Henry was pleased when Mr. Weston nodded in agreement.

"Of course, it won't matter to our customers that we dismissed the employee in question before this unfortunate...incident."

"Maybe it should matter that the person is dead," Fletcher said in his usual blunt manner.

Mr. Weston's mouth gaped before he quickly shut it, apparently thinking better of whatever he'd been about to say. "Right."

"The sooner we receive the descriptions, the better," Henry advised, trying hard not to smile at his sergeant's antics.

The man nodded curtly. "I will see what can be done and send word as soon as they're available."

"Thank you." Henry cleared his throat. "While we are here, there is something you should be aware of."

"Oh?" Mr. Weston looked between them.

"Digby was actually a *Miss* Clarissa Digby. A woman."

The man's eyes went wide with shock before he frowned, his disbelief evident. "That's...no. That's impossible. There has to be some mistake."

Henry pulled out the sketch in case he needed a reminder. "The victim had a youthful appearance and somewhat feminine features."

Mr. Weston shook his head severely as he stared at the drawing. "Yes, but—"

"He was a she," Fletcher interrupted. "Trust us. An autopsy rather reveals such things. There's no getting around it."

"Humph." The man's lips tightened as if to keep himself from arguing the point. "It's rather incredible to think none of us realized that fact."

"Is there a chance someone discovered the truth and...took offense?" Henry watched him closely but saw only genuine bewilderment.

"And killed him? I mean to say, her?" Mr. Weston considered the question for a moment. "Impossible. It is never pleasant to realize one has been duped, but to commit murder in retaliation? I cannot believe it."

"I would like to advise the employees who worked directly with her of the truth, to gauge their reaction all the same," Henry said lightly.

"As you wish." The man didn't seem to take in his words, still processing their news.

Henry tucked away the sketch and his notebook. "We look forward to receiving the descriptions of the missing items soon. Now if we could speak with those employees, we would appreciate it."

Miss Digby's supervisor, the short man who seemed to take offense at anyone taller than him, appeared the most surprised. "That can't be," he insisted. "I would have known."

"There is no question that she was a woman, but we are quite curious as to how no one noticed," Henry said with a lifted brow.

The supervisor scoffed, as if he was still unable to believe it. "He—I suppose, she—was gruff. Unfriendly, disinclined to converse with other employees. Kept to himself, was efficient with his work until I caught him stealing. Her," he corrected himself once again.

While the man was clearly shocked, he didn't appear angry, nor did the other employees show anything but surprise by the news.

Once they'd returned to the street, Fletcher glanced at Henry. "None of them appear to be an obvious suspect."

"Agreed." Henry rather wished one had so they had a lead to follow.

"At least now we know how Miss Digby came to have the notes in her pocket," Fletcher added. "Jewelry, eh?"

"Yes, but I'm not sure how much it will help, especially since we already questioned nearby pawnbrokers without success."

"Digby must've sold the items to an individual—if we're to believe the pawnbrokers." Fletcher grimaced. "I suppose that means whoever it was will be nearly impossible to find."

"Which puts us back to our original plan." Henry pulled out the sketches of the victim and handed one to Fletcher. "You work this side of the street, and I'll work the other. Meet back here in an hour. We'll decide which other streets to cover after that."

Fletcher had the right of it, Henry decided by the time luncheon had arrived—it was a rarity that they discovered much using this kind of questioning, and his inquiries today were just as disappointing.

"Anything?" he asked Fletcher when the sergeant returned.

"Nothing. Hard to believe we haven't come upon someone who recognized her."

Yet it only took a glance around to see how many passed through the area, making it easier to understand how a young 'man' without distinguishing features had managed to blend in. Between the pair of them, they'd shown the sketch to numerous people with nothing to show for it.

"Fish and chips, hot and ready!" a man called on the street corner, his cart with its small tin chimney emitting puffs of steam.

"Hungry?" Henry pointed toward the cart, his stomach growling at the appetizing scent. "Perhaps some sustenance will stir a few ideas."

First they showed the sketch to the food seller, who shook his head, before they ordered the hot meal served in paper. Neither of them was eager to return to what felt like a pointless task.

Henry sighed, stomach sated but hunger for knowledge left entirely unfulfilled. "Let's return to Scotland Yard and see what else requires our attention. With luck, the descriptions of the jewelry will provide us with a new avenue of inquiry."

"Good idea," Fletcher readily agreed. "Maybe working another case will clear our heads on this one."

"How's your uncle coming along?" Henry asked as they started toward the Yard.

Fletcher's uncle, Edward Clarke, had been promoted to inspector just over a month before, and gained his nephew's assistance with investigations from time to time.

Fletcher shook his head, his pace matching Henry's. "He's working a case involving the theft of a museum painting, but it's not going particularly well. The only potential suspects have solid alibis. Leads have dwindled to nothing."

"How frustrating." And a scenario familiar to Henry and every other detective.

They were both quiet on the remainder of the walk, each lost in their thoughts.

As they were about to enter the Yard, Constable Dannon stepped out. "Inspector Field. I was just coming to look for you. Sergeant Johnson received a message addressed to you—says it's urgent."

Alarm filled Henry, his thoughts flying immediately to Amelia. He hurried inside to the front desk where Sergeant Johnson oversaw things. "You have a message for me?"

"Here it is." Johnson reached into a drawer calmly and handed it to him. "Arrived a half hour ago. The scruff of a lad who delivered it said it was urgent."

The masculine writing on the envelope was unfamiliar, offering no exterior clues. Henry tore it open, aware of Fletcher, Dannon, and Johnson watching him with concern.

His gaze dropped to the signature at the bottom—Martin Tisdale. Mr. Tisdale? The man was a friend of his father's and someone Henry had known for a long time, but had not spoken to recently.

"Not bad news, I hope," Fletcher murmured.

Henry quickly skimmed the message, then read it again more slowly as his stomach dropped. "Actually, it is. The daughter of a friend of my father's is missing."

Eleanor Tisdale, whom Henry had known since her youth, had failed to return that morning after spending the night at a friend's after attending the theater. Mr. Tisdale had sent a carriage to collect her, only to be advised that she had never been there. He hoped Henry would help find her.

"Needless to say, her parents are worried." Henry couldn't imagine what might've happened. "I'll call on them and send word if I need you," he advised Fletcher.

Henry rushed out the door and hailed a hansom cab. The well-to-do family lived on the outskirts of Mayfair, and he had been to their home many times over the years, the Tisdales friends with his parents for as long as he could remember.

Eleanor, missing? It was unthinkable and terribly concerning.

It was rare for him to work on investigations in which he was familiar with the person involved. After all, it clouded one's judgement and reduced objectivity. But he would do all he could to help as both a friend and a detective in this case, at least until he determined his personal connection had become a disadvantage.

With luck, by the time he arrived at the Tisdale residence Eleanor would be home, and the entire trip would be for nothing.

He certainly hoped so.

Eleanor was a lovely young woman of nineteen years with her whole future ahead of her. She was headstrong but not unreasonably so, even if her parents occasionally thought otherwise. They had high hopes she would marry well, but Eleanor had confided to Henry over the Christmas festivities that she had other plans, though she wouldn't share any details.

He soon arrived at the familiar home and, from the moment he was shown inside, knew Eleanor had not yet returned. The somber attitude of the servants and the heaviness in the air were undeniable. He was shown directly to Mr. Tisdale's study, a book-lined space with dark wood paneling and a walnut desk with ornate detailing.

"Henry." The older gentleman stood and rounded the desk to shake Henry's hand with both of his own, his features pinched. He looked much older than his sixty years compared to the last time Henry had seen him. "Thank you for coming so quickly."

"Of course. There's been no word from Eleanor?"

"None at all." He shook his head as if hardly able to believe it. "I keep thinking there has to be some sort of mistake..."

"Your message said you thought she planned to spend the night with a friend?" Henry guided the shaken man to a chair and sat down as well.

"Yes. Eleanor and Caroline Walters were to attend the theater, something they've done together in the past. Eleanor said she would spend the night with her since it would be late, and they were sharing a modiste visit the next morning before she returned home." He rubbed a hand across his forehead as if a headache brewed there. "When she hadn't appeared by luncheon I sent the carriage for her, but the coachman returned without her, saying she wasn't there."

Henry's stomach twisted. That did not sound promising. "Did the young ladies attend the theater as planned?"

"No," replied the older man, worry etched across his brow. "No, it's worse than that. Caroline and her parents told the coachman they didn't know anything about it—that Caroline had no plans with Eleanor. Not for the theater nor spending the night nor the modiste. She...she lied to us."

Though Henry longed to offer reassurance that all would be well, he didn't want to give false hope until he knew more. "Do any of the servants know anything? Her lady's maid, perhaps?"

Her father shook his head. "She said Eleanor seemed especially excited for the evening when she helped her dress. But otherwise, the girl didn't notice anything amiss."

"Did you see any change in Eleanor's behavior the last few days?" There had to be a sign, a clue somewhere.

"No," came the reply, only for Eleanor's father to grimace. "Well...we have been arguing more often than usual of late, but nothing terribly serious. She is certainly in no hurry to marry, much to her mother's dismay."

Henry took out his notebook, knowing the sooner he learned all he could, the sooner they could find Eleanor. The urgency gripping him didn't bode well.

Hopefully this missing person case wouldn't end in murder.

Chapter Fourteen

HENRY FINISHED QUESTIONING MR. Tisdale, then spoke to a distraught Mrs. Tisdale, doing his best to keep his objectivity, treating the situation like any other case.

But it wasn't any other case. He pushed the thought down firmly. If a formal investigation was opened, he might have to remove himself, given his personal involvement. But that was a concern for later.

The coachman had delivered Eleanor to the residence of Miss Walters at seven o'clock the previous evening, and that was the last time anyone had seen her. The driver had been with the family for over five years and swore he'd watched Miss Tisdale enter the home before he drove away...yet it was an errand he'd completed numerous times, and he'd had no reason to linger in the cold evening air once she'd gone inside—or he *thought* she had.

"We don't want a scandal," Mr. Tisdale advised quietly. "The fewer people who know Eleanor is missing, the better. We can't have her reputation ruined merely because she decided to venture out alone."

"Do you think that's what happened?" Henry asked. Eleanor had an independent streak to be sure but, to his knowledge, had never acted recklessly. Leaving her friends and family, and overnight...

"Henry, you know Eleanor. She can be rather...strong-willed." Her father briefly closed his eyes. "But no, I didn't expect this of her. I fear she did something out of character and ran into trouble of some sort." Shadows lingered in his eyes when he met Henry's. "Why else wouldn't she have come *home*?"

That was a question Henry couldn't answer.

Mrs. Tisdale was beside herself with worry, and it took Henry several attempts to calm her enough to question her. A strand of hair had escaped her normally neat bun, and her eyes continually darted toward the door, as if hoping her daughter would arrive momentarily. She smoothed back the hair for a third time, then returned to twisting a ring back and forth on her finger.

Eleanor hadn't said anything unusual about the evening. Her behavior hadn't changed of late. No, she hadn't been secretly seeing anyone, to her mother's knowledge. No gentleman had caught her eye. Mrs. Tisdale insisted that such a thing would be impossible, as she accompanied Eleanor to nearly all social events.

Yet Henry had to wonder...

Sarah, Eleanor's maid, dabbed her red eyes as she spoke hurriedly to Henry, but had nothing helpful to offer either. The servant insisted she hadn't noticed anything different about Eleanor's actions, other than she'd been looking forward to attending the theater with her friend—not an uncommon occurrence. Henry was uncertain whether the maid's upset stemmed from the potential loss of her position if Eleanor never returned home or from true concern for her mistress.

"Does Eleanor keep a diary of any sort that might hint at her whereabouts?" Henry asked tentatively, knowing she would not thank him for this.

"Yes, yes, she does. Sarah, fetch Miss Tisdale's diary for the Inspector." Mrs. Tisdale shook her head, worry lining her forehead. "Eleanor will be appalled to learn that someone looked through it."

That was the least of their worries as far as Henry was concerned.

"Thomas isn't home?" Henry realized he hadn't seen Eleanor's half-brother, nor had his parents mentioned him. Thomas was Mrs. Tisdale's son from a previous marriage, with Eleanor being their only child together. The two had always got along as well as could be expected, from what Henry saw on the outside.

"He left for work as usual, but I sent him a message," Mr. Tisdale said. "I'm sure he will arrive at any moment."

Henry took the diary to read on the way to speak with Miss Walters. The worry clutching him had only grown since his arrival. Something felt terribly wrong about the situation, even if he didn't allow himself to rely on hunches or premonitions.

He'd advised Mr. Tisdale that he wanted to send for more officers to aid in the search, but the man had asked Henry to wait just a little longer. Though Henry understood the need for discretion, unless a helpful clue or better yet, Eleanor herself, arrived, a formal investigation would need to be opened.

The woman was, after all, missing.

He opened the diary as the carriage rumbled to the Walters residence. Eleanor's neat, feminine script was easy to read, and he skimmed several pages to get a feel for the sort of things she liked to write, before looking at the last page.

This evening will be the most exciting of my life, and I hope more evenings like it will follow.

Henry blinked. Had he missed a detail explaining this?

He flipped through the rest of the journal, but that was all she'd written. He re-read the pages following up to the last entry, and let out a long, deep breath of disappointment. Not particularly helpful. He stuffed it into his pocket to review later and alighted from the carriage at the Walters residence. He couldn't imagine what Eleanor had been thinking by doing this, and would be hard-pressed not to berate her soundly when—if—she was found.

The stately red-brick mansion was set back from the street by a wrought-iron fence and a precisely clipped box hedge. The covered portico with columns on either side of the front door offered protection from the elements. First impressions suggested the Walters were a well-to-do family, much like the Tisdales.

Henry again wondered whether the Tisdale's coachman had truly seen Eleanor enter the shadowed doorway or merely assumed she would do so once she reached the front door. How clearly would one see over such a distance, and in the dark?

He used the polished brass knocker to announce his presence.

"Inspector Henry Field of Scotland Yard, and a family friend of the Tisdales," he told the butler who answered the door. "I would like to speak with Mr. or Mrs. Walters."

"Of course, sir. Do come in," the servant advised, obvious worry furrowing his large brows, as if aware of the situation.

In short order, Henry was shown up the stairs to a high-ceilinged drawing room with pale blue wallpaper and a marble fireplace where the Mrs. and Miss Walters awaited him.

Henry introduced himself, thanking them for seeing him, and explained his personal connection to the Tisdales.

"I can't imagine what happened." Mrs. Walters shared a worried look with her daughter. "Eleanor is a dear friend of Caroline's and a frequent visitor in our home, but she wasn't here last evening—and we did not expect her."

"She did spend the night last month after we attended the theater," Miss Walters offered in a small voice. "We've...we've done that on occasion if we also had a shopping trip planned the following morning." She sent a worried look toward her mother. "Always with one of our mothers, of course."

"When was the last time you spoke with her?" Henry asked gently. It was clear how upset they both were about Eleanor's disappearance, something to which he could relate.

"We spoke privately last Thursday when she came for tea with her mother, and we sat in the window seat of the drawing room." Miss Walters released a shuddering breath. "There was no mention of us attending the theater again, nor did we make any other specific plans."

Henry's jaw tightened. No plans at all. That did not bode well. "Did she seem out of sorts in any way? Troubled or particularly animated?"

"She was in good spirits, I think—but not overly so." Again, Miss Walters glanced at her mother to see if she agreed. "It's hard to think back on it now."

The older woman nodded. "I don't remember her saying anything of note. Just the usual conversation with a little gossip."

"Did the two of you often attend functions together?" Henry asked, desperate to find some lead, some clue as to her whereabouts. "Balls and other social events?" He had never been part of that world, nor did he care to be, but he'd brushed up against it often enough to know of it.

"Yes, of course." Miss Walters frowned. "The Season hasn't truly begun, but we did so many times last year. But nothing interesting happened, sir. Just dancing, and chatter."

Henry was disappointed, if not surprised, by the lack of helpful information, though both women seemed very distressed. Surely if Miss Walters suspected where Eleanor was, she would've immediately said so when she knew how concerned Eleanor's parents were?

"We were so astonished when Mr. Tisdale came by and told us she was missing." Mrs. Walters shook her head, casting a pointed look at her daughter, clearly grateful she wasn't the one gone. "I just can't *imagine*."

Her daughter reached over to squeeze her mother's hand as if to reassure her.

Henry swallowed. There was one final line of questioning, and it pained him to ask it—but what sort of an inspector would he be if he did not consider it?

"Did Eleanor mention any gentlemen that she might have a fondness for?" He didn't want to make assumptions but had worked enough cases to know that there could be a dark side to romantic liaisons—even if he could not imagine little Eleanor, all bright eyes as she had always been as a child, running off with anyone.

Miss Walters lifted one shoulder in a half-shrug. "She has several gentlemen friends, but I wouldn't say anyone in particular had caught her fancy. In truth, and she won't mind me saying this, she didn't seem anxious to wed."

Mrs. Walters nodded with a wry smile. "On more than one occasion, she claimed there was more to life than being a wife, much to her mother's displeasure, I might add. I can't imagine she would change her mind on that without mentioning it to Caroline."

"Can you provide a list of Miss Tisdale's other friends?" Henry wrote down the names they gave, the number of them giving him pause. Of course, the Tisdales moved in different social circles, but to have so many 'close' friends...he would need assistance to question everyone.

"Might I speak with your lady's maid?" Henry asked, determined to leave no stone unturned. At their questioning look, he added, "Sometimes servants say things to one another that you might not hear."

There was the chance the two maids had shared a conversation that could prove helpful. He could only hope. In all honesty, panic was creeping in that he hadn't yet discovered anything helpful.

"If you think it necessary." Mrs. Walters nodded at her daughter, who stood to ring the bell.

While they waited for the lady's maid Henry continued with his questions, learning that Mr. and Mrs. Walters had three other children, with Caroline the youngest. Only one other sibling lived at home though she was betrothed, the wedding planned for June. Their other children were married and lived elsewhere. Mr. Walters was spending the afternoon at his club, and at present had no knowledge that his daughter's friend was even missing, though a note had been sent.

The lady's maid soon arrived, worry pinching her narrow face. Henry politely asked to talk to her alone, advising the mistress of the house and her daughter that he'd taken enough of their time. He would have also liked to speak with Miss Walters without her mother present as she might well be holding back information, but he could conduct a more thorough interview if an official case was opened.

For now, he wanted to speak with as many people who knew Eleanor as quickly as possible. In missing person cases, the first four and twenty hours were the most crucial, and that deadline was quickly approaching.

The two ladies reluctantly departed after requesting to be advised if Eleanor returned, or additional information regarding her whereabouts was discovered, all while the lady's maid stood anxiously waiting.

"How well do you know Miss Tisdale's maid?" Henry asked in what he hoped was a friendly tone, given the woman's nervousness, as the door closed and they were left alone.

"I wouldn't say we're friends, but we chat when the ladies call on one another."

"And is that often?" As if he hadn't already asked the ladies a similar question—but he had to get the woman to open up somehow.

"Quite often, yes." She lifted her nose. "Sarah tends to think she's an authority on nearly everything, which makes conversing with her mighty unpleasant at times."

Henry hadn't gained that impression but nodded all the same. Servants were people, and therefore their relationships could be as complicated as those in the upper part of the house.

"Did she mention anything different with Miss Tisdale of late? Someone new in her life or a new pastime that occupied her?"

"Not that I can recall."

After several more fruitless questions, Henry pushed to his feet, deciding nothing further could be gained from the household. He asked the lady's maid to let him know if she thought of anything, thanked her for her time, then took his leave.

He was anxious to return to the Tisdale residence, wishing he had more to show for his efforts. His heart ached for the family. With each moment that passed, he grew more concerned that Eleanor truly had found trouble and the situation wouldn't end well.

Chapter Fifteen

"I just don't understand!" The bewilderment in Mrs. Tisdale's voice was heart-wrenching, heightening Henry's own worry. "How could she have just disappeared?"

Henry wished he had an answer. Instead, all he could think of were the numerous people who had done just that. Some were victims of foul play. Others met with a terrible accident. The whereabouts of a few remained a mystery.

But some returned home safely. Those were the memories to which Henry held tight. But he couldn't give the Tisdales hope without reason when he didn't yet know what had happened to their beloved daughter.

"We will do all in our power to find her." That much he would promise. No more. No less. But in order to do so, he needed to open a formal investigation. And that required him to gain their permission to make this public.

"We must keep hope that she will return home of her own accord soon," Mr. Tisdale said as he patted his wife's arm with a trembling hand. "Sh-She will undoubtedly laugh that we were worried enough to send for Henry."

His wife sniffed, pressing an embroidered handkerchief to her streaming nose. "Do you truly believe that?"

"We must," her husband advised, though his tight expression looked anything but hopeful.

Henry waited a moment, then cleared his throat. He hated to increase their concern, but the clock was ticking—and he couldn't forget that he also had Miss Digby's murder to investigate. That trail was also growing colder by the hour.

"I would like to open a formal investigation," he advised in a low voice. "We need to broaden the search for Eleanor as quickly as possible, and the best way to do so is with more officers."

"Oh, dear." Mrs. Tisdale turned to her husband. "Is that truly necessary?"

Mr. Tisdale frowned. "Is it really, Henry? As I mentioned before, I hesitate to take action that would tarnish her good name."

If they didn't find her soon, her 'good name' would be the last thing they needed to worry about.

But Henry didn't say that. He didn't have the chance; before he could respond, the sound of voices echoed in the hall. He followed the couple's gazes toward the doorway, taken by surprise to see his own father striding into the room.

"Martin. Dorothy. I just received your message." His father glanced at Henry, concern deepening the lines on his face. "What do you know thus far?"

Henry slowly stood, uncertain whether to be pleased or offended by his father's arrival. Had Mr. Tisdale sent for him as a comforting friend...or because he didn't trust Henry? "Father. I didn't realize you were coming."

Thurmond Field, retired chief inspector and highly respected detective within Scotland Yard, continued forward to greet his friends before clasping Henry's shoulder. "I just returned home and came as soon as I read your note—is there any word of Eleanor?"

The worry that he would never live up to his father's good work and excellent reputation had plagued Henry since his promotion to inspector. He thought he'd overcome his doubts, in part because of Amelia's faith in him and his recent successes, yet here it was again.

The real Inspector Field, albeit retired, was now on the case, at least unofficially.

"None." Mr. Tisdale shared a look of apprehension with his wife. "We're so grateful for Henry's help, of course, but we felt certain you'd want to know. You've known her from a babe."

Henry put aside his concern. Now wasn't the time to allow his feelings of inferiority to arise. All that mattered was that more help had arrived, and he could think of no one better than his father to aid in the search. "I was just advising Mr. and Mrs. Tisdale that we need to open a formal investigation."

His father slowly nodded, clearly sifting through the advantages of doing so. "I agree. More officers looking for her is your best hope at this juncture."

"If the two of you both think that's necessary," Mr. Tisdale reluctantly agreed.

"I do." Henry gestured toward the door as he glanced at his father. "I'll send word to the Yard while Mr. and Mrs. Tisdale advise you of what we know."

He departed to write a message to Director Reynolds, requesting the assistance of Fletcher and at least two additional officers, then asked the butler to have it delivered to Scotland Yard.

While he held doubt as to whether he was the best person to lead this investigation, given his personal involvement, neither could he imagine walking away. There was no denying that his emotions made it difficult to think clearly, and he was already neck-deep in a murder investigation. Miss Digby deserved attention as well, though he had few clues to follow in that case as of yet. Still the idea of leaving the Tisdales with some other inspector to find Eleanor was impossible to consider.

By the time he returned to the drawing room, his father appeared even more grim.

"Little to go on thus far, eh?" His father lifted a brow as he held Henry's gaze.

"Very little. Miss Walters, Eleanor's friend, provided the names of other friends we can speak with." He consulted his notebook and shared the names with Mr. and Mrs. Tisdale, prioritizing the list based on their opinions. "Is there anyone else I should question?"

Henry intended to have a solid plan to conduct a thorough search by the time his men arrived. There had been no one to sound the alarm when Clarissa Digby went missing; she was a young woman without the resources and family pull of Eleanor Tisdale. Involving more officers now would hopefully lessen the chance of another young woman meeting foul play, no matter how upsetting the idea was.

His father proved helpful, reinforcing in his calm voice the importance of everyone in the household providing even the smallest detail about Eleanor's activities of late.

"Rarely is there just one piece of information that points in the proper direction," his father told the couple. "It's the compilation of clues that paints a map of sorts for us to follow."

Henry didn't miss his father's use of 'us'. He knew retirement from the police force had been a challenge for his father after spending so many years investigating crimes, and he always enjoyed it when Henry stopped by to discuss cases. There was no need to feel as if the Tisdales, or his father, had doubts about Henry's ability to manage the investigation.

Yet the concern resurfaced when his father asked for a word in private.

He followed his father into Mr. Tisdale's study and watched as he closed the door behind them.

"So. What are your impressions?" his father asked briskly.

Henry swallowed. Why did he feel as though he was now the one being interrogated? "Difficult to say when no one can think of anything suspicious that has happened in the past few days."

"Not even the lady's maid?"

"No, though I intend to have another conversation with her." In fact, he wanted to speak with several of the servants again. Never mind how ineffective the task felt when he wanted to take to the streets himself in search of Eleanor.

"Always good to confirm their statements, but surely you have a sense of some sort at this point," his father suggested.

Henry hesitated. Hunches weren't something he liked to rely on since he didn't fully trust them. His father and his grandfather, both of whom had retired as chief inspectors, were famous for following their instincts to bring cases to successful conclusions. Henry was only starting to listen to the voice in the back of his mind.

But this was his father he was speaking with, not the Director. His father surely had an idea as well. Comparing notes might lead to a break in the case.

"I tend to think that Eleanor arranged to have an unchaperoned outing, and it somehow went awry." Henry told him of the last entry in Eleanor's diary, frustrated by how little he'd learned given the number of people he'd interviewed. "Perhaps she met with a gentleman, or a friend her parents wouldn't approve of."

His father sighed, his expression pensive. "I thought the same. Dorothy has always kept a tight rein on her daughter...perhaps too tight. I noted a flash or two of rebellion in Eleanor's behavior during our last few visits. Of course, that is often the case in young people of a certain age." He sent Henry a pointed look.

"I never rebelled," Henry countered with the hint of a smile. "I prefer to think of it as testing the boundaries of parental guidance and limits."

"Hmmm. We shall have that discussion at another time, preferably with your mother in attendance." His father's dry tone and affectionate look warmed Henry. It was a relief his father had come. He needed another pair of eyes.

Once again, Henry was pleased he hadn't given in to the urge to tell his parents that he knew they'd adopted him. Whether he ever would remained to be seen. He'd found out by accident when he was twelve years of age, a blow to his dream of following in his father and grandfather's footsteps and becoming a Scotland Yard Inspector, their blood and brilliance running through his veins.

It had taken time to find the courage to still pursue that dream after the discovery. He quickly decided he would have to work harder to overcome any lack of natural inborn talent. He'd done exactly that, proving his success wasn't just because of his last name, and had quickly risen through the ranks to his present position—something not all of his fellow officers, Perdy among them, appreciated.

Henry was good at his job, but sometimes he still had to remind himself of that. Hearing it from others, especially his father, certainly helped.

"Was there anything in particular she did that caught your notice?" Henry asked curiously.

"If only I had paid more attention these last few months." His father frowned, clearly searching his memory. "An angry look at her mother on more than one occasion. A huff or two from the child when chided by her father. But no specific details that I can think of."

"It might not hurt for you to have a private conversation with Mr. Tisdale, perhaps over a heartening brandy," Henry suggested. "There's always the chance he would more readily share a pertinent fact with you than me."

"Right." His father nodded. "I might even speak in confidence with Dorothy from one parent to another to see what she might say. Your mother could be of help there as well."

"That's a fine idea," Henry agreed, grateful for his father's help.

"It sounds as if young Thomas should arrive at any moment. I'm sure you're anxious to speak with him," his father mused.

"Yes, I am, though I'm surprised he hasn't already returned home, given the circumstances."

"As am I. I admit, I'm not sure how well he and Martin are getting on of late." His father sent Henry a rueful look. "Henry, I have always wanted to work on a case with you, even if it is in an unofficial capacity, but I would've preferred it to involve lashings of diamonds easily found."

"Agreed." Henry clasped his father's shoulder. "I'm pleased you're here. Hopefully together, we'll find her."

"Why is it that I worry we won't?" his father asked, even as he placed his lined hand on top of Henry's.

His father's words remained in Henry's mind as he proceeded to question several of the staff again, including the coachman, the lady's maid, and the butler. Before he'd finished speaking to the butler Fletcher arrived, along with Constables Dannon and Stephens.

"Terrible to hear of a young lady missing," Fletcher whispered when Henry met the men in the hall.

"It is." Henry sighed. "And between us, the Tisdales have been friends of my family for a long time."

"No sign of the young lady, sir?" Constable Dannon asked.

"Unfortunately, no." Henry gestured for the three to follow him to the small sitting room Mrs. Tisdale had offered for his use and provided a brief update of what he knew thus far. Sadly, there was not much to relate.

"Can't imagine where she could have gone," Constable Dannon said, shaking his head. "It would've been getting dark by then. A young lady, out by herself? Gives me the shivers to think of what might have happened."

Indeed. What could she have been thinking, Henry wondered not for the first time. Miss Digby had been out at night by herself as well, though desperation might have forced her to do so. But why had Eleanor done it?

"I don't think I need to tell you to be careful what you say to anyone, including the family or the servants," Henry warned, though he knew he could trust the men, having worked closely with them on numerous cases.

"Of course not, sir," they all agreed.

Henry provided them with the address where Eleanor was last seen, and requested they search the street and the surrounding neighborhood. He gave them a description of Eleanor as well as what she'd been wearing, which her lady's maid had provided.

"Start with the nearby houses and work out from there," Henry directed. "A neighbor might have seen her standing near the front door and noticed where she went, if she got into a cab, if she met with someone. We are to avoid sharing her name with anyone at this time." He would do what he could to protect her reputation—but he also had to find her.

Henry's father joined them, greeting Fletcher warmly before listening to Henry's plan with several nods of approval. "Yes, excellent plan. Look for anything out of place along the street. Might be a broken fence or a bit of torn fabric. Learning what direction she went could prove vital."

"We'll keep a careful eye out," Constable Stephens reassured him.

"It could be a late evening," Henry warned the men.

Fletcher nodded. "Whatever it takes to find the young lady,"

"I'll join you as soon as I'm done here." Henry wanted to speak with Thomas before he did so, hoping Eleanor's half-brother might tell him something helpful. He had always been a steady thing, and Henry knew his parents relied on him. They'd lean on him now more than ever.

The men departed, leaving Henry to question the remaining staff, taking them through the last few days but learning little.

"Inspector Field?" The butler stood in the doorway of the sitting room where Henry was speaking with a footman. "Pardon the interruption, but Mr. Tisdale asked me to advise you that Mr. Ballard has arrived. They await you in the study."

"Thank you." Henry rose, wishing he could speak alone with Thomas.

He entered the study to find Mr. Tisdale behind his desk, Henry's father in a chair before it, and Thomas pacing before the fire. Tension gripped the silent room.

"Thomas." Henry walked forward to shake the other man's hand. It had been some time since he'd last seen him, as Thomas had been away with friends during Henry's last visit.

Thomas was nearly six years younger than Henry and refined in ways that Henry would never be. He was training to become a barrister like Mr. Tisdale had been and liked the finer things in life. Henry tended to think they didn't have many things in common, but liked him well enough, nonetheless.

"Henry." Thomas's grip was firm as he met Henry's gaze briefly. "Good to see you, despite these terrible circumstances."

"And you." Henry offered a small smile, hoping to ease the tension in the room. "I don't suppose you can tell us where your half-sister is?"

The younger man shook his head, running a hand along the back of his neck. "I wish I could. What could she have been thinking, to do something like this?"

Henry knew the two half siblings weren't particularly close. Thomas thought Eleanor spoiled, and she thought him a prig and far too full of himself.

Over the years as he'd watched them grow, Henry couldn't help but think they were both partly right.

The silence stretched long, but Henry didn't break it. Instead, he looked expectantly at Thomas, waiting for him to add to his remark.

"I spoke with her briefly yesterday morning as I was leaving for the day," Thomas said at last. "She was just coming down for breakfast."

"How did she seem?"

"Bored." Thomas's lips twisted. "Then again, she often felt as such."

"Oh?" Henry wanted more, and he tended to think Thomas knew something.

With a wary glance at his father, Thomas continued, "She...she mentioned that she wished to find employment. Paid employment."

Mr. Tisdale scoffed, waving a hand in swift dismissal. "Oh, that was Eleanor. She often said such things to cause a stir."

Thomas clamped his mouth shut, leaving Henry to suspect the young man felt he was the one being dismissed, rather than his words.

"What caused her to raise the subject?" Henry asked, ignoring the undertones of the conversation.

Thomas's reluctance to continue was obvious, but at last he said, "I…I may have mentioned that it must be relaxing to rise whenever one wishes and have so few responsibilities to clutter up one's day."

Yes. That would do it. "Did she take issue with that?" Henry pressed.

"Apparently, as that was when she mentioned finding employment."

"Of what sort?" Mr. Tisdale asked before Henry could, the tight set of the older man's jaw undeniable.

"I don't know." Thomas hesitated again before continuing, "I didn't ask. I was in a rush as I didn't want to be late to work. I only wished her luck and said she'd need it, given her lack of skills." He shrugged. "That was the extent of our brief conversation."

Henry's frustration grew, and so did the worry in the pit of his stomach. A glance at his father, who met his gaze, revealed the same concern. He couldn't dismiss the fear that Eleanor wouldn't be returning home. Ever.

Not so different than Miss Digby after all.

Chapter Sixteen

"A MESSAGE FOR YOU, madam." Fernsby held out a silver tray for Amelia as she sat in the drawing room late that afternoon.

She'd spent several pleasurable hours earlier volunteering with her Aunt Margaret at the school for the mudlarks and the other orphans that her aunt's church funded. Seeing the children flourish, including Agnes and Pudge with whom she was well acquainted, delighted her. The two girls had taken great pride in showing Amelia their writing and reading skills, which were coming along quite nicely. Their pride in themselves pleased her to no end.

"Thank you." Amelia set aside the book she'd been reading and took the missive, her stomach tightening as she recognized Mrs. Nettle's script. "From the medium. Again. How...intere sting."

"Indeed. The messenger is awaiting a reply if you wish to send one," the butler advised.

That only made her more nervous to see what Mrs. Nettle had to say, yet she couldn't deny a measure of curiosity and so opened the note.

Dear Mrs. Greystone,

I am holding a séance at my home this evening at eight o'clock for a widow hoping for a message from her late husband. Regardless of whether you decide to proceed with the article on my abilities, I thought you might find the evening of interest.

Regards,

Mary Nettle

Amelia sighed. Was attending wise? She had never been to a séance and didn't know whether she wanted to risk receiving a message she was unprepared for. Yet she was intrigued by the medium's skills, just as she'd told Henry.

Besides, it wasn't as if she had another pressing engagement to fill her evening. Perhaps seeing the medium at work, so to speak, would provide a definitive answer as to whether Amelia could write an article in good faith.

Mrs. Nettle may have located the body at the railyard, but Amelia still had pressing questions about her true abilities. If the séance included tricks or attempts at deception, then she would politely decline to write about it without a second thought.

Amelia's chest tightened. But she also needed to consider the other possibility: that the evening could provide support for Mrs. Nettle's claims of being able to genuinely channel the spirit world. As unsettling as that would be, it would also be fascinating in some respects.

Still, she hesitated, reading the message again. *A widow hoping for a message from her late husband.* Thoughts of Matthew crossed her mind, raising the concern that the séance might somehow involve her own personal situation.

No. There was no reason to assume anything of the sort would happen. And if the topic arose, she would quickly end it.

"Yes, I will send a reply," Amelia advised as she rose and walked quickly to her desk to write an acceptance to the invitation before she could think too closely on it. She handed it to Fernsby, not quite meeting his gaze. "I will be attending a séance at Mrs. Nettle's home this evening at eight o'clock."

Fernsby's eyes widened with surprise before he quickly masked his reaction. "Very well. I will request that Mrs. Appleton serve dinner promptly at seven o'clock, so you will have time to prepare."

"Thank you. Please advise Yvette that I would like her to accompany me, and order a hansom cab for us."

"Of course." Fernsby departed with the reply in hand.

Amelia walked to the window, drawing a deep breath as she considered the quiet street below. She need only consider the séance as an experiment of sorts. She was a woman of science, after all, and understood that in order to achieve results, one had to study the subject and consider various potential outcomes.

Surely it would be interesting, perhaps even entertaining to attend, especially when *she* would not be the focus. She'd be able to view both sides of the event—the medium and her client—with some measure of objectivity. With luck, doing so would provide more insight than merely speaking to Mrs. Nettle had. She could only hope that Mr. Nettle would not be in attendance.

Amelia could imagine what Henry would say. He wouldn't be pleased that she would be attending. His protectiveness was touching, something she appreciated.

But as she had learned these past few months, she couldn't allow fear to guide her life. Moving forward was important and since she didn't seem able to simply refuse the idea of the article and let it go, better that she deal with the topic head on. That would allow her to finally put the medium and her cryptic comments from her mind.

At least, that was her hope.

The remainder of the afternoon passed quickly into evening. Yvette, her lady's maid, assisted her to change into a plum-colored gown with a striped underskirt, instead of wearing her customary gray. The color served as a reminder that she was more than a widow, and that while grief would always have a hold on her, it didn't rule every moment of her day.

Not anymore.

"This color is very becoming on you, madam," Yvette said as she smoothed the folds of Amelia's skirts.

"Thank you." Amelia smiled, pleased she'd asked her lady's maid to accompany her. "I'm certain you're as weary of me wearing mourning colors as I am."

The maid grinned. "It is a nice change."

Amelia enjoyed a light dinner, her stomach tightening that had nothing to do with the food before her, before donning her cloak and gloves.

"The cab has just arrived, madam," Fernsby advised as she and Yvette descended the stairs.

"Thank you." It did not take the pair of ladies long to step out into the evening air, and Amelia smiled as she did so. "I take comfort in your presence this evening, Yvette," she told her lady's maid as they settled into the cab.

"I look forward to seeing what I can learn from Mrs. Nettle's staff." Yet the young woman bit her lip, clearly unnerved about the séance.

Amelia had advised the servant about the evening and what she hoped to accomplish earlier, including questions about whether the medium's claims of connecting with the spirit world were valid. Yvette had accompanied Amelia on a few similar 'outings of inquiry', as the younger woman liked to call them. She considered it a welcome challenge to learn whatever she could from fellow servants, something Amelia appreciated and encouraged.

Amelia blew out a long breath as the cab lurched forward. "The medium is an unusual person, and as I already mentioned, I can't say I care for her husband. I will be quite interested to hear your impressions on them both."

"If you wish for me to attend the séance, I will, madam." Yvette lifted her chin, suggesting substantial courage was required to make the offer.

"Thank you. I will make that decision once we arrive and have the chance to see where it will take place and what is expected. From what little I know, the number of attendees is sometimes limited by the spiritualist." A silent reminder to herself that this was an experiment of sorts did little to calm her rising anxiousness.

Amelia took a moment to think of both Lily and Matthew, allowing a happy memory of them to fill her mind and calm her. She was blessed to have had them with her for as long as she had, and thought they were at peace in the afterlife. She didn't need Mrs. Nettle's help to believe that.

The cab halted, and they alighted into the gloom.

"My goodness, but it is a black night, isn't it?" the maid murmured into the heavy quiet surrounding them.

No moon lit the sky, and the lantern on the hansom cab did little to penetrate the darkness.

"Luckily I have been to her home twice before, or I might be less certain of our destination," Amelia advised, even as she tightened her hold on her reticule with a wary glance around.

Taking a firm hold of her nerves and remembering her purpose, she requested the cab driver wait with the promise of a hefty tip, knowing it might be difficult to locate one in the residential neighborhood once the séance was over at goodness knew what time. She had the feeling she would want to return home afterward as quickly as possible.

Amelia led the way up the walk to the front door, where a solitary lantern lit the entrance. Before she could knock, the door opened.

"Good evening, Mrs. Greystone." The maid greeted her with barely a glance in Yvette's direction. "Mrs. Nettle is expecting you."

The maid took their cloaks, then led them up the stairs to a spacious drawing room where three ladies conversed with Mrs. Nettle in low tones. There were no men in attendance, including Mr. Nettle, leaving Amelia to wonder at the reason for an all-female gathering—even if she was relieved at his absence. Several candles lent a gentle glow to the room, and a fire burned in the hearth.

"Mrs. Greystone." Their hostess left the side of an older woman dressed in bombazine from head to toe to greet Amelia. "I'm so pleased you decided to come."

Amelia did her best to smile. "Thank you for the invitation."

"May I introduce you to Mrs. Dowey. She hopes for communication with her late husband, who departed this world only a month ago."

"I'm very sorry for your loss," Amelia murmured, noting the widow's pale face and worried eyes.

The woman nodded, pulling out a handkerchief to dab at her nose.

Mrs. Nettle turned. "This is her sister, Mrs. Chambers, and her niece, Miss Chambers."

"A pleasure to meet you."

The two ladies murmured a greeting in return, both looking nervous.

Mrs. Nettle wore a gown of navy blue that made her look especially pale, but perhaps she was nervous about the evening ahead, though she acted with confidence. There was a seriousness to her demeanor that differed from Amelia's previous visits. Was she to meet with a different Mrs. Nettle at every meeting?

Her hostess smiled. "I advised the ladies that you are considering writing an article on my abilities. Mrs. Dowey kindly agreed to you attending, with the understanding you won't share her name or the specific details of any information she might learn during the séance."

"Of course." Amelia nodded in agreement. "Thank you."

The medium glanced at the tall clock which stood in the corner. "We will begin in just a few minutes."

"I look forward to it," Amelia said with enthusiasm, determined to hide any unease, but didn't miss the way Mrs. Nettle's eyes narrowed in response. Perhaps she'd been a bit too enthusiastic.

Yvette followed the other lady's maid out, leaving the ladies to visit in a quiet, stilted manner, exchanging vague pleasantries about the weather, all keeping an eye on the clock.

Despite her similar focus, Amelia started when the clock chimed the hour.

"If you will follow me," Mrs. Nettle announced once the clock chimed for the eighth time. She led the small group down the hall and opened the door to a small sitting room.

Heavy red velvet drapes covered the windows and only a few candles lit the space. A round table draped in black cloth adorned by a trio of unlit candles on its center sat in the center of the room, surrounded by five chairs. One chair had a notepad and pencil placed before it, along with a single white rose, suggesting it was for Mrs. Nettle.

A narrow side table held an empty picture frame with a small gold bell suspended on a ribbon. Amelia couldn't guess its purpose. What she assumed to be a mirror on one wall was covered in black fabric, no doubt to keep spirits from being trapped within, a custom many in mourning performed. She had done so herself, not quite knowing in her grief why it brought comfort. She half expected a cabinet which supposedly helped spirits manifest, something she'd read in a book, but the room held few other furnishings.

"Mrs. Dowey, if you will sit to my right and your sister to my left," Mrs. Nettle directed as she closed the door and walked around the room to extinguish the candles until only a single one remained, adding another level of eeriness to the moment. Then she took the chair before the notepad and the rose, leaving Amelia and the niece to take the two vacant seats.

The medium waited for them to sit, then looked at each guest in turn, her shadowed features unreadable in the flickering flame. "I ask that you remain silent for the duration of our endeavor. Interruptions of any sort will not be tolerated. Is that understood?"

"Yes," each of them murmured, the tension palpable.

"I will call the spirit world momentarily and await a response," Mrs. Nettle said in a calm yet strong voice. Her confidence was remarkable. "Please place both of your hands on the table, palms down, and keep them there. Doing so helps channel the energy of any spirits. It is not uncommon to feel a faint vibration when they reach out, so please, do not be alarmed. Any loud sounds or abrupt movements will more than likely end our session."

The medium tightened her lips, and for a brief moment, Amelia had the strangest impression she was reluctant to proceed with the séance. Had Mrs. Dowey paid for her services? If so, how much?

But then— "Mrs. Dowey, please put your husband's ring in the center of the table."

The widow set a man's signet ring near the three unlit candles with a trembling hand, casting a wary look at the medium before returning her hands palm down to the table.

Mrs. Nettle closed her eyes and drew several deep breaths. Amelia found herself slowing her own breathing, too, but she wasn't about to close her eyes.

At last the medium opened hers, reaching for the matches before her. "Tonight, we call on the spirits for Mrs. Jane Dowey." She struck a match and lit the shortest candle. "We call for her husband, Mr. Matthew Dowey."

Amelia stiffened. Though the name didn't match her husband's exactly, just hearing his given name was enough to send a shiver along her skin.

Mrs. Nettle struck another match and the middle candle sputtered to life. "Spirits of the departed, we call you forth with only good intentions." She hummed a single note as she used a third match to light the tallest and final candle with slow, deliberate movements. The hum continued as she shook out the match and set it aside, placing her hands palms down on the table, eyes closed once again.

The process thus far was not so different from the fictional account Amelia had read. It had seemed trite and staid printed out on the page. She would be the first to admit it was far more unsettling to experience in real life.

After several tense and silent minutes, Mrs. Nettle started to sway gently back and forth in her seat, the monotonous hum unnerving.

Amelia glanced at the other ladies to find their reaction much the same, as evidenced by their wide eyes and wary expressions—yet in this instance, knowing she wasn't alone in her feelings brought little relief.

"Come spirits," Mrs. Nettle muttered. "Come." She drew out the last word into the humming sound again.

The room's temperature dropped noticeably.

Amelia pushed aside her growing concern and held tight to her scientific training. She needed to observe, rather than focus on her unease. It took a moment to notice the candle flames had not flickered despite the temperature change. Surely the change was caused by a sudden draft...or was it?

How very odd.

The table beneath Amelia's hands vibrated, causing chill bumps to run along her skin. Another glance at the other ladies showed they appeared as alarmed as she was, but no one said a word.

Mrs. Nettle's eyes remained closed, her face pale, the swaying continuing along with an occasional hum.

Mrs. Dowey's gaze darted around the room as if in search of her husband, her frightened expression undeniable.

"Mr. Matthew Dowey, come forth."

Suddenly the candle flames flickered, dancing to and fro. The temperature dropped even more and a hint of cologne wafted in the air.

Mrs. Dowey's mouth gaped, her eyes wide as saucers. She looked at her sister, who wore a similar shocked expression. The young lady beside Amelia clearly didn't know what to think, her worried gaze glancing between her mother, her aunt, and the medium who was still humming.

The table shook harder, drawing their attention, and the ring in the center moved—not merely a vibration but moving smoothly an inch across the tablecloth.

But it was merely caused by the table shaking, wasn't it?

Then the bell suspended by the ribbon on the nearby table dinged.

The medium stilled and her eyes flew open, pupils dark. She stared straight ahead unseeing for a moment before her head slowly turned to fasten on Mrs. Dowey. "Darling?" Her voice was a deep drawl, unlike her usual tone. "What is it? Why are you here?"

Mrs. Dowey's entire body trembled. She opened her mouth twice before she finally managed to speak. "Matthew? I-I miss you terribly. But I must know—where are your mother's diamonds?"

Amelia stared at her in disbelief and the widow's gaze flicked to her for a moment, as if feeling self-conscious. Of all the things the widow could've asked her late husband, that was what she wanted to know?

Then again, Amelia's question to her own Matthew would likely sound odd to those unfamiliar with their situation.

"Box," Mrs. Nettle said in the same deep tone.

"W-What box?" Mrs. Dowey asked eagerly.

"In the floor."

"Oh." The widow frowned as if still uncertain what that meant. Suddenly awareness dawned and the woman nodded quickly. "Yes, the compartment under your dresser. Yes, of course. I will look there." Tears filled her eyes. "Thank you, Matthew. I-I hope you are well."

Mrs. Dowey waited, clearly hoping for confirmation, but the table stopped shaking and the chill in the room eased along with the tension in the room, though it didn't disappear completely.

Mrs. Nettle blinked several times then looked about the room, her vague focus landing on Mrs. Dowey. "Did—" She paused to clear her throat. "Did he come through?"

"He did." Mrs. Dowey's chest heaved with emotion. "And he answered my question."

"Oh." Mrs. Nettle appeared relieved as she nodded, keeping her hands on the table, making Amelia wonder at her thoughts. "Good. Then we shall close."

The widow nodded even as she sniffed. "Thank you—thank you so much."

Mrs. Nettle didn't respond, only drew another deep breath, her gaze holding on the candles in the center. One by one, she extinguished them as she spoke. "Thank you, spirits. Thank you for coming to us this evening. Go in peace." At last she lifted her hands from the table and sat back in her chair. Though it was difficult to tell in the dim light, she appeared drained from the experience, the shadows beneath her eyes more pronounced. "You may remove your hands as well."

Each of them did so. Amelia couldn't help but smooth hers along the fabric of her skirts, as they tingled strangely.

Mrs. Nettle nodded toward the ring still in the center of the table. "You may take the ring."

"Thank you." Mrs. Dowey reached for it, only to draw her hand back in surprise. "Oh! It's very warm."

"Our connection must have been quite strong." The medium stood, a pleased look on her face.

Amelia rose even as the room chilled yet again. She glanced at the others to see if they noticed it, but they were speaking in quiet tones amongst themselves, their voices muffled.

She shook her head, trying to clear the sensation as she shivered. The bell chimed faintly, and a scent caught her notice—an achingly familiar one that smelled of child and sunshine, like crushed grass, clean sweat, and soap. *Lily*.

Amelia closed her eyes, drawing it in, desperate to hold onto it a moment longer even as her heart ached. How often had she gone into Lily's bedroom and caught that same scent? More times than she could count.

Until the scent had finally faded.

A lump filled her throat even as she shivered, light-headed and slightly nauseous. But she would embrace the odd feelings for another moment with Lily. She missed her so much, so very much.

The emotions swirling through Amelia had nothing to do with science or investigating the medium's abilities, but everything to do with her heart and a mother's unending love for her child.

Chapter Seventeen

"Mrs. Greystone? Are you well?"

Amelia opened her eyes to find the medium standing before her, the others gathered around as well, concerned looks upon their faces. "P-Pardon me?"

"You've gone pale. Do you need to sit down?" Mrs. Nettle asked, her brow creased with what appeared to be genuine concern.

A single breath told Amelia the scent—the moment—was gone, and Lily along with it. She drew a deeper breath which helped to clear her head, leaving her to wonder if she'd imagined the whole thing.

"I'm quite well. Thank you." Amelia managed a smile, hoping Yvette was nearby. The time had come to return home, post haste. "I must have stood up too fast, that's all."

Mrs. Nettle's eyes narrowed before she nodded, her attention taken by the widow, who was gushing with praise.

"You did a wonderful job. It was more than I could have hoped for," Mrs. Dowey said, still teary, as she and Mrs. Nettle moved toward the door.

"I felt rather faint earlier, too," Mrs. Dowey's sister murmured to Amelia. She leaned closer, her voice dropping to a whisper. "The oddness of the evening doesn't help. It certainly left me unsettled." The woman glanced at her sister. "I hope she finds what she's looking for, as I do not care to endure another séance. Quite unnerving." She shuddered, still uneasy.

"It was certainly...interesting." And like Mrs. Dowey's sister, Amelia preferred not to attend another.

Mrs. Nettle opened the door, revealing her maid and Yvette standing in the hallway. The sight of the familiar face lent Amelia strength, further easing the dizzy sensation but not her heartache.

After another round of thanks and farewell to the medium, Mrs. Dowey, along with her sister and niece, accompanied Mrs. Nettle's maid down the hall, their voices echoing in the small space.

Amelia made to follow, but Mrs. Nettle placed a halting hand on her arm.

"Mrs. Greystone, are you quite certain you're well?" the medium asked, concern darkening her eyes.

"Yes, thank you." Out of the corner of her eye, Amelia saw Yvette draw nearer as if she unwilling to leave her mistress alone with the woman, something she appreciated.

"I'm pleased to hear that." Mrs. Nettle glanced at the small table where her blank notepad still sat. She touched a shaky finger to her temple and blinked rapidly. "I am terribly sorry to ask, but do you have a few minutes? Something else is coming through."

"Coming through?" Amelia repeated as she shared a worried look with Yvette. Was it something or *someone*? Worry weakened her knees. If Lily or Matthew—

"A spirit." The medium's grip on Amelia's arm tightened almost painfully. "One we can't ignore."

Before Amelia could respond, Mrs. Nettle pulled her to the table and sat, then picked up the pencil in one hand and the white rose in the other.

Yvette drew nearer to where her mistress stood and sent her a questioning look. Amelia offered a subtle shrug, uncertain what the medium was about. Whatever Mrs. Nettle had in mind, Amelia was grateful the maid was at her side.

"Sit." Mrs. Nettle didn't look up from her chair, holding the pencil poised over the paper. "Both of you. Quickly."

She should leave. And yet something kept her there. Amelia nodded to Yvette, and they reluctantly joined her at the table.

The medium didn't close her eyes this time but glared at the paper as if expecting it to move. Then she started to draw marks on the page haphazardly, or so it looked to Amelia. Lines, some thick, others thin, a few curved, and several letters. None of it made any sense, but Amelia watched in fascination all the same.

"This is quite strong," Mrs. Nettle murmured, almost to herself, lifting the rose briefly to her nose. "Stronger indeed than Mr. Dowey's presence."

Amelia hoped that didn't mean Mrs. Nettle would fall into the trance-like state which had seemed to overtake her earlier. That had been rather alarming.

The medium's brow furrowed as her hand moved quickly in jerking motions, connecting some of the lines until a form lying on the ground became recognizable. "There's...there's been another death," she whispered, a tremble in her voice.

Another? Horror gripped Amelia as she glanced at Yvette, wondering if she'd heard correctly. The maid's face was pale, her attention riveted to the drawing.

"A-A woman." The medium added hair to the figure, long and flowing. "It's t-too late for her." Next came an irregular oblong shape, which she filled in with the pencil. "So much blood."

Yvette let out a tiny gasp, eyes wide with horror as she stared at the paper.

Amelia couldn't blame her. The news was terribly disturbing, made all the more real by the rough drawing the medium continued to work on.

The urge to hurry out the door and find Henry proved nearly overwhelming, but Amelia held herself still. She needed to know where the woman was, and if possible, what had happened to her. The more details Mrs. Nettle provided, the more helpful it would be to Henry. The thought of him, of working with him again, steadied her, and she forced herself to watch—and listen—with care.

The medium continued to write and draw, more lines and more letters. Again, she muttered to herself, then shook her head, pausing frequently as if to listen. To whom Amelia couldn't say, for the room was eerily silent except for the occasional scratching of the pencil on the paper and Mrs. Nettle's frenetic whispers.

Time stretched taut, each minute painful as Amelia desperately wanted to interrupt to ask the identity of the woman and her whereabouts. Instead, she directed her gaze to the notepad.

A door emerged in the drawing, made of planks and an old-fashioned lock near the handle. Overgrown weeds bordered it. At least, that was what Amelia thought they were. Then Mrs. Nettle drew a circle inside a square at the top of the paper, which had Amelia frowning as she tried to interpret the meaning of it.

Suddenly, the medium stiffened, then dropped the pencil and sat back in the chair, her breath coming quickly even as her shoulders slumped as if exhausted. "It's...gone."

Amelia hesitated, uncertain of her meaning. "The body?"

"The spirit," Mrs. Nettle corrected. She looked at the paper as if for the first time. "A woman. Murdered, it appears." Her gaze shifted to Amelia. "How terrible."

It was. If only the medium could warn people in danger rather than share where their bodies were. The morbidness of her ability was difficult to understand.

"Do you know who she is?" Amelia asked in a quiet, calm tone, much unlike the swirling storm of emotions within.

Mrs. Nettle shook her head as she stared at the drawing again, clearly on the verge of tears. "She's far too young to be gone."

"Where is she?" Amelia gestured toward the door she'd drawn. "Where is this?"

"I-I don't know. There's an old door."

An old door... Similar to the medium's previous description.

Amelia's attention caught on the circle inside a square near the top and she gasped. "Could that be the clock on the tower at King's Cross again?"

"Perhaps." The lack of certainty in the medium's tone as she stared at the paper was maddening.

"The same place where you told us the last body was."

"Is it?"

How did she not know? Her behavior was infuriating. "What of the letters?" Amelia asked urgently. Henry would want every last detail. "What do they mean?"

"I don't know." Mrs. Nettle ran her finger along one, then another, tracing them. "It couldn't tell me."

"The spirit?" Amelia asked, though she wasn't certain she wanted to know.

The medium nodded, looking away from the drawing.

Amelia hesitated but her curiosity overwhelmed her. "Who is the spirit?"

"I don't know." Mrs. Nettle pressed her palms over her eyes. "I-I've asked them all so many times not to contact me." Tears filled her voice. "But they won't listen." She sniffed as she dropped her hands to hold Amelia's gaze. "It's not that I don't want to help people, you understand. But why do they tell me about the ones who are already dead?"

That had been Amelia's thought as well. How frustrating it must be to see past events rather than true predictions. If one were going to have visions, surely seeing what could be changed would be preferable.

"Madam?" Mrs. Nettle's maid appeared in the doorway, eyes narrowing as she looked at Amelia and Yvette, obviously displeased they hadn't departed with Mrs. Dowey and her family. "The other guests have left. It is time for you to rest."

Amelia could see how weary the medium was. The woman could hardly sit upright in her chair. "Mrs. Nettle, may I take this drawing? I want to show it to Inspector Field to help him find the...young woman."

"Oh, no." The medium placed both hands protectively on the sheet. "I couldn't allow that. My husband would be most unhappy."

"It could aid Inspector Field in finding the body." Amelia had to hope he could make sense of the L and E repeated on the sheet more than she could, along with the capital D. "I will return it after I show it to him," she offered, hoping that would change her mind.

"Well...if you promise." She removed her hands, smudging some of the lines.

"I do." Amelia stood, and Yvette did the same. Their host made no move to hand it to her, so Amelia reached to take the sheet, hoping she wouldn't change her mind.

Mrs. Nettle's maid moved closer to place a hand defensively on her mistress's shoulder. "I will return as soon as I show your guests out."

Mrs. Nettle nodded, staring across the room.

"Thank you for...everything." Amelia wasn't sure what she was thanking her for, but it seemed like the polite thing to say. "Have a good evening."

"Y-Yes. Thank you for coming."

Amelia held tight to the paper, and within a few short minutes, she and Yvette were out the door and hurrying down the walk toward their waiting cab.

"I must notify Inspector Field," Amelia said firmly as they reached it.

"Of course. You could send him a message upon our return home," Yvette suggested, one hand on the door. "Fernsby would be happy to—"

"Time is of the essence." Urgency filled Amelia, and waiting any length of time felt impossible. She had to do something. "We will stop by his lodging house on the way home," she announced.

Never in her life had she called on an unmarried man, and it felt positively scandalous even to suggest doing so. Yet neither could she imagine returning home with the drawing in hand and waiting hours, perhaps until the morning for Henry to reply to a message.

The sooner he heard the news and saw the drawing, the better. And in all honesty, she welcomed the impatience rushing through her, easing the terrible ache of losing Lily that gripped her.

"Madam, it's nearly nine o'clock," Yvette said nervously.

Amelia lifted her chin. "It can't be helped." She gave the driver Henry's address and asked him to hurry. Then she climbed in with Yvette, the cab lurching forward before they were properly settled. "It's not far," she told the maid as she studied the dark street.

"I hesitate to mention this, but...well, I believe Fernsby would expect no less of me," Yvette began.

Amelia's chest tightened. "What is it?"

The maid drew in a deep breath and did not meet her mistress's eye. "Inspector Field's landlady might take issue with someone knocking on her door at this hour, especially when the caller is...female."

"Oh." Amelia stiffened, realizing Yvette was right. "That is an excellent point." As a widow, she was afforded some leeway, but this stepped out of even those bounds. "I'll ask the driver to assist us."

Yvette nodded, though it was easy to see from her worried expression that she was less than convinced about the wisdom of this errand.

Just over a quarter of an hour later, the cab halted and Yvette stepped out with Amelia directly behind her.

"It's just there to yer left," the cabbie pointed from his perch to where a lamp glowed near a door. "You want me to wait again?"

A faint light shone in some of the upper windows, but little could be seen of the building in the darkness. Would Henry still be awake?

"Excellent," Amelia said as she approached the driver. "If you would be so kind as to knock on the door and state that Inspector Field is needed outside—"

"Wot?" The driver stiffened with outrage, clearly having none of it. "I'm not leaving me cab or me horse to go knockin' on some door!"

"Sir." Amelia used her firmest tone. "My maid and I will remain here to watch over the horse and cab, but surely you can understand that *we* cannot request to speak with the Inspector."

"Why not?" the cabbie demanded.

"Because we are ladies, and he is an unmarried gentleman." Amelia allowed exasperation to color her tone. Anything to lessen this tension within her. "The matter is urgent."

"For Chrissake," the man muttered as he tied off the reins. "The things I do fer customers." He gestured toward the horse, which stood placidly, not looking as if it intended to go anywhere unless forced. "Ye'll need to hold her, just in case. Don't want her gettin' spooked."

"Of course." Yvette moved to the steed's head and took hold of the bridle, much to Amelia's surprise.

The cabbie stomped off to the lodging house, muttering as he went, and rapped on the door.

"I didn't realize you had an affinity for horses?" Amelia said to the maid, impressed by her complete lack of hesitation.

"My grandfather lived in the country and his neighbor had one. We rode it several times." She reached out to brush the horse's nose tenderly. "I have fond memories of those days."

"That sounds lovely." Amelia had ridden horses on occasion in her youth but rarely since. Her attention shifted to the partially open door where a woman stood, stretching around the cabbie to look in their direction.

"Who? Inspector Field? But he only just came in," the woman protested, displeasure sharpening her tone. "And his dinner half cold!"

"He's needed quick like," the driver told her, then turned away and stomped back to them, still muttering. "Urgent, apparently."

If the news she had to share weren't so dire, Amelia would've been amused by the scene.

Several minutes passed before the door to the lodging house opened again and Henry emerged, looking about before moving toward the cab.

"You wanted to see me?" he asked the driver warily.

"Henry." Amelia stepped forward.

"Amelia?" Astonishment laced his tone as he drew nearer. "Whatever are you doing here? Is everything all right?"

"No, I'm sorry to say it's not." The events of the evening threatened to overcome her. She had yet to determine if the precious moment when she'd sensed Lily had been real, but now wasn't the time to allow her emotions to get the better of her.

"What's happened?" He took her arm, holding it gently as if to lend his support, his handsome features reassuringly familiar in the faint glow of the carriage light.

"I've just come from Mrs. Nettle's home," she began, trying to gather her thoughts so she could deliver the news as concisely as possible. "And—"

"At this hour?" Alarm sharpened his tone. Henry glanced around, nodding politely at Yvette, but was clearly distressed by the news.

"She hosted a séance, which she invited me to attend. I'll tell you about it another time—it's what happened afterward that is of concern."

"Oh?"

Amelia shook her head. There was so much she wanted to tell him. Where to begin? "She asked Yvette and me to wait after the séance ended and the others left, saying there was more coming through." She paused, hoping she'd done the right thing by calling on him. "Mrs. Nettle has seen another body."

"No," Henry whispered, yet there was no denying the real dread in his tone.

"I'm afraid so." Amelia pulled out the paper, aware he wouldn't be able to see much in the dark. "Her drawing made me think of her last description of King's Cross with its clock tower."

Henry didn't respond, seeming more distressed by the news than she'd expected. "What else did she say?"

"That's it's a woman. A young woman."

"Dear God." Henry turned away, a hand running through his hair. "No—no, it can't be."

"What is it?" Now she was the one concerned, based on his obvious upset, something she'd only witnessed on rare occasions. "Henry?" She placed a comforting hand on his arm, waiting for him to face her.

He slowly did so, the sorrow in his eyes apparent even in the dim glow of the cab lantern. "I've spent much of the day and half the night searching for a young woman...a friend of the family...she's been missing since last evening."

Amelia gasped, her heart aching for him. "Oh, no." She longed to tell him this might be someone different, that Mrs. Nettle could be wrong. Yet the sinking sensation in her stomach said otherwise. But it wasn't within her power to keep from reassuring him. "We mustn't jump to conclusions. There are many young women in London, sadly many of them living dangerous lives. It might not be...we don't have any evidence that it could be..."

He straightened, head dropping back, to stare at the starless night sky. Did he hope to see something in the heavens that wasn't there? She knew that feeling all too well. "It's difficult not to."

She knew that feeling too. "I know."

With a beleaguered sigh, he met her gaze, the anguish in his expression clear, tugging at her. “Let’s have a closer look at the drawing.”

Chapter Eighteen

Henry insisted that Amelia and Yvette return home. In fact, he'd insisted on it several times—to no avail.

"This is a police matter," he told Amelia as they neared King's Cross in her hansom cab after he'd returned inside for his hat and coat, worry for her echoed in his concern for Eleanor Tisdale. "I appreciate you allowing me to make use of your cab, but you must go home."

"We will." She reached to take his hand in her gloved one and gave it a firm squeeze. "As soon as we see whether there's anything to discover at the railyard."

Anyone, he wanted to correct. The terrible feeling gripping his entire body told him no other word would do. Eleanor was behind that door, in the same place they'd found Clarissa Digby, his gut told him that fact. Would her skull be fractured in the same manner? Shattered into tiny pieces for no apparent reason?

The thought was inconceivable. Unbearable.

Yet the clear puddle of blood Mrs. Nettle had drawn beside the body suggested there was little doubt. If it proved true, Henry feared he might vomit—the first time since his early days as a constable walking a beat, when he'd come upon his first murder victim.

It no longer mattered if he didn't believe in Mrs. Nettle's supposed abilities. All that mattered was Eleanor.

"We will not borrow worry," Amelia ordered in a quiet tone, pressed up against his side in the small cab with the maid on the other side of her. "No purpose will be served to make any assumptions until we know for certain."

She squeezed his hand even tighter, belying her words. It was clear the same fear which gripped him held her in its grasp.

Blast it. How many times in the last few months had he wished he hadn't brought murder and danger to her doorstep? Yet here he was again, dragging Amelia into another murder investigation.

It had been easy to think he could allow her to aid him in his investigations in some manner. That it would be not only helpful but...enjoyable.

How foolish he'd been. How naïve. Henry longed to take back those thoughts and remove Amelia from this moment entirely.

Or rather, he *almost* did.

Her warmth against his side steadied him, something he would've denied needing until this evening. Her presence meant more than he could say. He rubbed a hand over his chest to ease the sudden ache. Amelia was coming to mean even more to him than he'd realized.

Now wasn't the time to consider how he felt about that, or whether her feelings might match his own, though he most definitely appreciated how much it helped to have something other than Eleanor to fill his thoughts for even a few minutes.

It didn't take long for them to arrive at King's Cross station, the place quiet this late in the evening.

Henry rapped on the roof of the cab as they approached the railyard, and the driver halted. Right. He had to put aside all personal feelings, and do his job. That was all he had to do.

"If you'll wait here—" he said determinedly to Amelia, one hand on the door.

"You are not going in there alone." Her firm tone suggested she wouldn't allow any argument.

Blast the woman, but she was brave. "It could prove dangerous," Henry began.

"All the more reason someone should accompany you." Amelia waved a hand for him to alight. "We should hurry, don't you think?"

Her distraction method was impressive. He recognized it for what it was, as he used the technique himself on occasion. Still, he stepped out of the cab and assisted her to do the same.

"Yvette, are you comfortable waiting with the driver or would you prefer to join us?" Amelia asked her maid quietly.

The young woman swallowed. "I will wait here. If you don't return in a timely manner, I shall request that the driver aid me in finding help."

"Excellent plan." Amelia nodded. She glanced at the driver, who heaved a sigh.

"I expect we can count on your assistance," Henry said to the driver with a nod.

"Yes, Inspector," the cabbie reluctantly agreed. "I'll keep watch and do as she says."

Henry retrieved the two lanterns he'd brought and quickly lit them, handing one to Amelia. "There was a break in the fence just over there." He nodded in that direction. "With luck, they haven't yet repaired it. Ready?"

"Yes."

He moved to the fence and followed it a short distance to where he'd noted the damage a few days ago. After handing his lantern to Amelia, he forced it open and stepped inside.

Amelia quickly followed, returning his lantern before holding hers aloft to look around. "A rather spooky place," she whispered in an undertone.

"It certainly is." He held her gaze for a moment, still torn about having her accompany him. Should he send her back to the cab? Should he have gone to the Yard? "Stay close. If anything happens—" He couldn't bear to finish the thought. What had he done?

"I shall scream loudly and run for help."

"Good." That was some small comfort. Henry started forward as quickly as he dared with Amelia's hand in his, stomach knotted with worry, taking care to step over any rail parts or tools lying on the ground and pointing them out to Amelia. The smell of damp earth, train smoke, and grease lingered in the air.

There was no sign of the watchman. Henry supposed he should've tried to find him before entering the yard this way, but the urgency clutching at him said otherwise.

It didn't take long before they stood at the top of the slope that led to the door of the abandoned tunnel.

"My goodness." Amelia stared at it, her voice barely audible. "It...it looks very much like what Mrs. Nettle drew, doesn't it?"

Her observation only made him more worried that they'd find Eleanor inside. Without a word, heart aching, Henry moved around to the side where the slope was less steep, trusting that Amelia would follow, carefully stepping only where there was no other footprint.

He held out his hand to aid her descent, and a moment later, they stood before the door. *This was it.* "Wait here."

"I would prefer to remain with you." This time her voice held a hint of uncertainty, her gaze darting about the darkness.

"I'm just going to have a look inside. The tunnel isn't very long, so I won't be far away." And if someone had murdered Eleanor or anyone else in there, he didn't want Amelia to see it.

"Very well." Her worried gaze held his, visible in the dim glow of the lantern. "I'll be right here if you have need of me."

Henry's heart squeezed at her supportive words. He didn't know what he'd done to deserve the blessing of her in his life, but he was grateful all the same. And he would not lose her.

Lantern in hand he opened the door, finding it much easier than the last time. Then he braced himself and stepped inside, holding the light before him.

Eleanor.

There was no denying the identity of the body lying on the ground, and Henry's stomach lurched in response, bringing unwanted bile to his throat. He recognized her instantly, though her pale hair was strewn about her face and shoulders, hiding most of her face. She was on her side, hands outstretched before her, wearing the exact gown her lady's maid had described.

And there was, indeed, a pool of blood before her, the metallic scent of it tainting the small space and stinging his nose.

Henry lifted the lantern higher to check the partial tunnel, though he already knew it was empty. Then he set the light down and bent low for a closer look, his heart aching and stomach churning at the horrible sight before him.

"Eleanor?" Why he bothered to say her name, he didn't know. Still, he gently brushed aside her hair and checked with fading hope for a pulse.

Her skin was cold, and it came as no surprise there was none. She must've been killed late last night or early this morning, based on the color of her skin. Some of the blood on the ground had dried, suggesting hours had passed since her murder.

How was he going to tell her parents of this? They would be devastated.

The door opened behind him and Amelia stood framed in the doorway, mouth agape. "Oh, no." Her horrified gaze flew to Henry's. "Is it...your friend?"

He nodded, still sick to his stomach from the loss, by what she might have endured in her final hours. His attention returned to her still form, needing to know how she'd died—and who had done this to her. "It's Eleanor."

Though he knew he should order Amelia out—she didn't need to see another body when she'd already seen more than her share—he couldn't. Not when her presence lent him strength.

He forced himself to focus on his job, the routine of it allowing him a small measure of objectivity. The blood on the ground before the body had him examining her chest, finding a bloody slit in the fabric near her ribs. Then he found another, this one higher, closer to her heart.

"Can you tell...how?" Amelia whispered, drawing nearer to hold her lantern to allow him to see better.

"Stabbed. Several times." That accounted for the significant blood loss. Henry eased back more of the hair from Eleanor's pale face, strangely relieved not to find any injuries there. That would be a blessing of sorts to her parents; they wouldn't have a bruised and bloody face to scar the memories of their daughter.

How he dreaded telling them.

"What would have possessed her to come here?" Amelia asked as she glanced about the space, taking care where she stepped.

"I have no idea." Henry hesitated to say more out of habit. It was rarely good practice to share details of an ongoing investigation; but this was Amelia, and she had proven herself trustworthy time and again. Besides, she had been brave enough to venture in here to lend him support. She deserved to know the few facts he possessed. "She told her parents she was attending the theater with a friend and spending the night with her, something they'd done in the past. The coachman left her at the friend's house, but it appears she never went in."

"Hmmm. Sounds as if she might have had something other than the theater planned with someone other than her friend."

"Yes, but what and who?" Henry shook his head, exhaustion starting to demand its dues after a long day. "There has been no trace of her until now."

Amelia sighed. "If only the medium foretold threats, rather than merely where to find the victims after the fact."

Henry couldn't agree more as he continued to stare at the young woman he'd known for nearly all of her short life.

The only thing he could do now was try to determine who had done this to her and why. Eleanor and Miss Digby both.

"Odd that both victims were found here, don't you think?"

The question had Henry blinking, bringing him back to the task at hand. Odd. Yes. "It certainly links their murders. Though the method is different, not many people know of this place." Had the victims been left here with the hope that no one would discover them? Another question he wanted answered.

"It—it almost looks as if she is clutching something in her hand." Amelia pointed to the one she meant, holding the lantern closer to allow Henry to look.

"A bit of fabric." He pulled it free and briefly studied it. "It could have come from the killer." He took a second look at Eleanor's hand. "She does have a torn nail and abrasions on her fingers."

"Good for her."

Henry glanced up, uncertain as to Amelia's meaning.

Her lips tightened. "Good that she didn't succumb without a fight. I-I hope she hurt whoever it was. Made him—or her—pay at least a small price for what they did."

He nodded, appreciating the sentiment, and wrapped the bit of fabric into his handkerchief before placing it in his pocket. After checking Eleanor's other hand, he searched around her body for any sort of clue.

"This appears to be a man's shoe print, based on its size." Amelia pointed to the ground just to the side of her.

"You are proving to be a very effective investigator," Henry advised with a wry smile as he straightened to take a look at the print, noting it was definitely a man's. The narrow toe and deeper heel indentation suggested it wasn't a work boot. "I'm pleased to see that you're already taking care to remain in one place."

Amelia glanced to either side of her, keeping her feet still as she'd done since coming into the space. "That did cross my mind. I was careful when I stepped inside as well."

"I appreciate that. Let me know if you see anything else of interest."

Henry found a second half-shoe print but little else. It appeared to be smaller than the one Fletcher had previously found, but measurements and better light were necessary to know for certain.

He returned his attention to Eleanor. If Amelia could return to the cab without going through the dark railyard alone, he would have asked her to leave. All he could do at this juncture was warn her in case she preferred to look away.

"I'm going to take a closer look at the body." He briefly glanced at Amelia, who nodded, but her expression showed curiosity rather than dread, and the words on his mind spilled out. "You are unique, Amelia."

Her brows lifted. "Oh? What makes you say that?"

"I cannot name any other lady of my acquaintance who would act as bravely as you have this evening."

Pleased surprise widened her eyes before the hint of a smile touched her lips. "I only wish the case wasn't so...personal to you."

He nodded, wishing the same. But of course, every victim he tried to gain justice for had a loved one; every single one.

At least her eyes were already closed. Seeing them wide with horror might've been too much to bear, and it was already bad enough.

Still, he studied her face for a long moment, memories passing quickly through his mind. Ones of her laughing, the look of disdain she'd mastered at an early age, the way her nose wrinkled when she found something distasteful.

He closed his eyes as a wave of grief rolled over him. It was too much after all.

The feel of Amelia's hand on his shoulder steadied him once again.

"I'm so very sorry, Henry." She paused a moment. "I can't help but think Eleanor would be relieved it was you who found her. She's in the presence of friends again."

The thought was strangely comforting. *Back amongst friends.*

Forcing his emotions back, Henry returned his focus to the procedures that were almost second nature, mentally logging the information he found so he could consider it later.

Signs of a struggle, given the state of her hands and tears in her pelisse and gown.

No reticule or personal belongings nearby.

Scuffs on the bottoms of her shoes.

A smear of dirt on her cheek.

Overall, not much to go on. He and Fletcher would need to return at daylight for a second look, especially outside.

"Come out of there at once!" a male voice demanded from outside. "I'm armed!"

Amelia stiffened with fright, gaze on Henry as if uncertain what to do.

He blew out a sigh. "The night watchman, I would imagine." She drew a relieved breath as he straightened. "Scotland Yard Inspector Field coming out," he shouted, then moved to the partially open door.

"Inspector Field?" A lantern thrust forward at eye level had Henry squinting in response. "Whatever are you doing here at this ungodly hour?"

"Unfortunately we have found another body."

"You don't say. How could that be?" The man finally lowered the lantern, allowing Henry to confirm his identity as Jolly, the same watchman he had met previously.

That was a question Henry wanted answered. How effective was the supposed watchman when not one but two bodies had been discovered at the railyard? The place was of good size, but it still seemed as though the guard should have seen something. Could the man be guilty after all? If nothing else, the fence should've been repaired to better protect the property—though of course he didn't yet know if that was how the killer and Eleanor had entered.

"I assume you didn't see anything out of the ordinary this evening?" Henry wasn't sure why he bothered with the query.

"Can't say that I have." The man shrugged nonchalantly, peering around Henry at the unmoving body just visible. "Made my rounds like usual. It's been a quiet evening—that is, until I noted the glow of light around the door just now." He leaned close, holding Henry's gaze. "It gave me quite the start, to tell you the truth."

"I'm sure." If only the man had seen something of the sort earlier. "Are you aware the fence remains in disrepair?"

The guard shook his head, clearly exasperated. "It was supposed to be taken care of this afternoon. Not sure why it wasn't."

Bother it all. Henry would have a word with Mr. Weston about it.

"W-What happened to them?" The man gestured with his free hand toward the doorway, his curiosity obvious.

"I can't say." He didn't trust the watchman not to tell everyone he came across about the details. Henry would do what he could to protect Eleanor's reputation and honor her memory, though it felt pointless now. "But I could certainly use your help."

"Of course, sir." Jolly's gaze flicked uneasily between Henry and the door. "I...I suppose we need to haul out the body."

"Yes, but first I need a constable." Henry wanted Fletcher, but a constable would have to do. He wasn't about to leave Amelia alone with Eleanor, nor would he allow Amelia to return to the cab alone. The watchman couldn't very well leave his post, nor did Henry trust him to remain and not disturb any potential evidence. "I have a hansom cab waiting near the break in the fence," Henry told the man. "If you could ask the driver to return with a constable or two, I would appreciate it."

"Of course, sir."

Henry waited for the man to depart, then opened the door for Amelia and assisted her to step out. Eleanor's reputation wasn't the only one he intended to protect. He paused to set his lantern inside the abandoned tunnel with Eleanor, not wanting to leave her in the dark. Then he took Amelia's lantern and offered his elbow.

She wrapped her arm tight around his, remaining quiet for a long moment, leaving him to his thoughts. While he appreciated having her at his side, he was equally anxious to remove her from the crime scene and send her home where he knew she'd be safe.

It didn't take long for the silence of the night to be broken by shouts in the distance, followed by a police whistle, then a second one farther away.

"How efficient," Amelia said with a smile.

In short order, Jolly returned with two constables, lanterns in hand. Henry ordered one to stand guard and the other to fetch a police wagon to take Eleanor to St. Thomas'.

He didn't bother to explain Amelia's presence and soon turned to meet her gaze. "I will escort you to the hansom cab," he told her. "It is past time for you and Yvette to return home. Mr. and Mrs. Fernsby will be beside themselves."

"Are you certain?" She sent a questioning look between him and the door as if doubtful Henry could manage without her, nearly making him smile. "I could send Yvette home with the cab and a message—"

"No need," Henry quickly countered. The night was going to be even longer—and more difficult—than he'd anticipated, but there was no need for that to be true for Amelia. Besides, he needed his concentration on his job, not on the woman whose safety mattered so much to him.

"Be sure to avoid trampling the crime scene," Henry directed the constable. "We need to preserve any and all clues that could be in the vicinity."

"You may count on me, sir." The constable nodded.

"Good. I will return directly."

Henry glanced one more time toward the door. *Bless you, Eleanor. May you rest in peace, knowing I will do everything in my power to find whoever did this to you and Miss Digby—and bring them to justice.*

Then he turned away, pressing Amelia's hand against his side, once again grateful for her steadying presence.

Chapter Nineteen

THE NIGHT WAS AS long and terrible as Henry feared it would be.

He accompanied Eleanor's body to St. Thomas' himself, giving strict orders for her not to be touched until he sent word to proceed. Henry wanted the Tisdales' approval before Arthur Taylor performed an examination, even though it wasn't required.

Then he made his way to the Tisdale residence, despite the late hour. Though tempted to wait until morning to tell Eleanor's parents, he decided it was unlikely they were sleeping soundly anyway. Delivering the horrible news wouldn't steal a night's rest from them.

The anxious butler, slightly disheveled and clearly in the middle of putting the house to bed for the evening, showed Henry to the study to wait while he roused the family. Mr. Tisdale descended first, wearing a nightrobe and a worried expression.

He took one look at Henry, then buried his face in his hands.

Henry gave him a few moments to absorb the shock before clearing his throat to formally state the message he hated to deliver. "I'm so very sorry, sir...but Eleanor has been found dead."

Some needed to hear bad news more than once before they fully accepted it, a lesson he'd learned over the years, having delivered it far too often.

Several moments passed before the older man managed to respond. "H-How?"

"She...she was stabbed."

"Good God." Mr. Tisdale reached out a shaking hand to a nearby chair to steady himself. "But why—where?"

Henry's jaw tightened. Telling this story was worse than he could have imagined. "I found her in an abandoned railway tunnel near King's Cross station."

The bereaved man shook his head, clearly confused. "What on Earth could she have possibly been doing there?"

"We don't yet know." Henry would only be guessing if he answered. Perhaps she'd left her friend's house and walked to King's Cross. It was only two or three miles, so was certainly possible. He intended to check the distance come morning. Or she might've hired a cab. Perhaps she'd ventured to the station to meet someone, or planned to take a train. And there was always the chance the railway station hadn't been her destination, that the killer had encountered her on the street where the Walters lived and taken her to King's Cross.

Theories, theories. He needed evidence.

Mr. Tisdale moved to drop heavily onto a chair, his face pale, looking far older than he had the previous day. "Whatever will we do?"

Henry hesitated. Not only did he have no answer, but he also didn't think Mr. Tisdale expected one. At least not from Henry.

A rustle of fabric from the doorway had Henry turning to see Mrs. Tisdale, also in her nightclothes, pause there. Her gaze darted between Henry and her husband, then her face contorted with utter grief before heart-wrenching sobs filled the silence.

Mr. Tisdale rose to take his wife into his arms and held her as she cried, the guttural, almost animal sound of despair making Henry's chest ache.

The couple's shared misery was enough to bring tears to his own eyes. He would have given them a few minutes alone, but they stood in the doorway, blocking his escape. He made do by looking away to give them a small measure of privacy, certain they'd have questions soon. It took some time, but their gushing tears temporarily eased.

Given the terrible news and the late hour, he shared only the basic details and answered the few brief questions they asked. The rest could wait until morning. To his surprise, Thomas didn't join them. Hadn't he been awakened, or had he chosen not to be with his mother and stepfather? Either option caused Henry concern.

Making his excuses, he left the two Tisdales in their shock. When Henry finally sought his own bed, he slept fitfully for a few short hours before rising early. He wanted to deliver the news to his own parents as well. The news had to come from his lips.

His father continued to be an early riser, despite his retirement several years ago, but he hadn't yet come downstairs when a maid opened the front door to Henry.

"I'll wait in the study," Henry said, after telling her he needed to speak with him.

He'd been there less than five minutes before his father joined him, doing much the same as Mr. Tisdale had: taking one look at Henry's expression before shaking his head, sorrow etching his face. "It's not good news then."

"I'm sorry to say it's not," Henry confirmed quietly, his father's expression making his chest ache once again.

"I was afraid of that as each hour passed without her return." His father clasped Henry's shoulder before embracing him briefly, then leaning back to look into his eyes. "Did you find her?"

Henry nodded. He hadn't told the Tisdales about the medium's involvement yet, feeling it would only cloud their grief. He intended to do so later that morning. He felt obliged to, despite his skepticism, though he rather wished he could keep the full story to himself, as he worried it would only cause harm.

"How was she killed?" His father gestured to the chairs before the cold hearth, and they both took a seat.

Henry shared the basics, knowing his father would ask what Mr. Tisdale hadn't.

He did so immediately "What made you look in the railyard?" His father frowned. "Did the watchman report something amiss?"

Henry sighed, still uncertain what to think of the medium's predictions. He usually tried not to share too many details of a case with his father. After all, he was retired and should spend his days thinking about things other than murder—but this one was personal to them both.

"About a week ago, a medium recently contacted my...my friend, Mrs. Greystone," Henry began, watching his father's puzzled expression. Clearly he didn't understand what that had to do with their conversation.

Henry told the story slowly, taking time to sort through his own thoughts as he spoke. The whole situation was ridiculous, yet without Mrs. Nettle's involvement, how would he have found Eleanor?

"Two bodies at King's Cross." His father stared across the room, brow furrowed, as if still taking in the information. "Interesting."

How often had Henry caught himself using that same word in the same manner? Perhaps he was more like his father than he realized. He took comfort in that.

Their longtime butler Stubbs entered the room with a tray, the scent of freshly brewed coffee filling the air. "Pardon the interruption, sir, but I thought coffee might be welcome."

"It is." Henry's father sat forward in his chair, as if eager for a cup. "For both of us, I would imagine."

"Yes, please." Henry watched as the butler poured then took the offered cup, knowing it would be better than the one his landlady had brewed. He couldn't linger long, but a moment of respite after the turmoil of the last day and night was welcome, especially when spent in his father's company.

After Stubbs departed with the promise to advise them when Mrs. Field woke, Henry's father took a sip before sending an inquiring look at Henry. "What do you know of this Mrs. Nettle?"

"Very little. She worked with another inspector on a case, and I spoke to him. He has nothing but praise for her and her...talents."

"Hmm. I can't say that I tend to believe in such things, but one must admit there are events in this world that are difficult to explain."

Henry nodded, having had the same thought himself. The memory of his conversation with Arthur returned. A presence, just out of the corner of one's eye...

"Your mother and I will call on the Tisdales later this morning. I'm sure they can use any and all support through this difficult time."

Henry blinked, brought back suddenly to the present. "Needless to say, they are devastated. I am hoping they will agree to a postmortem, though, of course, we will proceed with one regardless. Mr. Taylor might be able to provide helpful details, and we need every piece of evidence we can get on the case."

"I will advise them of the need for one as well." His father shook his head again. "Whoever did this must be found and brought to justice."

An even deeper resolve took hold at his father's words—to find the guilty party for both Eleanor and Miss Digby's sakes, and make them pay. It wouldn't bring back either young woman, but it was all that was within Henry's power to do.

And he couldn't dismiss the worry that the killer would strike again.

With the promise to be in touch soon to see how his mother was faring with the bad news, Henry went first to St. Thomas' to make certain Arthur understood the request to wait on the examination then hurried on to Scotland Yard.

Fletcher waited for him, obviously anxious to begin the day. “Back to the search?”

Henry shook his head wearily. “To a search of a different sort. I found Eleanor Tisdale’s body last night —and in the same location as Clarissa Digby’s.”

“No.” Fletcher heaved a sigh, his disappointment obvious. “How strange—though I confess that the worry of not finding Miss Tisdale alive crossed my mind in the middle of the night. Still, I wanted to hope her independent streak took hold and she was having a bit of fun.”

If only. “I wish that had been the case. I need to update the Director—will you join me so you have all the details as well?” At Fletcher’s nod, Henry led the way to the Director’s open office door and knocked.

“Morning, Field. Fletcher.” Reynolds set down the report he was reading and waved them in. He looked between them for a moment. “I can see you don’t come bearing good news, despite the early hour.”

“No, sir. I found the body of Eleanor Tisdale at the railyard in the same location as Clarissa Digby last night,” Henry began, before deciding he would have to mention Amelia’s involvement to avoid raising questions if it was discovered later. It couldn’t be helped.

He shared the details in a succinct manner, appreciating that the Director didn’t interrupt until Henry had completed the tale. He was careful to include the fact that he knew the Tisdale family well, as did his father, and hoped Reynolds wouldn't request him to remove himself from the case because of that.

"Sounds as if you need as much information as possible to solve this one," the Director said heavily. "One murder there is tragic. A second is suspicious. If we find a third, we have a real problem on our hands."

"Agreed." Henry nodded. "I intend to return to the railyard with Fletcher for a closer look, now that it's morning. I'll call on the Tisdales mid-morning to see if any additional information has arisen and confirm the need for a postmortem."

Reynolds slowly nodded. "Good plan. Can't say that I like the medium's involvement."

"Nor do I, sir." Henry cleared his throat. "You may remember reading that Inspector Robertson at F Division worked with her on a case. He says he would work with her again if the opportunity arose. Thought she was helpful and cooperative. And she has pointed us to two bodies in the last week, sir."

"Hmmm." The Director grimaced. "That doesn't make me feel any better."

Henry nodded. He felt the same way and knew Fletcher did, too.

The Director sighed. "I suppose her claim of being a medium is neither here nor there. It doesn't change our job, or the fact she's a potential witness who needs to be interviewed." Reynolds held each of their gazes for a long moment as if to make sure they agreed.

"No, it does not. Her servants confirmed her and her husband's whereabouts the night of Miss Digby's murder, and we'll speak with the medium and her household again." Henry stood, eager to get on with it as Fletcher did the same.

"We need to act with all speed, Field," the Director advised. "Find our murderer quickly."

"Understood, sir." Henry hid his irritation as best he could. Of course he intended to act with all due haste—that was how he proceeded on every murder case—but in this instance, he had the added motivation of the Tisdales being longtime friends, not to mention the worry the killer might strike again.

He stopped at his desk long enough to retrieve his hat, deciding his case notes would have to wait. Then he turned toward the door, Fletcher on his heels as a voice called out—

"Field."

Henry reluctantly halted at the sound of Perdy's call, unable to imagine what the other inspector wanted. "Yes?"

Perdy eyed them both, shifting on his feet. "I heard a rumor you were working with that medium woman." His lips twisted. "Watch your back. Don't let her lead you astray."

"What do you mean?" Henry stared, puzzled as to why the other inspector would raise the subject and how he knew anything about her.

"Just a rumor I heard." Perdy shook his head. "There's something odd going on there."

"What rumor?" Henry asked.

"That...that she's in league with the devil." Perdy gave a mock shudder, seeming unnerved by the thought.

Henry raised an eyebrow. "We will certainly keep that in mind."

He returned to his sergeant, and they continued out the door.

"What was that about?" Fletcher asked as he matched Henry's stride along the busy street.

"I have no idea. Maybe he's superstitious about the spirit world."

"Is it only me that tends to think that whatever Perdy says, we should do the opposite?"

A laugh nearly escaped Henry. "No. The thought struck me as well."

"Good to know I am not alone in that." Fletcher was silent for a long moment before he said quietly, "I'm very sorry, sir. About your friend. How terrible that you were the one to find her."

"Thank you." Henry's thoughts drifted to what Amelia had said the previous evening. That she thought Eleanor would be glad he was the one who had. "I hope I can find justice for her." He held his sergeant's gaze. "That *we* can find justice for her. And for Miss Digby as well."

Fletcher nodded somberly, his eyes fierce. "We will do all we can to make that happen."

They arrived at the railyard to find a repairman working on the fence.

"Let's hope that finally keeps the killer out," Henry murmured, though he wished they'd had a chance to examine the ground around the broken fence for possible footprints. Another avenue of clues gone.

"But will it keep him from striking again?" Fletcher mused. "What's to stop him finding another dumping ground—one we don't know?"

Henry had no answer. The difference between the two victims and the method of murder made for a puzzling case. However, their bodies had been found in the same place, and they were both young females with a rebellious streak—all connections and ones he would carefully consider.

Henry led the way to the gate of the railyard, surprised to find Mr. Weston crossing the open space.

The man paused as recognition dawned. "Ah. Inspector Field. I thought I might see you here today."

"Yes, another murder requires yet another visit." Henry didn't try to hide the reproach in his tone. "Good to see the broken fence is finally being repaired."

He knew his anger was misplaced, but he couldn't help it. A part of him wondered if the killer had forced both Miss Digby and Eleanor through that broken spot. If it hadn't been broken there, they might've managed to escape, or someone could have helped save them if not for the access into the railyard. Then again, the two women might have hoped to hide in the railyard from whoever followed them. Would he ever know?

"It is, after an unfortunate delay." Mr. Weston seemed entirely oblivious to the subtle dig. "Do you have any idea who is behind either of the deaths yet?"

As if murder cases were so easy to solve. "No, not yet. If you happen to have any suspicions, we'd be happy to hear them."

"Can't say that I do. I will leave the investigating in your hands." The other man smiled politely. "I hope to have a list, including descriptions, of the stolen jewelry this afternoon and will let you know when I receive it. For now, I must be going. Do let me know if I can be of further assistance."

With a nod, he departed.

"He is yet to be of any assistance, if you ask me," Fletcher muttered. "Wouldn't you think he'd be more concerned that a second body—and another woman—was discovered here?"

"I would, yes." He watched Mr. Weston hurry away, wondering what had brought the man to the railyard so early in the day. Was he now suspicious of everyone? "Why don't we see what more we can discover."

Chapter Twenty

HENRY AND FLETCHER SCOURED the abandoned tunnel as well as the area outside the door, coming away with one full shoe print and two halves—but no murder weapon. While the imprint didn't appear especially distinguishable, it was still a clue. They also found a few more strands of fiber that Henry thought might match whatever fabric Eleanor had held in her hand.

"Now we need only come across someone with torn clothing that matches the fibers, in the whole of London, hoping of course that they haven't changed since yesterday or dumped the torn clothing," Fletcher muttered, obviously frustrated. "Clues like this can be maddening."

"Something might come of it." Henry was equally frustrated but refrained from admitting it. One of them needed to remain at least outwardly optimistic.

Though he intended to ask Arthur Taylor to search for more fibers when he did the postmortem, Henry also wondered if Amelia might be of assistance. He remembered seeing a microscope in her laboratory. With that in mind, he returned to the repaired fence to see if any fabric had caught there, the most likely point of entry for the killer and his victims.

The repairman had departed, the ground near the area trampled by his boots. Henry focused on the iron fence, searching for any threads stuck to the rough metal. He found several, including a long strand of hair that might have been Eleanor's, but couldn't say whether the fibers matched what he'd already found. Still, he carefully placed them in a handkerchief to study later.

He left Fletcher to continue searching the railyard with additional orders to question any employees who regularly had business there. The sergeant was also to question those in the nearby shops to see if anyone had witnessed anything unusual.

Meanwhile, Henry returned with a heavy heart to the Tisdale home.

The sight of the boxwood wreath adorned with black ribbons on their front door gave him pause, a sign to callers that the house and its occupants were in mourning. It might be merely his own grief, but he felt a heaviness in the air as he lifted his hand to knock on the door.

He was shown to the drawing room where the drapes were drawn, another mourning custom, gratified to see his mother and father with the Tisdales. Shock and disbelief marked their faces, as did deep sorrow.

"Henry." Mr. Tisdale nodded but didn't rise from his chair. No doubt the poor man was exhausted.

Mrs. Tisdale inclined her head as well, her eyes red and shadowed, a handkerchief clutched in one hand.

Henry greeted his mother and father, the grief in his mother's eyes pinching his heart as he kissed her cheek. He detested seeing her sad and was grateful it rarely happened. The questioning look his father sent him was another hurdle. To admit he had nothing to report didn't sit well, even if he'd only discovered Eleanor's body late last evening.

At the slight shake of Henry's head, his father gave a subtle nod but showed no other reaction. That Henry expected to see disappointment on his face was something he needed to work on. His father knew better than most that investigations took time.

It was apparent from the silence of the room that they had no news to share that might aid the investigation. Though not surprising, it was still disappointing.

Henry cleared his throat, wishing he didn't have to mention what he needed to. However, there was no need for the ladies to hear the conversation. "Might I have a word?" He lifted a brow at Mr. Tisdale, followed by a pertinent glance at his father.

"Of course." Mr. Tisdale pushed to his feet, the effort nearly more than he seemed able to manage.

Henry's father also stood, but not before tightening his grip on his wife's hand before releasing it.

"If you ladies will excuse us?" Mr. Tisdale didn't wait for a response but shuffled to the doorway, Henry and his father following.

Their host led the way to his study and closed the door behind them. The drapes were drawn there as well. Mr. Tisdale went directly to the sideboard, where a collection of crystal decanters awaited. "Excuse the early hour, but support of some sort is required." He lifted a decanter with a trembling hand, only to have Henry's father take it. Mr. Tisdale glared at him, clearly expecting an argument.

Henry's father smiled sadly. "Allow me." He took the crystal decanter and poured three measures into the waiting glasses.

Though Henry opened his mouth to protest, now wasn't the time. In all honesty, a stiff drink might be just what they all needed, given the terrible circumstances.

He took the glass from his father with a shared look of understanding, which did more to revive him than the drink could offer. But he didn't miss the fact that Mr. Tisdale needed this moment even more. If the whiskey would bolster the man's spirits, however temporarily, Henry was all for it.

His father, who always seemed to know the right thing to say, lifted his glass and waited for them to do the same. "To Eleanor. A lovely lady of grace and good humor."

Mr. Tisdale's hand trembled even more as he lifted his glass. "To my beautiful d-daughter," he said, his voice cracking. "May she rest in peace."

"To Eleanor," Henry added, his voice thick. "Her smile and laughter will be dearly missed."

Their host's eyes filled with tears as he tipped his glass, draining it completely. His father did the same, leaving Henry to follow suit.

The liquor burned a path down his throat all the way to his stomach, nearly causing him to cough. Sipping whiskey at Amelia's was a far cry from this. Luckily he maintained his composure, unsurprised his father did the same.

Mr. Tisdale, empty glass in hand, made his way to a chair and sank into it. "Thank you," he said weakly. "I needed that."

"As did we," his father added, moving forward to take the glass and set it aside. "Now then, there are a few things we need to discuss."

Mr. Tisdale looked between them with a weary expression. "And what might those be?"

Henry took the chair before their host and held his gaze. "It is imperative that we have a closer look at Eleanor to discover exactly what happened. It could help us find who did this." He deliberately left out the words postmortem and examination, as well as body. While Mr. Tisdale's agreement wasn't needed as this was a murder investigation, Henry wanted it all the same, something he tried to gain whenever possible. It felt especially important in this case, given the length of time the two families had been friends.

"Oh?" The man frowned. "I don't understand—"

"Martin," Henry's father interrupted. "We have been friends long enough that you are familiar with the investigative process. We need every bit of evidence we can get to find the guilty party. He must be brought to justice, you know that. A postmortem is a requirement in this type of situation."

Henry hid a grimace at the blunt language, waiting to see Mr. Tisdale's reaction.

"A—a postmortem!" Mr. Tisdale straightened for the first time since Henry's arrival. "You can't be serious. Why would I want her cut—"

His father waved a hand to halt the tirade. "First of all, the important part of Eleanor is no longer here. Her soul is in a better place. You know that as well as I do. Second, we *must* find who did this to her." He waited until Mr. Tisdale met his gaze. "Martin, listen to me. Eleanor was not the killer's only victim."

"What?" The grieving man looked between them. "Not the only—you can't be serious."

"We are," Henry interjected before his father could say anything else. "Another young woman was murdered several nights prior, the body left in the same location."

"Good God." Mr. Tisdale ran a hand over his forehead, as if uncertain what to think. "How terrible."

"Whoever it is could strike again," Henry's father warned before Henry could. Though retired, the older man clearly hadn't lost the ability to convince others to agree with what he wanted.

In truth, Henry appreciated seeing him in action. He had been a constable in a different division when his father had retired as a chief inspector, so they had never worked a case together. Still, he couldn't help but send him a questioning look, wondering how far he intended to take the tough language. There was a risk of pushing Mr. Tisdale too far.

"Another young lady could be killed?" The outrage in Mr. Tisdale's expression was touching. "That's—that's unacceptable!"

"We must work quickly to prevent that," Henry added in an effort to support his father's reasoning. "The clock is ticking. Every minute matters."

"Yes, of course." The older man pressed his lips tight, clearly torn about the subject. "I will speak with her mother and tell her...tell her we must do all we can to help."

"That is much appreciated. The sooner, the better." Henry nodded as he stood. "Thank you. And with your permission, I would also like to speak with a few members of the household again."

One of the footmen had been clearly uncomfortable when Henry questioned him the previous day, and Eleanor's lady's maid might have more to say now that her mistress had been found dead. In truth, finding Eleanor's body opened a whole new set of inquiries, many of which involved the same people.

Mr. Tisdale frowned as if perplexed by the request. "You've spoken with everyone at least once already. Is that really necessary?"

"It is. I have a few additional questions for several." He paused for a moment. "Including Thomas."

Henry noted his father stiffening out of the corner of his eye.

"Thomas?" Mr. Tisdale stared at him in confusion. "Why?"

"He was one of the last to have a conversation of any substance with Eleanor. He might have some insight into her thoughts, her decisions. It is important I review the details more closely with him."

A missing person investigation was one thing, but a murder was quite another. Finding Eleanor's body meant deepening the questions he'd asked of those who'd been in contact with her.

Including Thomas.

As an only child, Henry found sibling relationships interesting. He knew older brothers tended to treat their younger sisters with a certain amount of disdain, or, at the very least, disinterest. In the case of Thomas and Eleanor, the span of years between them and the fact that Thomas had a different father added further complexity to their situation.

But unlike most of his cases, Henry had the advantage of knowing the family prior to the investigation. While he didn't care to think Thomas capable of murder, he also knew from experience that when emotions ran high, the meekest person could change in an instant—becoming someone that no one, including themselves, would have recognized.

And it hadn't escaped Henry's notice that Thomas had been absent once again upon his arrival. Didn't he feel compelled to support his parents in any way possible, including spending time with them while the household adjusted to the loss? Wouldn't he want the comfort of their presence as well?

"I see." Mr. Tisdale sighed. "Well, I'm sure that can be arranged."

"That would be most helpful," Henry replied politely.

"I can tell you he won't be happy about it." Their host slowly stood. "But I'm certain you're accustomed to dealing with difficult personalities."

Henry shared a look with his father, who lifted a brow, as if also wondering what Mr. Tisdale meant.

Their host rang the bell and the butler soon appeared. "Please advise Thomas to join us."

"Of course, sir."

They waited in silence for Thomas's arrival, a silence that grew more uncomfortable with each minute that passed. At last, his father cleared his throat. Before he could speak, Thomas strolled into the room.

"Here, as requested," he announced as he looked between them.

"Henry has a few more questions for you," Mr. Tisdale moved toward the door. "I'm certain you will give him your full cooperation."

"Questions?" Thomas glared at Henry, his irritation obvious. "Surely he asked me enough yesterday."

Henry nodded, determined to remain polite and remember grief revealed itself in many different ways. "Just a few. They won't take long."

Henry's father started toward the door, pausing to clasp Thomas's shoulder. "I'm very sorry about your sister."

"Half-sister," Thomas corrected, only to have his eyes dart toward his stepfather as if realizing his error too late.

Mr. Tisdale glared at his stepson, lips pressed together with disapproval. "Even now, Thomas?" He shook his head and took his leave without another word.

Thomas's expression tightened. Remorse flashed across his features, but no apology emerged. Henry's father sent a worried look at them both, then followed Mr. Tisdale out the door.

Henry waited to see if Thomas would attempt to explain what had just happened. Was it a result of grief, or was something more going on?

Thomas heaved a beleaguered sigh and turned to face Henry. "What do you want to know *now*?" he asked, irritation coloring his tone.

Henry considered the younger man for a moment. "Have problems arisen between you and other members of the family?"

Anger stirred in Thomas's eyes, but he quickly dropped his gaze. "Nothing out of the ordinary. Father is less than pleased with me at least once a week."

"Oh?"

The younger Tisdale gave a one-shouldered shrug before turning away to glance at the closed door as if he'd rather be anywhere but there. "You know how it is with parents' expectations."

Henry didn't; he had always been fortunate that his desires for his life aligned with that of his parents for him—but decided to let it go for the moment. How lucky he was that he and his own parents were on good terms.

"I wanted to review your last conversation with Eleanor again." Henry withdrew his notebook from his pocket and flipped to the page where he'd jotted down Thomas's previous answers.

Thomas snorted as he threw himself onto a chair. "Am I to be accused of her murder?"

Henry looked up to hold his gaze. Perhaps he should follow his father's bluntness on this occasion. "Did you kill Eleanor?"

The young man glared. "No."

"Did you have anything to do with her disappearance?"

"No!" Exasperation had the man stiffening. "Shouldn't you focus on whoever might have done so instead of bothering us?"

Us? His word choice was interesting when he'd shown so little loyalty or affection for his family in the last four and twenty hours.

"Do you have anyone in particular in mind that I should speak to?" Henry asked, keeping his voice calm.

The young man sneered. "I think Caroline knows more than she's letting on. Someone caught Eleanor's attention, and one would have to assume Mother wouldn't approve of him."

Excitement danced up Henry's spine. A lead? "You don't have any idea who that was?"

"No, but I haven't accompanied Eleanor or attended the same gatherings as her for well over a year or more. Your time would be better spent asking someone who did."

"Such as Caroline," Henry suggested mildly.

Thomas shrugged. "Or one of Eleanor's other friends. She had plenty of them. Surely one knew what she was doing and who she was doing it with."

"She hadn't shown interest in any of your friends?"

"No."

The clipped and rather rapid answer made Henry wonder, but he had enough for now. He wouldn't push harder with Thomas until he had reason to do so—but neither was he ready to proclaim him innocent.

Chapter Twenty-One

Amelia returned home that afternoon from a thankfully cheerful errand, a pleasant sense of anticipation filling her. In truth, she'd needed a distraction to clear her mind from the previous evening's events.

"Was your outing successful?" Fernsby asked as he closed the door behind her and took her damp cloak.

"It was. The bookshop has promised to fulfill my request by the end of the week."

A story in a scientific journal she'd read that morning mentioned *The Principles and Practice of Medical Jurisprudence*, which outlined forensic science methods, a relatively new field. She couldn't think of a better way to aid Henry than to learn more about those methods, so she could apply her own background in chemistry and science to the task of seeking justice. She might not typically be allowed to accompany him as he worked on cases, so she needed to find another way to help.

The few murders they'd come upon together had been a result of unfortunate circumstances. While she had learned much from observing Henry, viewing crime scenes firsthand was an unsettling, often shocking, experience, as it had been last evening. Only afterward had she been able to reflect on his actions and consider how he approached the setting.

But if she could learn more about using modern scientific methods to analyze clues, surely she could be of assistance, even in an unofficial capacity?

Seeing his anguish when they'd found Miss Tisdale had touched her deeply. Of course, Henry being Henry, he'd hidden his emotions well, but not well enough. She'd still noted the subtle signs of his upset.

How fortunate she'd been at his side to lend support, even if seeing the poor woman's body had been distressing. Not for the first time that day, she wondered how Miss Tisdale's parents were faring.

As disturbing as murder investigations could be, something she knew firsthand, she was determined to help Henry in any way she could. It provided her with purpose, the challenge of solving a puzzle—or at least trying to—proving impossible to resist.

Amelia paused to study Fernsby with concern. "I truly am sorry that Yvette and I worried you and Mrs. Fernsby last evening." She'd apologized upon their arrival and again this morning, but wouldn't soon forget how concerned and weary the older couple had been by the time the cab delivered them home.

"It is quite all right. The unfortunate and unforeseen circumstances left you with no choice." The understanding in his expression allowed Amelia to think he truly had forgiven them. "It was quite an eventful evening for you both."

"Rather too eventful." She wondered how Henry's day was proceeding. Had he found any additional clues? Was Clarissa Digby's murderer the same as Eleanor's—was there the risk of another victim? She was tempted to send him a message to ask if she could examine the bit of fabric found clutched in Eleanor's hand, but didn't wish to overstep her bounds.

"Are you inclined to attend another séance?" her butler asked with a curious look.

"In all honesty, I'd rather not." She couldn't help a shiver that had little to do with the cold rain coming down outside. Those few moments when she'd felt Lily's presence were ones she'd never forget, though she remained uncertain whether she'd simply imagined it. "While I've yet to be convinced about the authenticity of such things, there was an unsettling feeling to the gathering." Amelia had shared a summary of the evening with Fernsby and his wife, but not the sensation of Lily's presence.

"I would be quite curious to know if the widow found success with the message her late husband supposedly provided," the butler said as he brushed the rain from her cloak. "The diamonds, I mean."

"As would I." She pondered her options. Asking Mrs. Nettle seemed unwise, for a variety of reasons. "I suppose it would be terribly rude of me to inquire."

"Hmm. That's difficult to say." When Amelia looked askance, Fernsby added, "If the widow didn't object to you attending the séance, which was for her singular purpose, would she mind your inquiry?" He paused with a frown. "And if the medium still hopes for your article about her, wouldn't she want to be proven right?"

"Those are both excellent points. You have given me something to consider, Fernsby. I should've thought to ask the widow's address last evening."

Fernsby's eyes twinkled as he held Amelia's gaze. "Our Yvette did just that while sitting with the servants."

"How clever of her." She smiled in appreciation. "Please ask her to provide it to me. Then I will send a message to Mrs. Dowey to ask."

Learning if the séance had been successful might not aid Henry, but it would certainly help to confirm the medium's abilities to Amelia and allow her to finalize her decision about writing an article.

Yet how could she not when Mrs. Nettle had directed them to the location of not one, but two bodies? Did a spirit have a tie to the abandoned tunnel and take umbrage at having murder victims deposited within it?

Or was there a more sinister reason that Mrs. Nettle had 'seen' the location?

Though the task made her uneasy, she supposed interviewing Mrs. Nettle for *London Life* could also aid the murder investigation if the medium told her more about how she'd learned about the victims' location. But Amelia's goal with the article wouldn't be to prove or disprove the medium's abilities solely, but rather to shed light on her process and the possibilities it presented; to take the readers along with her as she looked into the life of a medium and considered the possibility of a connection to the spirit world.

It appeared that her decision was almost made.

"Shall I bring a tea tray to the drawing room?" Fernsby offered as Amelia started up the stairs.

"That would be most welcome. Thank you, Fernsby."

She was soon settled at her desk with a cup of tea to note some of her observations thus far regarding the medium and the séance while Master Leopold lounged on his favorite chair by the window. While many of the articles she wrote took a straightforward approach, this one would be more challenging. Writing down her impressions thus far would help organize her thoughts.

She also penned a message to her editor at *London Life* to advise him that she had decided to write the article after all. An explanation exactly as to why would have to wait until they met again.

A pleasant hour passed before she heard voices in the foyer. Feminine, which suggested at least one particular visitor. Amelia tidied her notes, placed the cap on her ink, and rose just as her aunt appeared in the doorway.

"Aunt Margaret, how kind of you to call," she greeted her with a smile, genuinely pleased she'd come.

"I brought Louisa with me for a visit." Aunt Margaret glanced over her shoulder toward the empty doorway, before leaning closer. "Before she joins us, might I inquire as to whether Inspector Field has heard anything regarding...the matter I recently brought to his attention?"

Amelia offered a sympathetic smile, wishing she had news to share.

Her aunt had enjoyed the company of a gentleman and believed the relationship would continue into the future. It had been only natural for her to offer to lend him funds when he'd mentioned his former employer hadn't yet paid him. However, the scoundrel had taken the money and left for the Continent without a word.

Amelia had encouraged her aunt to speak to Henry about it to see if anything could be done to get her money returned as it had been a substantial sum. Henry had sent word to several of the police stations along the Channel to watch for the man, so he could be questioned when he returned to England.

"I'm sorry, but he didn't mention it when I last saw him," Amelia advised. "I shall ask when I next see him."

"Thank you, dear." Aunt Margaret shook her head, obviously disappointed. "Perhaps nothing will come from it." Before she could say anything more, a large woman appeared in the doorway, clearly out of breath after ascending the stairs.

"Miss Elmcroft, it's been an age." Amelia reached out with both hands to briefly clasp her gloved ones. "I hope the day finds you well."

Louisa Elmcroft was several years younger than Amelia's aunt and had been a friend of hers for as long as Amelia could remember, having been raised in the same village before Miss Elmcroft moved to London nearly half a dozen years ago.

"It...does," the woman returned the greeting with a smile, then pressed a hand to her ample chest. "Allow me to...catch my breath. Apparently I took the stairs too quickly!"

Miss Elmcroft was a spinster, as was Aunt Margaret, and the pair often enjoyed each other's company, especially now that they both lived in London. Though younger than her aunt,

Miss Elmcroft had always struggled with her health, something that frustrated her to no end as it limited her activities.

The woman took several deep inhales, her cheeks rosy in a round face framed by brown curls. "There we are." She smiled warmly. "I couldn't resist joining your aunt when she mentioned calling on you. It's been too long."

"I'm so happy you did." Amelia turned and gestured toward the chairs. "Please have a seat."

Miss Elmcroft settled her large frame on the settee, smoothing the skirts of her mauve silk gown. "Your aunt tells me you've been writing articles for a periodical. How did I not know that before now?"

"I shall have to send you the next copy within which I appear. It has been quite enjoyable and allows me to indulge my curiosity about a variety of subjects." Amelia shared writing about all manner of things, from the ravenkeeper at the Tower of London to orchid collectors.

Aunt Margaret glanced toward her desk. "Oh dear. Were you working on an article when we interrupted?"

Amelia hesitated, uncertain whether she wanted to talk about it, given the difficult circumstances. Then again, her aunt shouldn't be too surprised to learn her niece was involved in yet another murder investigation—since she'd already been embroiled in several. "I am at the beginning stages of interviewing a medium."

Miss Elmcroft's eyes lit up with interest. "Do tell! Which one?"

"Mrs. Mary Nettle. Are you familiar with her?" Amelia asked with surprise.

"I don't believe so, though I have attended several séances."

Aunt Margaret stared at her friend in surprise. "You have? Goodness, whatever for?"

"I hoped to communicate with my grandmother the first time. I loved her dearly, you know." The woman paused as if to consult her memory. "The second time was for a friend of mine. The third one, I hoped for a sign from my father."

"And were any successful?" Amelia couldn't help but ask. Though spiritualism of all kinds was quite popular, she didn't personally know of anyone interested in it. Or at least, she hadn't thought she did.

The older woman sighed. "I thought I felt my grandmother's presence that first time, but I didn't receive anything with the next two."

"Yet your interest in the field remains?" Amelia's aunt asked with a doubtful look on her face.

Aunt Margaret was a practical soul, and Amelia didn't think she put much credence in anything involving divination or the spirit world.

"Most assuredly." Miss Elmcroft nodded with no small measure of enthusiasm, which sent her curls bouncing. "In fact, I have several friends who swear by mediums."

"Have they received *proof* of contact?" Amelia truly did find the topic intriguing, even if she wasn't comfortable with it.

"Proof? One insists she felt a hand on her shoulder." Her guest leaned forward as if to share a secret. "A *cold* hand."

"Hmmm." The doubt in Aunt Margaret's tone sounded just like Amelia's mother when certain subjects were broached. Amelia held back a smile at the thought. Her aunt studied

Amelia. "And what has been your impression of the medium you're interviewing?"

"Well, she has proven...interesting."

"How so?"

Amelia hesitated. "She has directed the police to the location of two murder victims." That wasn't anything more than would probably be reported in a news sheet within the next day or two. Fleet Street always seemed to discover such things, regardless of whether the police wanted them to.

"The police?" Aunt Margaret's brows rose. "Does this involve Inspector Field, perchance?"

"Yes." Amelia's cheeks warmed under her aunt's scrutiny.

"Do not tell me you are involved in yet another murder investigation." Aunt Margaret's astonishment would have been nearly comical if not for the seriousness of the subject.

"In a very limited manner." Amelia wasn't about to admit she'd been with Henry when he found the last victim. She wasn't certain her aunt would be able to endure it.

"Murder?" Miss Elmcroft's jaw dropped, but from the interest gleaming in her eyes, it was from curiosity rather than horror. "Do tell."

Luckily Fernsby entered the room with a fresh tea tray, saving Amelia from having to reply until she gathered her thoughts.

It wasn't that she didn't like speaking of the investigations, but she knew her aunt worried about her putting herself in danger again. And then there was the fascination Miss Elmcroft displayed. That also made her uncomfortable.

Not for a moment could Amelia forget that her husband had been the first murder victim she'd known, or that she'd subsequently known several of the other victims. For other people, it was a story. But it was her life.

She poured tea while her aunt selected a sandwich, her other guest's plate remaining empty.

"Amelia, I had no idea you were living such a fascinating life as a widow," Miss Elmcroft began after taking a sip of tea, clearly eager to continue the conversation. "Tracking down murderers!"

"I don't think fascinating is the proper term," Amelia began awkwardly. "I was familiar with several of the victims, so it is painful to speak of."

"Your late husband, of course. I am sorry. But there were others you knew?" Miss Elmcroft's gaze remained fixed on Amelia, clearly hoping for more information.

If the woman weren't a friend of her aunt's, Amelia would've left it at that and changed the subject. But as it was... "My husband's murder brought me in contact with a Scotland Yard Inspector. Then I interviewed the ravenkeeper at the Tower, who was unfortunately killed."

"My goodness. Two people you knew were murdered."

Amelia shared a look with her aunt, reluctant to admit to just how many murder victims she could name.

"There are more?" Miss Elmcroft asked, her teacup halting in midair as her mouth gaped.

"Yes," she admitted, more than a little reluctantly now. "A mudlark, then another case involving two of my late husband's business associates."

"Two?" The woman set her cup down with a clatter, appearing shocked by Amelia's admission. "I cannot imagine."

"You are lucky in that regard," Aunt Margaret added, pausing to select a biscuit from the tray. "Amelia has been in danger on more than one occasion." Her gaze held on her niece. "And I do hope that is not the case with the new investigation."

"Nothing of the sort." Amelia took a bite of a cucumber sandwich, deciding the time had come to change the subject. "Enough of me. Tell me what you've been doing of late, Miss Elmcroft."

The lady stared at the plate of biscuits with a yearning expression. "I am embarking on a new journey."

"Oh?" Amelia waited, unable to imagine what that might be. A journey? As far as she knew the woman rarely travelled, though she longed to, hampered by her health challenges.

Her guest nodded. "I recently read a fascinating book about fasting, written by a female physician. She operates a sanatorium that promotes hydropathy and fasting to cure a variety of diseases and promote general health. I venture there on the first of May."

"A sanatorium?" Amelia shared a worried look with her aunt.

Miss Elmcroft nodded again, this time more vigorously. "Hollowgate Heights offers modern methods to regain health in a picturesque setting."

The phrase sounded like something from an advertisement.

"Quite courageous of you, dear," Aunt Margaret said, setting down her half-eaten biscuit. "But I wonder if such a drastic move is necessary."

Miss Elmcroft heaved a sigh as she retrieved her cup. "I have tried everything else. I'm weary of not being able to do everything I want. Of enduring stares while out shopping. Of not being able to sit comfortably at the theater." She bit her lip, her angst visible in her face. "Life is passing me by. If I don't take action now, I may never have the opportunity to enjoy this world. If I'm not meant to have a husband or a family, then the least I could have is a full life, especially when I have the funds to do so."

Amelia's heart went out to her, having experienced a few of those questions herself after the changes in her own life. Where was a woman's place in the world if she was neither a wife nor a mother? "I applaud your determination, but I must ask if you have fully investigated the results of previous patients? It does sound rather drastic."

"I have spoken with two former patients and read the accounts of numerous others." Miss Elmcroft's smile returned, full of hope. "The reports are glowing. A stay there has not merely changed their lives but given them a new one. How could I not consider trying this when the results are exactly what I want?"

How indeed? It all seemed very convenient, and Amelia's doubt remained. "I hope you find exactly what you're seeking."

"Thank you." The anticipation in Miss Elmcroft's expression was undeniable. "Advances in science are truly remarkable, aren't they?"

Amelia agreed, though she knew not all scientists kept the best interests of others in mind. She need only think of the mudlarks to know that. Perhaps she would mention the name of the sanatorium to Henry to make sure all was well with the establishment. But then, perhaps she was becoming overly suspicious of everything these days.

There could not be murder around every corner...could there?

Chapter Twenty-Two

After another hour spent at the Tisdale residence speaking with several servants, Henry left his parents continuing to offering comfort and himself headed to St. Thomas', relieved to escape the heaviness of the mourning household.

The black armbands the servants wore, the drawn drapes, the covering of mirrors, not to mention Mrs. Tisdale's gown of unrelenting black and the tension between husband and stepson were all vivid reminders of the family's loss. But none of that compared to Eleanor's parents' deep grief.

Their fragility and sorrowful expressions, as well as that of his own parents, made Henry more determined to find who had killed Eleanor, as well as Miss Digby, with the hope that finding justice would bring the grieving families some measure of peace. And perhaps if the killer could be stopped today, lives would be saved.

He'd learned nothing more from the servants; their replies to his queries, including those of the lady's maid, remained unchanged. He'd already sent a message to Arthur to proceed with the postmortem, but felt compelled to explain the urgency of this particular case. Disappointed to find Arthur's office empty,

Henry entered the examination room with caution, hoping he wouldn't see Eleanor lying on the cold slab with Arthur's scalpel poised above her.

To his relief, the surgeon worked on an older man with a balding head. *Thank goodness.* An assistant Henry hadn't seen before stood by the surgeon's side with a board clip in hand and pencil working madly.

"Henry! I thought you might stop by based on the number of messages you've sent in the past few hours." Arthur, holding a scalpel as expected, paused his work to study him. "Is all well?"

Henry sighed, careful to breathe through his mouth to avoid the worst of the stench in the unwelcoming room. The surgeon's question reminded him why they had become friends. "Not really."

"Oh? Give me a moment." Arthur set down the scalpel and walked to the nearby basin to wash, murmuring instructions to the young man who pulled a sheet over the body as Arthur dried his hands. He then removed his leather apron, leaving his torso in his shirtsleeves, and gestured toward the door. "Let us have a breath of fresh air and you can tell me about it."

"If you have the time, I would appreciate that," Henry admitted.

"Of course." Arthur paused by his office to don his jacket and hat, then led the way out of the building and onto the street. He looked both ways before walking in the opposite direction from Scotland Yard, which wasn't far away. Rain threatened yet again but was holding off at the moment. "Am I right to presume you have a personal connection to the latest victim?"

"She was a longtime family friend." Henry matched his pace to Arthur's. "My parents and her parents have been friends for decades."

"I'm terribly sorry." Sympathy shone in Arthur's eyes. "Were you the one who found her?"

"Yes, after spending yesterday looking for her."

"Even worse. How terrible to end a search with such poor news. Where was she?"

Henry told him of the medium, the railyard, and the abandoned tunnel.

"My. That is quite the tale." Arthur shook his head. "How odd to hear this case is connected to Miss Digby, and that the medium knew of both. I can't say I would have guessed the two were connected, though I have yet to examine Miss Tisdale." Before Henry could ask, Arthur added, "She's next on my list."

Henry nodded, pleased to hear it. "The sooner the better. The methods used were quite different, but the location of the bodies suggests the same killer."

"The victims seem a world apart as well. I assume Miss Tisdale was from an affluent family, but it appeared Miss Digby was most definitely not."

Henry sighed. "Right. Perhaps more a situation of opportunity for the killer, with the victims being at the right place at the right time."

Arthur grimaced. "Or the wrong place at the wrong time."

"Yes. Quite." Henry shook his head. "I don't know that Miss Tisdale's parents will be satisfied until we learn not only who killed her and why—but also the reason she was in the area." A little beyond his purview.

"So you're feeling extra pressure," Arthur suggested.

Henry shrugged, pausing as they walked single file to avoid passersby before resuming their conversation. "I want to know for myself, in all honesty. She has—had an independent streak, but never to this extent, from what I know."

His friend's jaw tightened. "She shouldn't have had to pay such a high price for one evening of escape from parental supervision."

"No, she shouldn't. It's not fair." Such a ridiculous thing to say when life so rarely was.

"It's not." Arthur halted and held Henry's gaze. "I am sorry."

"Thank you." Henry attempted a smile. "I appreciate you listening."

"Of course. I only wish I could offer more than sympathy."

"Perhaps you can once you complete the postmortem. Any information would be helpful at this juncture."

"I will do my best."

"You always do, and that is something for which I'm grateful." Henry cleared his throat as they resumed their walk. "There is one other issue." As much as it pained him, he had to ask.

"What might that be?"

"I need to know if she was...violated." Saying it made Henry realize how much the idea distressed him. "I'm assuming Miss Digby was not since her clothing appeared to be in order, and you didn't mention it." The idea that someone could—

"Ah. A logical question. You're right, Miss Digby was not, but I will see what I can discover." Arthur stuffed his hands in his pockets. “Have you considered what you will do if there is evidence of that?”

“How do you mean?” Henry frowned. “I still intend to find whoever killed her and make them pay for both victims.”

His friend’s gaze did not waver. “Yes, of course. But will you tell her parents? Or yours?”

Henry drew a sharp breath. “I suppose I hadn’t thought that far ahead.” Would he be able to? Should he?

“Once the edge has worn off their grief, they might ask.” Arthur shrugged. “You might have the choice to tell the truth, or lie. Something to consider.”

“True.” Henry shook his head. “If they do, I would have to tell them the truth.” He considered the situation more carefully. “I need to know, for the investigation...and I think they would want to know too.”

“Very well.” Arthur halted and turned back toward St. Thomas’ as rain began to fall yet again. “Then I shall get on with it. Expect a full report come morning.”

“Thanks, Arthur. For both the support and the conversation.”

“The pleasure is mine.” He glanced at Henry with a smile. “By the by, the wife is quite anxious to meet you.”

“She is?” Henry couldn’t hide his surprise. While he knew Arthur was married, the idea of his wife having any interest in Henry was baffling.

“Apparently she’s been following your recent successes in the news sheets and has become quite a fan.” The teasing glint in Arthur’s eyes suggested he didn’t mind. He pitched his voice in a decidedly feminine tone. "He saved the Queen, Arthur. The Queen herself! Can you believe that? I simply must meet him!"

Henry laughed, hardly able to imagine it. "I don't believe you."

His friend grinned. "Then you must meet her so you can see for yourself. She's beside herself to think you and I have become friends."

"You surely jest. But I would be honored to meet her." An idea came to mind. "Perhaps the two of you and Mrs. Greystone and I could meet for dinner at a restaurant." In fact, he should inquire as to whether Amelia would like to meet Fletcher and his wife for dinner one evening soon as well.

Arthur frowned. "Are you certain? In all honesty, few are eager to meet a surgeon who performs postmortems. It doesn't make for good dinner conversation."

Henry chuckled. "I don't suppose. However, I must warn you that Mrs. Greystone is an unusual woman. She is a chemist herself, and is no stranger to dead bodies. She would undoubtedly enjoy learning more about your work, though perhaps it would be best to save that discussion for after dinner."

"I'm sure I'll try to hold back!" Arthur laughed, clearly under the impression Henry was teasing him.

"I am quite serious," Henry advised wryly. "You shall see for yourself. She is...refreshing." He said the words with both satisfaction and pride, more than pleased they were courting.

"You are truly taken by her then?" Arthur lifted a brow.

Warmth spread through Henry's chest as he considered the question. "I am." Even the thought of her lifted his spirits considerably.

"Intriguing. I look forward to meeting the lady who caught your notice enough to lure you away from the Yard."

"That's entertaining to hear, for I have thought much the same of you and your examination room."

Arthur chuckled. "My wife is a very patient woman, much to my relief."

"We must plan an evening together then. I would like that." How much more enjoyable those kinds of outings would be as part of a couple rather than a single gentleman.

But it was more than that. Sharing the experience with Amelia was the reason it would be delightful.

"Saturday evening next?" Arthur asked.

Henry nodded, pleased to have something specific to look forward to. "Allow me to consult with Mrs. Greystone and advise you if that date is acceptable."

"Excellent." Arthur's expression sobered as they neared St. Thomas' door. "I shall send word as soon as possible about the results."

"Thank you." Henry found himself torn, both anxious to hear and yet reluctant to.

Arthur clasped a hand on his shoulder. "And know I will take great care with Miss Tisdale and treat her with the utmost respect."

Henry's throat tightened. "I appreciate that more than I can say."

"Be well, Henry. Don't forget to allow yourself time to grieve. I look forward to better times ahead, including our dinner."

Henry drew a deep breath and nodded. "I will do the same."

With that he took his leave, feeling more himself after the brief respite with a friend. He walked to a cab stand and directed the driver to Mrs. Nettle's address; he had questions for the medium and hoped she could shed more light on how she'd learned about both victims. Though Amelia would've accompanied him if asked, she would surely be weary after the previous evening's unsettling events, and Fletcher had been called away to assist in a nasty attack related to a burglary.

At Mrs. Nettle's home, he asked the cabbie to wait and strode to the familiar door to knock.

The same maid as before answered. "I'm sorry, Inspector, but Mrs. Nettle isn't home. I don't expect her to return for several hours."

"It's imperative I speak with her as soon as possible," Henry advised, impatience filling him. "I will call again later. Please tell her to expect me."

The maid nodded but was rather quick to shut the door.

With a frustrated sigh, Henry requested the driver to take him to Scotland Yard, hoping Fletcher might have returned by now. Whether he'd learned anything helpful remained to be seen.

Henry mulled over the next steps to take, one being speaking to Caroline Walters again, preferably without her mother in attendance. While in the area, he wanted to determine the most likely path Eleanor might have taken to King's Cross. Though Fletcher and the constables had spoken with many who lived on the street, now that they knew which direction Eleanor had walked, they could take a more concentrated approach. And of course he couldn't forget Clarissa Digby, the reason this whole adventure started. What jewelry had she stolen? Who had she sold it to—had she allowed herself to walk the streets of London as a woman at any point? Who had wanted her dead?

He entered Scotland Yard, but a glance about didn't reveal Fletcher. Constable Dannon sat at a desk, muttering to himself as he worked on a report.

"Have you seen Fletcher?" Henry asked as he neared.

"Can't say that I have." The constable sent an irritated look in Henry's direction. "I've only just arrived."

"What has you in such a foul mood?"

The man glared. "I just spent the worst hour of my life with a cabbie who not only didn't know where he was going, but has no right to be driving anything, especially a hansom cab."

"Oh?" Henry smiled with amusement, almost feeling sorry for the driver, whoever he was, given Dannon's grumpiness. "Memorizing some 25,000 streets is not for the faint of heart."

"Good thing the responsibility of ensuring these drivers know where they're going falls to us, otherwise we'd have even more accidents on the streets."

"I assume he didn't gain his Knowledge?"

Dannon shook his head. "Didn't know more than two of the 320 runs. I told him to consider a different occupation." The constable tipped his head toward the doorway. "Ah, there's Fletcher just now."

Henry turned to greet the sergeant striding in. "Learn anything?"

Fletcher looked just as morose as Dannon. "Nothing, other than no one seems to know why Mr. Weston was in the railyard this morning. Otherwise, seems like both the killer and his victims were invisible."

"Disappointing. The medium wasn't home and won't be for several hours, so I have yet to question her. Meanwhile I think we should visit to the Walters residence."

Fletcher nodded, sending a questioning look at Dannon, whose foul mood was impossible to overlook.

"Another Knowledge of London failure," Henry explained as he turned toward the door.

"That explains it." Fletcher grimaced as he followed Henry. "I've had my share of those."

Henry's mind had already left the Yard and was instead focused on the task that lay ahead of him. "Now we know Miss Tisdale's destination after being left at the Walters, I'd like to question the neighbors in that direction to ask if they saw her."

"Good idea. Trace her path between her friend's house and King's Cross station." Fletcher held the door for Henry. "Someone had to have noticed her."

One could hope, but as they knew, that wasn't always the case. A busy city like London, everyone with their own problems? It was astonishing how invisible a person could be. "We can't forget Miss Digby, but since we know so little about her actions the night she was killed, it feels more effective to focus on Miss Tisdale for the moment."

"Agreed. Doing so will hopefully lead us to the killer of them both."

They took another cab as Henry didn't want to waste time, and the steady rain made walking less than pleasant. The afternoon was passing more quickly than he'd like. Henry left

Fletcher to start questioning the neighbors as he knocked at the Walters' residence.

"Miss Caroline isn't receiving callers," the butler advised swiftly, clearly not remembering him.

"I am not a caller," Henry corrected him, holding out his warrant card.

The contrite butler directed him to wait in a small reception room near the door. Nearly a quarter of an hour later, Mrs. Walters bustled into the room, her expression one of distress. "We weren't expecting you to call again so soon, Inspector."

Henry didn't bother to apologize. "I'm assuming you have been advised of the unfortunate news regarding Miss Tisdale." At her nod, he continued, "I would like to speak to Miss Walters again, and verify the whereabouts of everyone in the household at the time Miss Tisdale was left at your door."

The woman's mouth gaped as she clasped her hands tightly before her. "Why? I'm certain you can understand how upset my daughter is. Surely it isn't necessary to cause her further distress. As for the servants, they had nothing to do with thi s...situation."

How could she be so sure? "It won't take long to verify the staff's alibis to remove them from suspicion, and I only need a few minutes of Miss Walters' time. I'm sure you would like to do all you can to assist us in finding the killer and help bring justice to Miss Tisdale and her family."

Mrs. Walters stiffened in response before potent remorse tightened her features. "Of course. Of course, her poor parents...allow me to hurry Caroline along." She bustled out much the same way she'd entered, leaving Henry to pace the room once again.

In short order, the woman returned with her daughter, who had clearly been crying.

"I am very sorry for the loss of your friend, and I apologize for disturbing you during this difficult time," Henry began quietly as he pulled out his notebook.

Miss Walters nodded, holding her arms as if bracing herself, a handkerchief clutched in one hand.

He had to be clinical, despite the woman's distress. Eleanor deserved that much.

Henry referred to the list of friends Miss Walters had provided and pressed her for the names of any gentlemen with whom Eleanor often spoke with.

"Eleanor was well-liked and spoke with many people everywhere she went," the young woman advised, clearly reluctant to provide more names. "But none would harm her."

Henry bit back a remark stating that *someone* had. However, it was not his intent to upset her further. "I'm sure you can understand we are speaking with everyone who knew her in an effort to solve the case."

Miss Walters nodded, tears filling her eyes. "Of c-course." After much consideration and worried glances in her mother's direction, she provided the names of three men who had been especially friendly with Eleanor.

Though far from satisfied with the brief list, Henry thanked her, resolving to return to speak with her again if necessary.

Next he spoke with several servants and verified an alibi for nearly all of them. Unfortunately no one had seen Eleanor arrive or depart, nor had they noted anything suspicious in the area of late.

After a painful hour of interviews, Henry had gained all he could. He walked along the street and soon found Fletcher, who had been unsuccessful in learning anything as of yet. They split up the next few houses, frustrations rising.

Henry knocked on the second door and was delighted when the lady of the house confirmed she'd seen a well-dressed young lady walking along the street in the fading light two evenings ago.

"It caught my notice as she glanced behind her several times as if worried whether someone was following her, though I didn't see anyone." The lady frowned. "I hope she arrived safely to wherever she was going."

"Unfortunately, she did not," Henry said heavily. "Do you happen to know what time you saw her?"

"How terrible." She pressed a hand to her chest, her upset obvious. "It must've been near seven o'clock, as we had dinner soon after I saw her. I watched her until she moved out of sight down the street, but thought no more of it. I'm so sorry to hear trouble found her."

After leaving his card and asking her to notify him if she remembered anything else, he made his way to the next house, thoughts swirling.

Trouble had, indeed, found Eleanor. If only Henry could determine who and why.

Chapter Twenty-Three

"Henry, I'm so pleased you called." Amelia's heart thumped as anticipation filled her at the sight of him standing in the doorway that evening.

"I hope I'm not interrupting?" he asked politely as his gaze held on her in a most delightful way.

"Not at all." She set aside her book and rose to greet him, pleased to see he'd left his coat and hat with Fernsby. That had to be a sign he could stay for a time.

Though she appreciated his warm smile, underneath the warmth he looked exhausted. The shadows beneath his eyes suggested the investigation was not going well. No doubt he was working long hours, and his personal involvement surely meant he wasn't sleeping well.

"You are never interrupting." She took his hands in hers, needing the contact and thinking he did as well.

Henry rubbed the pad of his thumbs over her hands, sending a little shiver along her skin. "I'm pleased to hear that." Still, his warm brown eyes searched hers as if to make sure. A hint of distress lingered in their depths, causing her to release one of his hands to cup his cheek.

"I can see you've had yet another long day. May I offer you a drink?" Hope rose that she might be able to coax him into staying for dinner which would be served soon.

"I would like that very much."

Amelia released him, smiling when he followed her to the sideboard to watch her pour. After handing him a glass and taking her own, she led the way to the fire where Fernsby had just added more coals to chase away the evening chill.

"Any progress on the case?" she asked, only to frown. "Or perhaps you'd prefer not to discuss it." She enjoyed hearing about his work but could understand if he wanted to talk of something else instead.

Henry sighed. "Some, but not as much as I'd like." He waited for her to take a seat, then sat in the nearby chair, prompting Amelia to decide to rearrange the furniture so they could more easily use the settee while still enjoying the warmth of the fire. She would much prefer to sit at his side.

"Any is better than none, though I'm sure you'd prefer more." She waited for him to take a sip before asking the question on her mind all afternoon. "How are Miss Tisdale's parents faring?"

The answer was visible across his expression. "As well as can be expected, I suppose, but they are devastated. It's as if the smallest task is nearly more than they can bear. I'm sure Miss Digby's mother is in a poor state as well."

Amelia nodded, remembering those days all too well. "My heart goes out to both families."

"As does mine. My parents spent a considerable amount of time with Eleanor's parents today, doing what they could to help."

"How kind of them. I'm sure that's exhausting for them as well."

"Yes, they both looked it when I left earlier." Henry paused to take another sip, seeming to slowly sort through his thoughts. "The postmortem has been completed, so I'm hopeful the report will provide more information come morning, though Miss Digby's was of limited help."

Amelia swallowed down the revulsion of a loved one being cut up in such a manner, something she'd experienced when Matthew had been killed. "A necessary part of any murder investigation," she reminded herself.

"Luckily my father was there to help them understand that. I also had another visit with Eleanor's friend and have a list of acquaintances that I intend to speak with tomorrow, starting with the gentlemen."

"Logical when it seems a man's strength would be needed to commit the murders and move the bodies into the tunnel," Amelia mused, too easily able to imagine it.

Henry shifted his gaze to stare at the glowing coals. "Most definitely. I have yet to determine whether she walked all the way to King's Cross and, if so, why. A neighbor of the friend saw her walking along the street shortly after the coachman said he'd left her at the door." He shook his head. "I keep thinking of Miss Digby, too, but we know so little about her movements thus far, that it feels more helpful to focus on Eleanor."

They continued to discuss the investigation with Amelia asking gentle yet probing questions. She doubted any of them were helpful but hoped speaking of the details would allow Henry to sort through his own thoughts.

Yet she wanted to do more than that.

"I know this is an unusual request," she began tentatively, "but I wondered if I could take a closer look at the fabric we found in her hand under my microscope?"

Henry smiled as he set aside his glass and reached into his pocket. "I confess that is one of the reasons I came by." He withdrew a handkerchief and unfolded it to show the scrap of material.

Amelia was more than flattered that he'd intended to ask her. She shifted to the edge of her seat. "Would you like to join me in the laboratory now for a preliminary look?"

Henry's eyes lit with interest. "I should like that very much."

She rose, cheeks heating as she realized it was an odd thing to suggest when a suitor called. Was there another woman in London who would suggest such a thing?

"What is it?" Henry asked with a curious look as he stood as well.

Amelia couldn't help but smile. "I was just thinking I should think of more suitable activities for when you call. Looking at evidence under a microscope is a rather unusual one." And hardly romantic.

He laughed, once again reminding her he didn't do that often enough. "If you think that is unsuitable, I have another for your consideration."

"Oh?" Amelia led the way out of the drawing room, only to pause at the sight of Fernsby at the foot of the stairs, looking up at them. "Is something amiss, Fernsby?"

"I only wanted to inquire as to whether I should set another place at the dinner table."

She looked back at Henry with a wry smile. "He read my mind. May I invite you to stay for dinner?"

His answering smile pleased her. "Thank you. It would be my pleasure."

"Thank you, Fernsby," Amelia called down, smile still in place. "We will be in the laboratory until dinner."

"Very well, madam." The butler bowed, seeming not to find anything unusual about that, God bless him.

They climbed the stairs, Amelia pausing to look back at Henry. "You were saying—something else unusual?"

"I have become friends with Arthur Taylor, a surgeon at St. Thomas'. He and his wife expressed interest in dining with us."

"That sounds lovely." How delightful it would be to spend an evening with another couple.

Henry cleared his throat carefully. "Just to clarify, he is the surgeon who performs postmortems."

Amelia halted before the laboratory door and turned to look at him, her interest caught. "Oh, really? It will be quite interesting to speak with him and his wife." At his laugh, she lifted a brow. "What is it?"

Her companion's eyes sparkled. "I told him you wouldn't mind his occupation, but I don't think he believed me."

With a frown, Amelia opened the door to the dark attic space. "Why would I? Mind, that is?"

"I suppose some people have expressed distaste about his occupation, making him cautious," said Henry with a shrug. "Would you be available Saturday after next? It is the date they have suggested and I...I admit, I am eager for the two of us to go."

Heat, joyful and hopeful, tinged Amelia's cheeks. "Yes. Yes, I look forward to it."

She lit a lamp near the door and Henry assisted her to light several more, looking around with interest even though he'd been in the room a few times before.

"I can see why you find it pleasurable to spend time in here," he said as he returned to her side, where she had uncovered her microscope. "It is a special space."

Amelia met his gaze, surprised to hear that when Matthew had rarely set foot in it. "I agree. I enjoy it very much."

Admiration filled Henry's expression as he studied the long table, rows of beakers, and the plants near the window which were her latest experiment. "It is full of possibilities."

"I like to think so." That Henry saw the same thing she did pleased her. She moved a lamp closer to the microscope, pausing to look at him. "I am hoping to put it to even better use soon."

"Oh? How so?"

"I have ordered a book on forensic science processes." She held her breath as she waited for his reaction.

"Truly?" His lips parted, but nothing else emerged as if he were speechless at the idea. An emotion washed across his face, only to pass too quickly for her to tell what he might be thinking.

"Is that...all right?" she asked nervously.

"It is." Henry blinked several times. "I am touched you would take such an interest in the field." He reached out to press a hand on her forearm, his hold gentle and more than welcome. "Very touched. Thank you."

She smiled, more pleased than she could say. "Good. Prepare to be inundated with questions, as I know you are well-read on the recent developments in the field."

"I confess to a certain fascination with the topic. Investigative techniques are improving almost faster than police procedures can be updated, though many are slow to trust in new methods."

"I look forward to many interesting discussions, over many dinners." Amelia's mood lifted even further at the thought. "Now then, let us see what we can discover from what Eleanor clung to."

Amelia used a pair of tweezers to retrieve the sample from the handkerchief, placed it on the glass plate of the microscope, and adjusted the focus. "It looks to be a bit of dark gray wool as you probably already noted."

"Is there anything distinguishable about it?" Henry asked, hope tangible in his voice. "I am not familiar enough with the making of wool to know if that's even possible to determine."

"Nor am I, though I have several items that I can compare it to." Amelia studied it for a moment, slowing her breathing to focus on the delight of the science, before stepping aside for Henry to have a look.

He did, his expression puzzled when he finally straightened. "Interesting, but I'm not sure what I'm looking at. There appears to be a strand of hair on it."

Pleasure that he had also seen it filled Amelia's chest. "I noticed that as well. It's close to the color of Eleanor's but straighter than what I thought hers was. However, this is only a fragment, so it's difficult to tell if it matches. Can you obtain a sample of hers to better compare?"

"I'm sure that can be arranged. I found additional threads on the fence, but I'm not sure what they're from." He pulled another handkerchief from his other pocket and opened it. "See?"

They spent several more minutes studying the samples from all angles, agreeing the fabric appeared to be of modest quality and that the one piece of hair on it did not look like Eleanor's.

"Would you mind if I cut a corner of the material to continue studying it?" she asked. It was, after all, evidence in a murder.

"Of course."

After Amelia trimmed a small piece, she glanced at the clock. "Dinner should be ready, and I would prefer Fernsby didn't have to climb the stairs to advise us of it."

"Not many who employ servants would worry about such things." Henry smiled. "Another example of how thoughtful you are."

Her cheeks heated yet again under his close regard. "It takes little effort to be kind. I only wish others would see the same."

"As do I."

She covered the microscope and set it aside while he extinguished the lamps, thinking how their time together in her laboratory might not have been especially romantic, but it made her feel even closer to him. "Shall we?"

Dinner was enjoyable, as expected. The few times the conversation halted it was in companionable silence, making Amelia realize how much she enjoyed spending time with Henry, even if they weren't involved in a meaningful discussion. His mere presence was enough.

"Have you advised Mrs. Nettle that she was right about another body being in the same location?" Henry asked as Fernsby cleared the soup bowls.

Amelia glanced at the butler, aware of how unusual the topic was for the dinner table. He didn't bat an eye. "No, I didn't. In truth, it didn't cross my mind. Should I?"

"I called at her residence twice today to question her, but the maid insisted she wasn't home." Henry frowned. "It's concerning that she knew the location of both victims, not to mention that it was the same place."

"That crossed my mind as well. In all honesty, I don't know what to make of it." She held Henry's gaze, hesitating to speak plainly. Yet the time she'd spent in his company these last few months had proven she could. "I know you confirmed her and her husband's alibis for the night Miss Digby was killed, but I still wonder if she is somehow involved."

He didn't look surprised by the remark, suggesting it had entered his mind too. "I wonder the same, but I have yet to discover any evidence other than Mrs. Nettle telling us where to find the bodies. And there's the fact that she did so in a previous case and that killer was found." His lips twisted. "I intend to question her again to see if any other clues can be gained."

"I should very much like the opportunity to accompany you if you decide to speak with her," Amelia said, taking a deep breath. "I am proceeding with the article about her and her abilities."

"Oh?" He lifted a brow. "Will you cast her in a positive light?"

"I intend to leave that for the readers to decide. I do think the topic of divination is worth exploring." She paused as Fernsby served the main course—thin slices of roast beef served with potatoes, carrots, and gravy.

Henry sighed in appreciation. "How kind of Mrs. Appleton to make one of my favorite meals on such short notice."

Amelia laughed, genuinely amused. "I must ask her if she *predicted* your arrival. Perhaps she has the gift of divination and never told us. Do you think that's possible, Fernsby?"

The butler smiled as he poured the wine. "I shall inquire. It would certainly explain her ability to so effortlessly prepare the perfect dishes on so many different occasions with little to no warning."

Once he departed, Amelia sent Henry a considering look. "Have you ever encountered anyone else who performed divination?"

"I can't say that I have. What of you?"

The memory had only recently returned. "My father employed a dowser to find water to dig a well."

Henry leaned forward. "And? Was the person successful?"

"Yes." She paused as she took a bite, savoring the tender beef as she tried to remember the details. "Everyone expected that he would be, and the whole process was completed in a very matter-of-fact manner."

"Did you watch him?"

She nodded. "My curiosity was insatiable. He used two stiff wires with bent ends that he held in each fist. He walked back and forth on the property until the tips of the two wires touched."

"Fascinating. I have seen a picture of a dowser, but it showed a small branch being used."

"From what little I understand, the method and tool depend entirely on the diviner." Amelia shook her head. "I wish I had paid more attention, though I must have been only seven or eight at the time. The man allowed me to hold the wires, and they did seem to move of their own accord. I was quite intrigued by the experience."

"I'm surprised your father would put credence in such things, given his interest in science."

"Isn't it fascinating how often superstition and science combine in such a practical way? Is not magic just nature unexplained?" Amelia paused to gather her thoughts. "I don't think it would be so terrible to realize that some things are beyond our ability to truly comprehend." She lifted a brow, hoping Henry might agree. "Not all we witness can be explained."

He considered her words for a moment, then sighed. "I must confess that I prefer facts and logic. Perhaps we don't have all the answers, but when it comes to murder investigations, I need at least a few to provide justice for the victims."

They continued to converse, eating the delicious meal slowly as if in silent agreement to savor their time together as much as the food, and for as long as possible. Amelia was pleased to see how much more relaxed Henry became as the evening progressed. The past few days had been difficult, and taking a small break from that would surely be good for him.

She couldn't have been happier that they agreed she would accompany him for another visit to Mrs. Nettle's, especially after the unsettling night of the séance. She told Henry of the evening and that she'd sent a message to Mrs. Dowey to see if the information she'd received had been helpful, but had yet to receive a reply. Though it was on the tip of her tongue to share that she had felt Lily's presence during the séance, she did not. More than likely she'd imagined it, even if the mere memory of the moment made her heart ache.

Regardless, she would hold tight to the comfort it had brought rather than question whether it had truly happened.

One thing she knew for certain—she didn't envy the medium her skill of divination or all the perils it brought.

As far as Amelia was concerned, it seemed more a curse than a gift.

Chapter Twenty-Four

EARLY THE FOLLOWING MORNING, Henry stopped by St. Thomas' to get the promised report from Arthur, his stomach twisting in anticipation of hearing the details.

"The knife was a straight blade, between four to five inches long," the surgeon advised as he reviewed the report in his office. "Three stabs in fairly quick succession, one of which struck the lower left ventricle of the heart, proving fatal due to hemorrhaging. Death would've been relatively quick, and without much pain."

Henry nodded, taking some comfort in that, regardless of whether his friend told the truth.

"The killer didn't use much finesse," Arthur added.

"Meaning?"

"Possibly a lack of experience in wielding a knife. The blade wasn't particularly sharp." He sent Henry an apologetic look before continuing. "The abruptness of the wounds could have also been caused by hurrying, I suppose."

"Hmmm." Interesting information, but unlikely to help him find the killer.

"The wounds aren't deep, suggesting the killer used little force. Again, that could be a result of inexperience or a lack of commitment to the task. Clothing obstruction could also be a factor."

Henry nodded, an image of the crime slowly taking hold. He usually welcomed that, the picture helping him to better understand what happened, but not when Eleanor had been on the receiving end of the knife.

How terrified she must've been in those final moments. She and Miss Digby both.

The thought had kept him awake at night.

"I'm not sure what to make of the two different methods used to kill the victims," Henry mused. "I doubt I would've connected them, if not for the location of the bodies."

"And the medium's involvement."

"Right," Henry agreed dryly. He still didn't like that. "I'm hoping to question her again later this morning."

"A wise idea." Arthur cleared his throat. "As to your other query, regarding any violation..."

Henry held his breath, hoping to hear the news he wanted.

"There wasn't any."

"She was not assaulted sexually?" Henry wanted to confirm it; needed to hear it said plainly to keep at least that image from his thoughts. "You are sure?"

"Positive." Arthur handed him the report. "I suppose that's a bit of good news."

"It is." The tension in Henry's shoulders eased, but it wouldn't disappear completely until he solved this case. *If* he solved it. He didn't care to consider that possibility. "I'm relieved to hear it. I only wish you'd found something definitive that could lead me to the killer. Perhaps another conversation with the medium will help."

"I hope she provides you with more clues than I did," Arthur said with a rueful look.

"Mrs. Greystone is accompanying me on the visit."

"Oh?" His friend's brows rose in surprise. "Mrs. Greystone—and the medium?"

Henry tried not to notice the surprise. "I'm hoping her presence will be beneficial. She will have the advantage of being able to ask a variety of questions as part of her interview which might sound accusatory coming from an inspector."

"Ah." Arthur nodded. "Clever of you to approach the meeting from a different angle."

"I suppose I thought it more efficient than clever." Going together to Mrs. Nettle's would allow him to watch over Amelia while she asked her questions, some of which might answer his.

He couldn't deny how protective he felt of Amelia, especially as he knew the topic of spiritualism distressed her—and for good reason. Though she'd spoken about the séance with a casual air the previous evening, he had noted the tension in her expression, making him wonder what she'd left out of the tale.

It made an odd sort of sense that Amelia might be more susceptible to the spirit world—if there was such a thing—considering the losses she'd endured. That Mrs. Nettle seemed to realize that vulnerability was concerning, but there were several possible explanations for how that had occurred. The medium might have heard about it from a friend of Amelia's or read of her husband's murder in the news sheet. Her awareness of

Amelia's grief didn't prove—or disprove—the medium's supposed abilities.

He took some comfort in that fact, unprepared to declare Mrs. Nettle's divination skills as fact despite her pointing to the two murder victims.

"And Mrs. Greystone looks forward to dining with you and your wife, as do I."

"Excellent." Arthur smiled. "It will be a fine evening."

"Can I request a few strands of Eleanor's hair to compare to those found at the scene?" Henry asked, forcing his mind back to the task at hand.

"Of course." Arthur handed him the report and stood. "I'll just be a moment."

Henry quickly scanned the report, his wish that some small detail the surgeon had failed to mention would leap off the page to provide a clue going unfulfilled.

Arthur returned and handed him a small envelope. "Here you are. I hope answers present themselves in a timely manner, and the guilty person as well."

"As do I. Thanks, Arthur." Henry took his leave, pausing to check his watch. He had almost two hours before he and Amelia were to call on Mrs. Nettle, so he returned to Scotland Yard to find Fletcher pacing the entryway.

"There you are," the sergeant greeted him with a nod. "Young Marcus has finally come through for us."

"Marcus?" Henry had nearly forgotten the boy's promise to help. "How did you discover that?"

"I stopped by the Royal Arms, where we agreed to leave messages, on the way here this morning."

"Excellent work. And?" Anticipation filled Henry at the sparkle in Fletcher's eyes.

Fletcher puffed out his chest. "He has the name of someone who might have provided Miss Digby with the wad of notes we found in her pocket."

Henry smiled with satisfaction. "Clever lad, eh?"

"He is indeed." Fletcher nodded, a hint of pride in his expression. "The man we seek, Scranton, spends a fair amount of his days doing business at the Queen's Slipper—by King's Cross station."

"Excellent work. We should have just enough time to venture there before I call on the medium to question her." Henry reassured himself there was no harm in leaving out the fact that Amelia was accompanying him. Time enough to decide if it was necessary to mention it.

They caught a hansom cab to King's Cross and easily found the Queen's Slipper. Despite its regal name, the place had a rough look to it. The few patrons inside did as well, staring at Fletcher's uniform with obvious distrust.

The barkeep approached with a wary look and a lifted brow.

"We're looking for information," Henry began, keeping his voice low, "about a man named Scranton who's said to be a frequent customer here."

The barkeep was unimpressed. "Yeah? Wot yer want him fer?"

"We have a few questions regarding a recent purchase he might've made." Henry wished they had more specifics to better allow them to press for answers.

The barkeep shook his head, his disbelief obvious as his gaze held on Fletcher's uniform. "And you think he'd be eager to speak of it?"

Henry weighed their options, trying to determine the best chance to not only meet the man but convince him to tell them what he knew. Perhaps some of Fletcher's bluntness would serve them well. "His choice to buy and sell stolen goods isn't of interest to us today." He made no promises, naturally, that it wouldn't be in the future.

With a scoff, the barkeep turned away.

"But the two recent murders in the area make it imperative that we speak with him," Henry added.

The man turned back, eyes narrowed. Henry couldn't tell if it was in anger or surprise. "Are yer accusin' 'im?"

"No, but we know he met with the first victim just before that person was killed." That was purely conjecture, but also a logical guess thanks to Marcus' help. "He might know something that could be useful."

"Humph." The noncommittal response was less than reassuring. "I'll see if 'e's 'round. An ale while you wait?"

The not-so-subtle suggestion had both Fletcher and Henry quickly agreeing.

The barkeep poured them each a glass, took Henry's proffered coins, then strolled toward the stairs, greeting a couple of customers along the way as if he had all the time in the world.

Impatience stirred in Henry as he reached for the drink. He'd spent more time waiting in a pub with a drink in hand than he cared to count. Sometimes it paid off, but often it didn't.

Fletcher sighed as he glanced toward the other patrons. "Do you suppose they know what we're about?"

"I would say yes." Henry took a sip. "You?"

"Most definitely. One of them slipped upstairs the moment we entered. Tall man. Dark hair. Worn cap, mended on its left."

And that was why Henry liked working with Fletcher. He noted things Henry missed, leaving Henry to focus on other matters.

They spent a long ten minutes waiting for the barkeep to return. Henry had nearly decided they'd have to return later as Amelia was expecting him soon when the barkeep descended the stairs with another man in tow.

"Looks like an interesting character," Fletcher muttered under his breath before draining his glass.

"Indeed."

The grizzled man of forty or fifty wore a perpetual scowl, based on the wrinkles in his face. They reminded Henry how often his grandfather had told him his face would stay that way anytime he wore a similar expression and the wind changed.

The new arrival paused at the foot of the stairs, stared at them for a long moment as if taking their measure, then finally tipped his head, covered by a low cap, toward a dark corner where a single table sat.

Henry ordered a pint then brought it and his own glass with him as they joined the other man at the table.

Scranton, for that was who he had to be, sat on the edge of his chair as if he thought he might need to bolt.

Perhaps he did.

Henry slid the drink and a silver coin across the table. "We're looking for information about an individual who sold you some valuables earlier this week." The medium's words popped into his head of their own accord. *Could she have been right?* "Including a ruby ring." Henry didn't miss Fletcher's look of surprise.

Scranton stilled, suggesting the description had struck a chord. Henry didn't know what to think about that. "Wot of 'er?"

Now it was Henry's turn to be surprised. "You *knew* she was a woman?"

Scranton cackled, revealing a row of crooked yellow teeth. "In my line of work, you learn to pay careful attention to such things." He pushed the coin away but took the drink. "Money won't 'elp ye to learn anything from me that I wouldn't tell ye otherwise."

Henry nodded in appreciation but left the coin where it was. "So what can you tell us about...her?"

The petty criminal drank deeply, wiped his mouth with his sleeve, then shrugged. "She'd been seen in the area off and on, sneakin' into the railyard like the thief she was."

"Did everyone know she was a woman, even though she dressed like a man?" If so, it was a little mortifying. After all, at first glance, he and Fletcher had been fooled.

"Don't fink no one else did." His gaze shifted across the room as if remembering. "She were clever with it." He nodded. "That was one of the reasons I agreed to...work with her."

"Was she nervous that night?"

"Course. She'd've been a fool not to be, comin' into a place like this at night on 'er own, not to mention tryin' to sell things what weren't 'ers."

"Mostly jewelry?" Henry guessed.

He nodded. "Truth be told, she had good taste."

"Do you happen to still have any of it?" Henry asked with a raised brow. "It could prove helpful if you do."

Scranton shook his head. "I'd be stupid to 'old on t'such things, and I ain't stupid."

Fair enough. Time to drill down on the specifics. "What time was the meeting?"

"Half past seven."

"How long did it last?"

"No longer than it had to."

"Meaning?"

Scranton shrugged. "Five to ten minutes."

"Then what?"

"She left. Didn't stay fer a drink or nofink. Just 'eaded straight out."

Henry leaned forward, resting his elbows on the table to hold the man's gaze as frustration mounted. "Can you tell us anything else? Anything she said or how she looked? Anything that could help us find who killed her."

Scranton's scowl returned. "Wish I could. The girl had spunk, I admit. A rare trait these days."

Henry had to agree. "Thank you for your time." He pushed to his feet, only to pause when Scranton tapped his fingers encased in fingerless gloves on the table, unease in his eyes.

"Some say there's been a man lingerin' about, watchin' from the shadows."

"Oh?" Henry's interest immediately piqued, though he didn't allow himself to become excited. Often rumors like that spread when people grew nervous, especially after not just one but two murders had taken place in their neighborhood.

"Wears a cloak instead of a jacket. Don't talk to no one. Always shows up 'bout the same time at night."

Henry shared a look with Fletcher, wondering at his thoughts, before looking back at Scranton. "Every night?"

"Not so often as that."

Of course not. It would never be that easy. "Big? Small? Rich? Poor?" He wanted to shake a few more details loose, if possible.

"Middle."

"What does that mean?" Fletcher asked before Henry could.

The man shrugged again. "Neither tall nor short. Neither rich nor poor."

"Any distinguishable features?" Without something more to go on, the lead would be nearly impossible to pursue. A man, middling height, middling wealth? London was full of them.

"Nah. Never had that close a look."

It was infuriating, and it could be nothing—or it could be the very man they were after. "Send word if you learn more or tell the local constable." Henry held the man's gaze. "It is likely he'll strike again unless we can stop him first."

A muscle twitched in the man's grizzled cheek. "I was afraid ye might say that. No one wants 'nother murder 'ere."

Henry nodded. On that, they could agree. "And while we're about it, I would caution you to think twice before dealing in stolen goods. No good can come of it."

Scranton almost smiled before reverting to a scowl. "I'll keep that in mind."

Henry almost returned the smile. "Thank you for your time, Mr. Scranton."

He and Fletcher stepped out of the pub, pausing to look up and down the street as Henry blew out a long breath. "More helpful than I anticipated. Remind me to thank Marcus and pay him for his help."

"I will. Interesting that Scranton saw through her disguise, when so few others did." Fletcher hesitated as his gaze met Henry's. "Though someone was clearly watching her—someone with little description of note. Almost sounds as if we have a specter on our hands."

"From the way Scranton described him, it certainly does. A cloaked figure hiding in the night. Very concerning."

"Enough to give you the shivers if you believed in such things." The sergeant pulled Miss Digby's sketch from his pocket. "Perhaps it would be worthwhile for me to make a few more inquiries in the area while you're meeting with the medium. I will ask about the mystery man as well and see if Mr. Weston has the jewelry descriptions we requested."

"Excellent idea. Let us hope one of us can learn something more this morning."

An undeniable sense of urgency gripped Henry, confirming time was of the essence.

Who was going to be the third unwitting victim?

Chapter Twenty-Five

"I CERTAINLY HOPE MRS. Nettle has something helpful to tell us," Henry said as he assisted Amelia to alight from the hansom cab outside the medium's home.

A flutter of nerves rolled through her. "You mean something other than where another body is?" Amelia asked, sending him a pointed look. She still didn't understand the woman's odd talent and didn't care for the way it unsettled her.

"Yes. That," Henry replied succinctly with a wry smile. "And since this is the third time I've called to speak with her in the past four and twenty hours, I will be happy if she's finally at home. I thought perhaps she was avoiding me." He bid the driver to wait, tucked Amelia's hand beneath his arm, then raised a brow as he met her gaze. "Ready?"

"Yes." Better that she didn't dwell on the dread weighing down her limbs. After all, it wasn't as if Henry were dragging her along—she did want to speak with Mrs. Nettle again. She *needed* to for her article. Unfortunately, the reminder didn't ease her reluctance.

Thank goodness for Henry's comforting presence at her side, and the faint sunlight piercing the low clouds. Surely the gray skies and recent rain accounted in part for her unsettled mood.

Or perhaps it had more to do with the murder investigation of two young women who had not deserved to die.

"Going to see the medium?"

Amelia turned to see an older woman walking toward them from down the street. She glanced at Henry for reassurance before nodding. "Yes, we are."

The woman wore widow's weeds from head to toe, but her grim expression was what caught Amelia's attention. "You don't want to hear anything she has to say. She's evil, you know. Evil." The woman's gaze shifted briefly to Mrs. Nettle's front door. "She and her husband both."

In addition to distaste, her tone also held a hint of fear and sent shivers along Amelia's skin.

"Why do you say that?" Henry asked mildly.

"She claims the dead speak to her. Nothing good can come of such things. That she earns *money* from it makes it unholy." The woman walked closer, pitching her voice low as she sent another wary glance at the front door. "She preys on the desperate. Her husband is no better." Her lips tightened. "His smile comes easily enough, but I see the evil in his eyes. God will, too, and soon."

"Did Mrs. Nettle try to contact one of your loved ones who passed?" Amelia asked with curiosity—even if it was a rather personal question. Perhaps the woman's disapproval of the couple stemmed from a failed attempt to contact a family member.

"I told her, I told her doing such things was unnatural, but she insisted on it." She gave a mock shudder. "The only thing I felt was cheated. She took my money without any sign of my

Jacob. If I were you, missus, I'd keep my distance." Without another word, she hurried along the street.

"Well then." Amelia drew a slow breath, her unsettled feeling only increasing. "A disgruntled customer. At any rate, she's not the friendly sort of neighbor, is she?"

"Definitely not." Henry watched the woman go. "I am all the more eager to hear what Mrs. Nettle can tell us. I would like to meet her husband as well."

Amelia nodded but secretly hoped Mr. Nettle wasn't home. She had no desire to deepen that acquaintance.

Henry knocked on the door and the same maid answered, greeting them with a cool demeanor as she bid them to enter. She requested they wait in the hall while she advised her mistress of their arrival.

Amelia reviewed her questions for the medium, aware Henry also had several. This was her third visit to the residence and she intended it to be her last. If she didn't have enough information to write a proper article after today, she would forgo it. Her editor would understand if she changed her mind again.

They waited in silence. Amelia found the quiet of the house unsettling, the faint murmur of voices in another room eerie rather than comforting. It seemed the neighbor's warning had bothered her more than she realized.

Henry caught her gaze, sending her a silent questioning look as to whether all was well.

She gave a nod and a small smile in answer, comforted that he knew her well enough to sense her mood. She was not alone.

The maid returned. "This way, please." She led them down the hall to the same reception room from their first visit. The medium was seated at a table by the window, with paper and pen before her.

"How kind of you to call," Mrs. Nettle said as she rose to greet them with a polite smile. She gestured toward the chairs before the chill empty hearth, and they all took a seat. "Although I am assuming this isn't a social call. What brings you to my door?"

Henry pulled his notebook from his pocket, as if to confirm the reason for the visit. "I have several questions regarding the recent murders."

The woman's eyes darkened with concern as she looked between them. "The—the young lady was found as I foretold?"

"Yes, unfortunately." Henry pulled out the medium's drawing from within the pages of his notebook and unfolded it. "Some of my questions pertain to this."

The medium frowned, her gaze holding on the sheet. "I had requested that it be returned as soon as possible. It is far too easy for such things to fall into the wrong hands."

"And I will see that it's returned to you once the cases are solved." Henry studied Mrs. Nettle long enough to make her uncomfortable, based on the way her expression shifted from displeasure to wariness.

Amelia intended to remember that technique when questioning someone, though she doubted she could perform it with the same effectiveness as Henry.

"Tell me. What do the letters on the bottom represent?" He pointed to a capital L and E, which were repeated. "And this one, as well." He tapped a large capital D that she'd written three times with enough force to crease the paper.

Mrs. Nettle stared at the letters as if confused about how they'd come to be there. "I don't know. I don't remember writing them."

Amelia stared at the woman in surprise, unable to mask her feelings. "But I saw you do so. I thought perhaps they somehow referenced the victim." They didn't match the location where they'd found Miss Tisdale, but surely they held some other meaning.

The medium's eyes widened. "Are those her initials?"

"No," Henry answered swiftly, leaving Amelia to wonder at his quick reply. The E could have possibly represented Eleanor's given name, but no T was on the sheet for Tisdale.

So were they the initials...of the murderer?

Mrs. Nettle's focus returned to the drawing with a puzzled expression. "I don't know what they mean."

Henry set the sheet beside him, a hint of impatience in his movements. "Where were you prior to the séance you held here that Mrs. Greystone attended?"

Mrs. Nettle stiffened, clearly taken aback. "Home preparing, of course. Séances take time and effort."

"How so?" Amelia asked, hoping Henry wouldn't mind the question. Surely the answer would help both of them. "For my article, you understand, Mrs. Nettle."

The woman's expression remained stiff. "Rest and meditation to clear my mind. Cleansing of the air in the room where the séance will be held. Gathering the items required. All manner of things."

"What of the previous day and night?" Henry asked calmly.

"I was at home then as well. My husband and our servants can verify that." Her eyes grew wide, her expression one of disbelief. "Am I a suspect yet again merely because I told you where to find the deceased?"

"You must admit, your particular knowledge of the situation is...unusual." Henry's logical tone made it sound as if it would be impossible for anyone to believe otherwise.

"I told you, I cannot control what the spirits share with me." She clasped her hands before her, lifting her chin. "Would you prefer I keep the messages I receive to myself?"

"I would *prefer* to know precisely how you obtain the information. How are we to know you didn't kill the victims?" Though his tone remained calm, the question was anything but.

Amelia swallowed, watching the two of them avidly.

"Because I didn't! I wouldn't—murder? I was here the entire time." Her voice rose in outrage, her face flushed. "Ask my husband. My maid or the other servants."

Henry pressed, "Did the killer tell you where he left the victims?"

"No!" She shook her head. "The spirits told me." She glanced at Amelia. "Mrs. Greystone can verify that."

"I can't confirm how you knew it or why you drew those letters." Amelia didn't appreciate the medium trying to use her as a witness, even if the back of her neck prickled uncomfortably. The cold. The buzz of the table. The scent of her child...

"I channel the spirits, but not everyone can hear them." Mrs. Nettle's exasperation was more convincing than her words. "I rarely leave the house. I often find it distressing as I have no idea when the spirits will contact me. I have few visitors other than clients, and don't often communicate with anyone except those from the other side. Who would tell me of a murder, if not the dead?"

Henry studied the woman, as if processing her information. Perhaps he was wondering if Mrs. Nettle honestly expected him to believe her explanation.

Amelia would guess this was one of the strangest interviews he'd ever conducted. The thought might've been amusing—if not for the fact that they were speaking of murder.

"What of your husband?" Henry asked politely. "Where was he the last three nights?"

"Home, of course. As he is every night. I will attest to that, as will our servants." Mrs. Nettle gave Henry an accusatory look. "Is this line of questioning a result of something our neighbor, Mrs. Johnson, said? My maid saw you speaking to her upon your arrival."

"She doesn't seem to appreciate your divination ability." Again, Henry looked at the medium expectantly, his voice level, and polite, but unrelenting.

The woman heaved a sigh. "You can't believe anything the widow has to say. In truth, I fear she's gone a bit crazed since her husband passed."

Amelia waited, but Henry didn't say anything further on the subject.

Mrs. Nettle's stiff posture eased. "Who was the young lady who died?"

"The spirits didn't provide you with a name?" A mix of anger and grief flashed across Henry's face and Amelia fought the instinct to take his hand in comfort.

"No. That rarely happens." Mrs. Nettle either didn't pick up on Henry's sarcastic tone or chose to ignore it.

"Did the spirits witness the murder?" Henry asked.

Amelia looked at Mrs. Nettle, curious about the answer. The question should have crossed her mind as well.

The medium hesitated, as if uncertain how to explain it. "It felt...felt as if the young lady called out as she passed into the afterlife." She frowned. "I think she wanted her body found, so it wouldn't be left in that dark place forever. She was alone."

"The victim communicated with you?" Henry's eyes narrowed, his confusion evident.

"No. The spirits heard the victim, and they shared it with me."

Amelia leaned forward. "How soon after she died?" she asked, intrigued despite herself.

"I couldn't say." Mrs. Nettle glanced at Henry. "I had the impression she hadn't been in the space for long, but time is of little consequence in the spirit world."

Henry neither confirmed nor denied the timing, and he had yet to mention Eleanor's name. Amelia understood his protectiveness since he'd known the young lady so well—and, as always, the fewer details he shared about any investigation, the better.

"Please describe the information you were given in as much detail as possible." Henry poised the pencil nub above his notebook, prepared to write down every word.

"But I already did." Mrs. Nettle looked at Amelia as if asking her to verify that. "Didn't I?" She pointed to the drawing beside him. "It's all there—there was an old door, a dark room beyond it, and the letters. Isn't that all?" She sent Amelia a questioning look.

"You don't remember?" Amelia asked gently, finding it hard to believe.

Mrs. Nettle stared at the paper in confusion. "Not precisely." She shook her head. "Much of it's a blur."

"Like being in a trance of sorts," Amelia mused. The medium's struggle to remember, as well as the frustration that she couldn't recall more, seemed sincere. At the very least, it made her more believable than the dramatic version she'd presented to them during their first visit. A completely different performance.

"You could say that," the medium said with a wry smile. "I only wish I could tell you more. That I could've prevented the death." She pressed a hand to her forehead, her breath coming quickly, and face going pale. "I'm sorry, I...I'm not feeling well."

Amelia shared a worried look with Henry, but he watched Mrs. Nettle as if doubtful of her claim.

"Would a drink of water help?" Amelia shifted to the edge of her seat, wondering if she should ring for the maid. Or was this an act to avoid answering Henry's questions—or something more?

Mrs. Nettle released a heavy sigh and wilted in her chair. "Yes. P-Please."

Before Amelia could do more than rise, the maid bustled into the room. "Madam? Is all well?"

"I need to lie down, Ida." Mrs. Nettle's voice was little more than a whisper.

"Of course. Allow me to see your guests out, and then I will assist you to your bedchamber." The maid leveled the two of them with a glare that suggested she believed them to be at fault.

Amelia stepped forward "Can I offer assistance of some kind?" She sent Henry a worried look. She couldn't dismiss the guilt filling her, though he didn't appear to feel the same.

"You should go," the maid ordered.

"Yes, please go," Mrs. Nettle breathed, her eyes fluttering closed. "Now."

Well, that left them with little choice. Amelia glanced at Henry who reluctantly nodded, tucking the drawing with its unanswered questions into his notebook while she reached for her reticule.

"We will see ourselves out," Amelia advised politely. "You have our best wishes for a quick recovery."

With one last glance at the medium and the concerned maid who hovered over her, they took their leave. The front door snapped shut behind them and the cool April air made her face tingle as she blew out a low breath, more than relieved to escape the tension of the interview.

"Another dramatic act or genuine?" Henry murmured as they walked toward the cab.

"I think mostly genuine." Amelia tended to assume others were telling the truth, but she supposed Henry had witnessed enough falsehoods that he had a better sense of such things. "What do you think?"

"Perhaps somewhere in between. Were our questions making her ill or the spirits?"

"Both," Amelia suggested, surprised when Henry nodded in agreement.

"At least that's what she believes. Then again, she truly seems to believe spirits talk to her," he added.

Amelia didn't reply until they were in the cab once again, her mind churning. "You still doubt her ability to communicate with those in the afterlife?" She didn't know what to think. The medium had pointed them to the whereabouts of two bodies, and there had been that moment when she'd felt Lily's presence.

Henry sighed, his gaze pensive as he held hers. "I remain doubtful, yet neither can I explain her knowledge."

She shook her head. "Not when she's provided the location of two murder victims."

"I hoped she would tell us that the spirits who communicated with her had witnessed the murder," Henry admitted. "At least then we might learn more about what happened—or what she believed had happened."

"I thought that question clever." Amelia truly admired his skills as a detective. "Yet that seemed to be the moment the conversation turned."

His slight smile suggested the compliment pleased him. "I wonder if she feels a continual connection with these spirits or if it is only when she allows them in."

"It sounds as if it is more under their control than hers. Can you imagine being suddenly immersed in visions whenever a spirit chose to contact you?" She shook her head. "No wonder she remains at home most of the time."

"It would be rather inconvenient."

The amusement in his tone helped to lighten her mood. "I doubt she would appreciate another visit from us."

"She might have to endure it until I have some straight answers, or another clue emerges." Henry took Amelia's hand in his as the carriage rumbled down the street.

The warmth of his touch calmed her. "That she knew of the deaths and the whereabouts of the victims does make her look guilty. And in such an odd location—I wonder how many of the aborted tunnels there are. It must've been frustrating for the men digging them to be told they'd been working in the wrong place for whatever reason."

"Indeed." He watched the passing scenery for a moment, still holding her hand. "The location near the railway station makes it too convenient for anyone to slip in and out of the area."

"Unfortunately so. The killer doesn't necessarily have to be someone who lives or works nearby when they can come and go on the train."

"Right. Hard to know where to look for the guilty person."

Amelia bit her lip. "If Mrs. Nettle contacts me again, shall I respond? Perhaps try to ask her more questions—for my article?" Though the idea made her uneasy, her desire to help Henry overrode that instinct.

His face was a picture of worry. "I wouldn't wish to cause you concern. I know speaking with her is difficult."

"It is, but finding who killed the two women would make it worthwhile." She believed that without a doubt. "Stopping him from killing again...and I need more information to finish the article." Never mind that she would set it aside without a second thought if not for the murders.

He turned toward her, his gaze sweeping over her face. "Not if it places you in danger. Please don't forget that for a moment."

His obvious concern touched her deeply, which only made her want to help him more. "I won't," she reassured him, deeply touched by his worry for her.

The cab soon rolled to a halt in front of her house. Part of her wished she could accompany him to wherever he went next, but before she was tempted to ask if it might be possible, Henry had stepped out and offered his hand.

"Thank you for your help," he said as he walked her to the front door. "Again."

"I wish our conversation could've led to more."

"As do I, but we will find who did this regardless."

Amelia wondered whether he said that to reassure her or himself. Both, perhaps. "Did the postmortem provide any helpful information?"

Yes, she was grasping for reasons for him to linger, but she only felt a little guilty about it.

Henry's brow furrowed. "Not particularly. Someone not especially skilled with a knife."

The idea had her frowning. Had that made poor Eleanor's death more painful? Had her end been slower because of it? She did her best to hide her alarm, not wanting Henry to stop sharing those kinds of details with her.

All victims always had her sympathies, but in this case she'd seen Eleanor's body for herself. Knowing the young woman had been a friend of Henry's somehow made it worse.

"I hope today provides you with new revelations." She turned to face him once they reached her door as another thought occurred to her. "Oh, one note of interest. The woman who hired Mrs. Nettle for the séance I attended has replied to my query as to whether she received the information she wanted, if it proved helpful."

Curiosity flickered in Henry's eyes. "And?"

"She did indeed find what she was looking for." Amelia wasn't sure what to make of that. "As I mentioned previously, it was quite specific."

Henry sighed. "I confess that the idea of communicating with spirits is foreign to me. If I can't see or hear something for myself, I have difficulty believing it."

"Finding evidence has been part of your job for many years. A job you're very good at."

"It's important to me."

"Which is one of the reasons for your success," Amelia offered with a smile. "It matters to you."

"It does." He sighed. "At first, it was because I was eager to follow in my father and grandfather's steps, but I have realized it's more than that. I enjoy the work and the challenges it presents. I like to think I have honed my skills, but there's more to learn."

Amelia nodded. "I enjoy learning new things, and I think you do too."

"I do," he readily agreed. "But this case and its ties to...divina tion, and spirits, and mysticism—it has tested me in unexpected ways. I have yet to determine what to believe."

The tension which had built at Mrs. Nettle's was finally starting to melt away. "I feel much the same, which is why I'm pleased that we are seeing this through together."

Henry's slow smile had her smiling in return. "As am I."

Chapter Twenty-Six

THOUGH FRUSTRATED BY HOW little he and Amelia had learned from Mrs. Nettle, Henry temporarily set aside his additional questions for the medium and shifted his focus to those he *could* demand answers from.

Often conducting a thorough investigation meant circling back to those he'd already spoken with to see if new information surfaced.

One of the few at the top of his list was Thomas Tisdale.

There was something about his behavior that felt out of place. Henry had both the advantage and the disadvantage of having known him for many years: an advantage because he could sense a change, yet a disadvantage because Henry might be allowing his personal feelings to color his impressions of the man. Completely setting aside his familiarity with Thomas was impossible, but he would do his best to view him objectively.

Henry had considered transferring the case to another inspector once again, but had dismissed it almost immediately. He wanted to be the one to bring Eleanor's killer to justice. And clearly the Director had no issue with Henry leading the investigation.

He called at the Tisdale residence after leaving Amelia's, surprised to learn Thomas was out, something that made little sense when the family was in mourning.

"Do you have any idea where I can find him?" Henry asked the butler, preferring to avoid bothering Mr. and Mrs. Tisdale. Surely Thomas wasn't expected to return to work so soon.

"Please allow me to inquire," the servant said politely. After a few minutes, he returned. "The coachman took him to his club." The butler provided the name and address, and soon, Henry was on his way.

Henry had heard mention of the Mercury Club once or twice before. It was a relatively new establishment frequented by younger barristers, journalists, and other professionals who prided themselves on engaging in spirited conversations about innovations, politics, and other controversial topics. The club was located just off the Strand near Charing Cross, and Henry arrived shortly thereafter. He eyed the modest exterior, wondering not for the first time why some men sought such places. As for himself, he cherished time alone—or with Amelia—far more than debating current affairs with others, who often liked to argue just for the fun of it.

He opened a heavy wooden door to find a large statue of Mercury, the fleet-footed god of travelers and merchants, as well as thieves and tricksters, complete with his winged helmet, taking up half the foyer. The interior beyond boasted polished oak paneling and generous leather chairs, the entrance guarded by a muscular man in a fine black woolen suit.

"May I help you?" he asked with a lifted brow, suggesting he knew with a glance that Henry was not a member.

Henry inclined his head in return. "I would like a word with Mr. Thomas Ballard, and I am told he's presently here."

"The club is for members only." There was no hint of apology in the man's tone.

Henry gave a tight smile and held up his warrant card for him to view. "Scotland Yard Inspector Henry Field, on official business."

Concern tightened the man's features as he hesitated. "Allow me to see if he's here."

Henry felt certain the man could consult the ledger before him to know, but he only nodded politely and waited as the man departed into an adjoining room.

Several minutes later, Thomas strolled into the foyer to greet Henry as if he didn't have a care in the world—yet the black armband he wore suggested otherwise.

"Henry." Thomas cocked his head to one side as he studied him. "Or perhaps since you are clearly here in an official capacity, I should call you Inspector Field?"

"No need for such formality." He bit off the phrase 'between friends'; he didn't know if he considered Thomas one and tended to think the feeling was mutual. "Is there somewhere we can speak in private?"

Thomas glanced about. "Probably easiest to find a quiet corner. The club isn't that busy at the moment." He led the way into a large room with numerous tables, only a few of which were occupied, and continued toward a trio of chairs grouped around a low table to one side. "This should do, eh?"

"Certainly." Henry looked around as he took a seat, noting the political cartoons framed on the nearby wall next to an elegant sconce. "Nice place."

"It has proven a refuge at times." Thomas slouched in the chair, more at ease than he had been at home. "You have more questions?" He offered a brief half-smile. "I wouldn't want to waste your valuable time with pleasantries."

Henry considered him for a moment, wondering what had changed Thomas into this pricklier version of the young man he used to know. "I can imagine that things are especially difficult at home right now."

Pain dulled Thomas's eyes for a moment. "You could say that."

Tragic events set a line in people's lives, marking all else as before or after. The murder of a family member was one of those terrible markers.

Henry nodded slowly. "I would guess that was the case even before Eleanor's death." Based on his observations during his time at the house, both Thomas and Eleanor had been unhappy and somewhat dissatisfied with their lives. How had he never noticed before?

Thomas stared across the room before at last looking at Henry. "Moving in that direction, at any rate." He shook his head. "My disagreement with my stepfather seems paltry now, yet we can't quite seem to move past it."

That certainly explained the tension between them that Henry had noted. "Disagreement over what?" Henry asked, keeping his notebook in his pocket. Hopefully that would encourage Thomas to talk.

It did. "His expectations for me and my career. I have come to realize that I don't wish to be a barrister, but he refuses to listen. He thinks I'm being obstinate and determined to disappoint him. That I'm allowing myself to be influenced by the wrong people." The young man gestured toward those in the club.

Henry was lucky to have never had such a disagreement with his own parents. His father had been pleased when Henry had told him he intended to join the police force, yet had also warned him of the trials and tribulations, saying he wanted Henry to make the best decision possible.

At the time, Henry had worried that his father was subtly discouraging him because of his unspoken adoption, but now he could see it for what it was: fatherly advice he would have shared no matter what career Henry pursued.

So, Thomas no longer wished to be a barrister. "What made you change your mind?" Though it might not be directly related to the case, he wanted to better understand the change in him.

"A friend, who told me my skills lay elsewhere." Thomas drew a deep breath. "And…Eleanor."

"Eleanor?" Henry was eager to hear more of their relationship, but worked hard to keep his tone casual even as excitement grew.

"She told me I was terrible at arguing and reminded me I tend to retreat when differences of opinion are shared." He looked around the room again, his eyes unfocused. "That was one of the reasons I joined this place, with the hope it would improve my ability to debate."

"And?"

"I still detest it."

"What of the law itself?" Henry asked, though it was hardly his place to offer career counseling, nor would it aid the investigation. "Do you still enjoy that? If so, there are other types of law you could pursue."

Thomas gave a lazy shrug. "Some, though the research can be tedious."

"Most jobs have their share of work that could be described as such."

"Even the exciting world of criminal investigation?" A wry smile curled Thomas's lips.

Henry allowed himself to return the smile. "Most definitely. At times during an investigation, it's impossible to believe I'm getting anywhere."

"Then you suddenly save the Queen."

"Helped to save her," Henry corrected, knowing he could never have done so without Fletcher's aid. "One of many." He'd made an educated guess on that case and was grateful—and relieved—it had turned out to be correct. Perhaps the first time he had truly trusted his gut.

"Always so humble." The other man's sarcastic tone grated on Henry's nerves.

"Just being honest," Henry said. Thomas would do well to improve his outlook. The younger man had opportunities spread before him, all with the safety net of his parents beneath him, but seemed determined to feel sorry for himself and wallow in unhappiness. Clarissa Digby hadn't. That ennui was nothing Henry could fix.

The time had come to get down to business. "Thomas, where were you the night Eleanor disappeared?"

Her half-brother stiffened, heat glinting in his eyes. "I already told you."

"Tell me again," Henry asked politely.

"With friends."

Of course he was. "I will need specifics, including timings, and the names of those you were with."

"Whatever for?"

Henry waited a beat. "That's how we conduct investigations. No stone unturned, and everyone must be accounted for." He leaned forward as if to impart a secret. "That's how we saved the Queen, by doing the tedious work."

Thomas scowled, clearly not appreciating the subtle dig. With some reluctance, he provided a basic schedule of both the night she'd gone missing and the following day until Henry and Amelia had discovered her body.

For this part, Henry did retrieve his notebook. While he'd asked before, he hadn't pressed for this level of detail, but now he needed to. Not for a moment could he forget the sight of Eleanor's lifeless body in the abandoned tunnel. While he detested the idea that Thomas could have anything to do with it, he needed proof—needed to absolutely rule him out.

"How familiar are you with King's Cross station?" he asked next.

"Not very. I don't take the train often." The young man's eyes narrowed as he once again stared across the room. "You know, I can't imagine why Eleanor went there."

"She didn't mention any new friends?"

Thomas shifted his attention back to Henry. "If she had one, especially of the male variety, she wouldn't have told me."

"Why not?"

The other man lifted his hand only to drop it. "Our...confidences were limited."

"But you just mentioned that she advised you not to become a barrister," Henry pressed. "Surely that suggests a certain closeness."

"Oh, she said it in passing when we were speaking of something else." Thomas shook his head. "We didn't attend the same functions, so as I told you before, other than Caroline, I couldn't say who her friends were."

"Did you notice any change in her behavior of late? Did she act differently in any way?"

To Thomas's credit, he at least seemed to give the question consideration. "No. Not that I noted."

"What was her relationship with your parents like?" Henry felt certain Thomas knew more than he was saying, but whether it was relevant remained to be seen. What question could unlock the puzzle that this young man presented?

Another shrug. "She found their suggestions amusing and their thinking old-fashioned."

"Oh?" Henry prompted when Thomas didn't say anything more. "What gave you that impression?"

"The condescending smile she offered each time they offered an opinion."

Henry nodded. He remembered that smile. "I suppose many young ladies that age feel a certain disdain for their parents' advice." He thought most people her age did, but preferred to avoid insulting Thomas when the man was finally sharing a little information.

Thomas leaned forward. "Eleanor more than most, I would say. Family dinners had become something I avoided once it was clear Father and I were not of the same mind, but the few I did join made it seem as if her relationship with them was deteriorating even more rapidly than mine."

Deteriorating? "Did you speak to her of it?"

Thomas scoffed. "Yes, and that was when she said I was ill-suited to be a barrister."

Henry had the impression that his sister's criticism hurt. Surely that suggested some affection between them. Unless Eleanor had managed to anger him and he'd killed her in a fit of rage, he didn't think Thomas was the killer.

Still, he intended to verify his whereabouts during the time in question to be sure.

Henry glanced at his notes, unable to think of anything else he needed to know at the moment, then closed the notebook. "I won't take up any more of your time."

Thomas watched as Henry stood. "Am I cleared of suspicion?" He seemed amused by the idea.

It was a hard question to answer. "Depends on whether any of the details you provided are inaccurate."

"Sounds like a waste of time when the real murderer is out there somewhere." Thomas shifted in his chair, a hint of anger tightening his face. "Perhaps I should do some searching of my own for the killer."

"I would advise against it. Rather tedious and occasionally dangerous work."

Thomas's lips tightened.

Henry turned to go, only to look back at the younger man, unable to help himself. "Sometimes we need a reminder that life is full of possibilities if we only open our eyes to see them. Often, it's naught but a matter of perspective."

"And what is that supposed to mean?" Color stained Thomas's cheeks, whether from temper or embarrassment, was impossible to say.

Though Henry didn't know why he bothered when his suggestions would more than likely fall on deaf ears, he continued, "You are a lucky man with opportunities all around you, Thomas. Perhaps instead of searching for what's wrong in life, you might focus on what's right. I'm very sorry about your half-sister's death, but I hope you use it as motivation to find what you're looking for and appreciate the love and support your parents so obviously want to give you. It's something all of us need, regardless of our age." He paused, wondering if Thomas had heard any of what he'd said. "And consider lending them some of yours. They're going to need it in the weeks and months ahead."

With a final nod, Henry strode out of the club. Why he'd felt compelled to offer unsolicited advice when he hadn't been completely honest with his own parents, he couldn't say. His adoption often stood between them, even if they didn't realize it, the information weighing heavily on him. Would telling them he knew clear that weight—or merely shift it from him to them?

If only he knew.

Chapter Twenty-Seven

"Field, there's a telegram for you," Sergeant Johnson called out as Henry returned to Scotland Yard that afternoon. "And a young man came by and asked for you. Seemed rather desperate to speak with you, but wouldn't give his name or talk to anyone else." Johnson frowned. "He only said he'd stop by again soon."

"Thank you." Henry took the telegram, pondering who the visitor could've been and what he wanted with little success. He had to hope the man would do as he said and come to the Yard again. Henry continued toward his desk, hoping Fletcher had returned with more answers than he'd managed.

He wanted to find out who Mr. Nettle was employed by. An investment bank, wasn't that what Amelia had said? He also intended to send a constable to speak to Mrs. Nettle's maid and any other servants at their residence to verify the couple's whereabouts on the evening of the second murder. He'd already done that himself after Miss Digby's body had been found, but it wouldn't hurt to confirm their alibis again. Sending an officer in uniform would bring home the importance of the inquiry while allowing Henry to pursue other avenues of the investigation.

Not that he had many at this point.

Clarissa Digby. Eleanor Tisdale. Two women living very different lives, but who had ended up in the same place.

Who had taken them there? And why?

A glance around the office showed Fletcher was still absent. Henry settled at his desk to read the telegram, noting it was from a police station in Folkestone, a town near the English Channel.

He couldn't help but smile as he read that they were holding a Mr. John Tinton for questioning at their station at Henry's behest. Amelia would be even more pleased to hear the man who had taken advantage of her aunt had been found.

"Good news, eh?" Inspector Duncan asked as he entered the office and paused beside Henry's desk. "I'd like to receive some of that myself."

"More or less good. Amusing, at any rate." Henry tapped the telegram. "The Folkestone police have detained a potential conman who's just returned to England, and are holding him overnight for questioning."

His colleague raised an eyebrow. "What scheme is he accused of?"

"Taking advantage of a middle-aged woman by romancing her, taking her money, and promptly leaving the country."

"A very ungentlemanly thing to do." Duncan frowned.

Henry couldn't agree more. "Quite. He played on her sympathies by saying he was short on funds due to a delayed payment from his former employer."

"So she lent him funds until his circumstances improved," the other inspector suggested with a sigh. "But of course, as they were so friendly, there was no written agreement about the particulars."

"Only verbal," Henry confirmed. "Her word against his. Then he left the country without a word."

"Leaving her heartbroken and short of funds." Duncan shook his head. "Unfortunate, and far too common."

"Indeed. It would please me to no end if the man found his conscience and repaid the lady—or ladies, if this is a frequent scam." That would make Amelia happy, too, though he wondered if she would think that enough. Her sense of justice might demand more. At the very least an apology and an admission of wrongdoing, and Henry was inclined to agree. Whether they would receive any of that seemed unlikely, despite the scoundrel being held by the police.

Duncan looked thoughtful. "Who knows what he might confess to after spending a night in jail?"

"That is my hope. The constable says Mr. Tinton is quite distressed at having been detained. He claims to have no knowledge of the woman or her complaint."

To Henry's further amusement, the telegram reported that the constable thought the man was lying, and added that he would do all in his power to help Mr. Tinton see the error of his ways.

"Hmmm. I worry he spent the money while abroad," Duncan said with a lifted brow.

They could only hope not. "That crossed my mind, too. Or he may be flush with cash, having used the same ploy on another woman."

"You're probably right." The other inspector nodded gravely. "Once they get away with it, they do it again."

"So it seems. The victim is the aunt of a friend of mine, which makes it especially frustrating that little can be done to punish the man." Of course Amelia was much more than that, but he was hesitant to tell anyone other than a chosen few about her and his growing feelings. He and Duncan had become better acquainted of late, but it was too soon for confidences in Henry's mind.

The man crossed his fingers. "I shall hope for a positive result."

"What case are you working on that has you less than optimistic?" Henry asked as he set aside the telegram.

"An angry lord and stolen jewelry which seems unlikely to make a reappearance."

Henry's interest was caught. "Any tie to King's Cross or the railway in general?"

"Not that I know of."

That would have been too easy. "Unfortunate. That might have provided another piece of the puzzle for my murder investigations."

"Sorry I couldn't be of more help." Duncan heaved a sigh. "I'd best get on with my report." With a nod, he walked to his desk.

Henry wrote a brief reply to the constable's telegram which included a few details to mention to Mr. Tinton, with the hope it would stir his memory and loosen his lips. Fletcher arrived by the time he returned from the telegraph room, and the sergeant shared the limited results from his inquiries near the Queen's Slipper.

"A few have noted a stranger lurking in the shadows. He never enters any of the pubs and has only been seen after dark." Fletcher shrugged as he sank into a chair. "Could be nothing more than a rumor created by those who live and work nearby to explain the murders. Could be a man thrown out that evening by the wife. Could be a different man each time. They don't want to think it's one of their own who has killed twice."

"True." Henry nodded. "Yet there could be something to it."

Fletcher sighed as he smoothed his generous moustache. "I thought you might say that. Should I plan on spending the next few nights in the area to search for anyone who doesn't seem to belong there?"

Henry considered their choices. "It's difficult to find someone who doesn't appear at the same time or place."

"We can alert the local constable, but I don't think that will be enough. The chances of him spotting the person and knowing he's our man are slim."

Constables were expected to make their designated rounds at the pace of two and a half miles per hour, with sergeants overseeing their progress. The system was relatively efficient, given the size of each area and the population density, but that still meant each constable had a lot to watch over.

"Why don't we each take an evening?" Henry suggested after some thought. "The time of death for both victims was estimated between eight and ten o'clock. We'll provide the constable with the limited information we have and ask him to remain alert, especially during those hours near the railway station."

Despite his plan, he felt less than hopeful. Every day which passed without identifying the killer lessened the chance of finding him...and increased the chance he'd claim another victim.

"I'll advise the constable, then have an early dinner with the missus and tell her we're in for a few late nights," Fletcher said with a nod. "I can take a turn this evening. Who knows? Maybe one night is all it will require."

Henry lifted a brow, surprised by the optimistic statement, even if his sergeant was only feigning it. "You may be right. I suppose stranger things have happened. I'll keep watch tomorrow evening." He considered the plan, preferring they go together to watch one another's back, but it might be a week or more before they found anyone suspicious, if they did. Taking turns would be the wisest approach. "Don't take any unnecessary risks if you happen to come upon him. Assume he's armed, and dangerous. The goal is to bring him in for questioning."

"Right." Fletcher patted the truncheon attached to his belt. "I'll bring this along, even if I don't wear my uniform."

"Better if you don't. You'll draw less attention from everyone that way." Henry also intended to wear clothes that would help him fit in.

"What of you?" Fletcher sent Henry a questioning look. "I hope you'll have a weapon of some sort, at least for defense purposes."

Henry rarely carried one, having seen too many situations escalate when weapons of any sort were drawn. Given the danger he'd faced of late, he'd had second thoughts about his choice.

Fletcher leaned forward with a twinkle in his eye. "You have more than yourself to think about now that you're courting a lady."

Though his friend spoke in little more than a whisper, the remark struck Henry. He and Amelia had never spoken directly of the dangers of his job, though he knew she worried, from a few comments she'd made. That was only natural, and he'd had more than a few concerns about her safety on several occasions over the last six months. He never took undue risks. After all, he had his parents to consider, and every intention of living to a ripe old age.

Now perhaps he had another reason to reach that goal—and with someone beside him.

"Might be a good idea to carry a knife in your boot." Fletcher sat back in his chair, as if his work was done after mentioning the idea. "Did our medium have anything helpful to share?"

"No." Henry rubbed the back of his neck, frustrated. "She doesn't remember writing the letters on the drawing, nor does she know what they stand for. When I pressed her for more, she suddenly started to feel ill and demanded that we leave. Whether her illness was real or imagined, I don't know."

The sergeant shook his head. "Impossible to guess what the initials mean without a hint."

"It is." Henry had spent several sleepless hours the previous night, trying to determine what they could represent. D for Digby perhaps? E could be for Eleanor, of course, but L? What did that mean? And why use the first name's initial in one case but the surname's in the other?

Fletcher pulled a paper from his pocket. "Here's the list of stolen jewelry, along with descriptions, from Mr. Weston. I didn't tell him we know who Miss Digby had sold them to since Scranton already got rid of it all."

"We will handle that as a separate matter. The murders take precedence for now."

"Right." Fletcher shifted his chair a bit closer and pitched his voice low. "Now then, onto far more important matters. Have you given any more thought about my suggestion of a romantic evening with Mrs. Greystone? Mrs. Fletcher thinks you should take the lady to the theater. Says most ladies would enjoy that."

Henry couldn't remember the last time he'd attended a play. He and Amelia had dinner with Arthur and his wife to look forward to, but he also wanted to do something with just the two of them. "That might be a good idea. I'll give it some thought."

"Good. I'll tell the missus you're taking her suggestion to heart." Fletcher appeared amused by the thought, as was Henry.

"Please thank her for me," he said with a smile. "I clearly need all the assistance I can get. Perhaps the four of us can dine together soon."

Surprised pleasure lit Fletcher's eyes. "We'd like that. We'd like that very much."

Inspector Clarke entered the Yard, and the sergeant spent a few minutes conversing with his uncle, leaving Henry to provide a brief update to Director Reynolds, who looked less than pleased by the lack of clues. So was Henry. His superior didn't offer any suggestions that Henry didn't already have in the works, so all he could do was proceed.

Henry departed to look in on the Tisdales again. Though he didn't like the idea of calling on them without having made progress on the case that he could share, he wanted them to know he was doing everything possible to find who had killed Eleanor.

Mr. Tisdale looked worse than the last time Henry had come by, a mere shell of his former self, but managed a smile at the sight of Henry. "Good of you to come by again, Henry."

"I hope you and Mrs. Tisdale are coping as best you can." Henry nearly grimaced at the phrase as he stepped into the somber drawing room, yet he couldn't think of anything else that would offer comfort.

"We're trying. She's resting at the moment."

Henry bit back the suggestion that Mr. Tisdale should do the same, given the shadows beneath his eyes.

"It's still so difficult to believe." The older man shook his head. "A nightmare from which we can't wake."

"A terrible one," Henry murmured, heart aching for them.

"The funeral will be in three days," the older man added. "I would appreciate it if you could come. Your parents have already confirmed their attendance."

"I'd be honored to be there." Henry cleared his throat, hoping he'd find who did this before then. "I can assure you, we're continuing to do everything possible to find the guilty party."

Mr. Tisdale nodded. "I have complete faith in you, Henry."

An ache filled Henry's chest, and the weight of responsibility to solve the murders increased tenfold. He couldn't bring back Eleanor, but he could offer her parents justice. The same for

Miss Digby and her mother. Whether that brought them a measure of peace was up to them.

But first he had to find who had taken their lives.

After promising to keep them apprised and bidding Mr. Tisdale goodbye, Henry departed, glancing up and down the street as impatience simmered within him. Daylight was fading and the workday ending, yet the thought of returning to his rooms at the lodging house held no appeal. Nor did he want to share his upset with Amelia.

Fletcher would be insulted if Henry joined him to patrol the area near King's Cross later this evening—but there was another place he could watch.

He stopped for a quick bite at a pub, then made his way toward the Nettle residence. He couldn't move past the fact that the medium was the connection that bound the murders together. Had the killer done his terrible work before Mrs. Nettle received her premonition...or at her bidding?

While he intended to question Mrs. Nettle again in the morning, regardless of whether she had recovered, and visit her husband's work to learn more about him, watching the house this evening to see if anyone came or went might provide insight.

Or it might be a complete waste of time.

It didn't take long to find a tall fence across the street and down a few houses from their home, where he would be mostly hidden in the shadows with a clear view of the residence. Watching here felt better than spending the evening pacing his rooms. He could use the time to run through the investigation in his mind and determine his next steps here, just as easily as there.

A fence post next to a bush provided a place to lean against while he studied the house in the fading daylight. The street was quiet, lights coming on in the houses one by one. A few people walked along the pavement, returning home after a long day of work. Luckily no one passed by or seemed to pay him any mind.

One man he watched moved up the walk to the Nettle residence and inserted a key into the lock. Unfortunately Henry didn't get a good look at him aside from noting an average build, a black jacket, and a bowler hat atop a head of pale hair. He quickly disappeared inside.

Come the morrow, Henry would take a hard look at Mr. Nettle, even though his wife insisted he had been with her that evening. The constable Henry had sent to their home should have verified their alibis with the servants earlier.

Henry shifted on his tired feet. The evening was going to be long and uncomfortable...but it was a small price to pay if it helped him find Eleanor and Miss Digby's killer.

Chapter Twenty-Eight

"SHALL I RETURN LATER to dust, Mrs. Greystone?" Yvette asked from the doorway of the laboratory, holding a rag and a feather duster.

"No, I'm done here." Amelia had taken time after breakfast to have another look at the torn piece of fabric Eleanor had held. She hadn't intended to remain there long, since she'd already examined it several times without gaining any further insight. If only her book on forensic science had arrived, she might know better what to look for.

Henry had left the samples of Eleanor's hair with her the previous day, and she had confirmed the hair on the bit of woolen fabric was not the young woman's.

So could it have come from the killer?

The question was enough to make Amelia shiver, even if it didn't bring her and Henry any closer to identifying him.

"Are you sure you're finished?" Yvette glanced around the room, its tall windows letting in the weak spring sunlight. "It's no problem."

Normally Amelia closed the door when she didn't want to be disturbed, but she'd left it open since examining the bit of material yet again had seemed pointless. Still, she hadn't resisted doing so.

"I'm sure." Amelia heaved a sigh, gesturing toward the microscope. "The lady we found dead at the railyard had a bit of fabric in her hand. I keep looking at it, hoping to find something that could help Inspector Field find who killed her."

Yvette drew closer, looking at the microscope with open curiosity. "Impossible to think you could learn all that from a bit of fabric, isn't it? Not unless you found a piece of clothing with a hole in it the same size."

"The fibers in the piece might help identify where it was made, but I don't have much to compare it to." Amelia smiled at the puzzled look on the maid's face. "Would you care to take a look?"

Yvette's eyes went wide. "Oh, I wouldn't want to bother you." She glanced over her shoulder nervously as if expecting Fernsby or his wife to arrive to tell her she was doing precisely that.

"You aren't. Just place your eye near the scope, and you'll see what I mean." Amelia tapped the top of the microscope. Well, why not? Most people would find it odd for a lady of any class to use a microscope. Why not a maid?

Yvette set her cleaning supplies on the floor and stepped closer to do as Amelia instructed, carefully wiping her hands on her apron. She leaned forward to look, only to gasp and jerk back. "What is *that*?" She stared at the small plate of glass which held the fabric in disbelief, then looked up at Amelia. "It looks like a spider of some sort."

Amelia grinned. "Those are the threads of the fabric magnified. Have another look, now that you know what to expect. You can see the individual fibers of the threads. It's actually quite fascinating, don't you think?"

Yvette tried again. "It almost appears to be strands of hair. To think that bit of fabric looks like that up close." She leaned back with a smile, brown eyes bright with interest. "Thank you for letting me see it."

"Of course." The maid's reaction gave Amelia an idea. "I wonder if the children at the school my aunt's church runs would like to visit my laboratory."

"That's a fine idea, madam." Yvette bent to retrieve her things. "They would surely enjoy it as much as Maeve did while she was with us."

Maeve, the daughter of the murdered ravenkeeper, had assisted Amelia with a few simple experiments and had been fascinated by them. Which reminded her—she really must reply to that endearing note the child had sent her. "You're right. I should've thought of it sooner. I shall send a message to my aunt and see if we could arrange for the students to come."

Yvette nodded, her attention already shifting to the tables and shelves in the room that needed dusting. "I'm sure they'd be thrilled to, madam."

Amelia took one more look at the swatch before placing the cover over the microscope. Staring at the fabric and wishing there was more to learn from it wasn't going to help. The strand of hair didn't match Eleanor's, so it could very well be the killer's—but that didn't help them find the person. It was maddening to feel like progress was being made that could lead them nowhere.

She turned toward the door to see Fernsby at the threshold with a silver tray in hand.

"A message has arrived for you, madam."

Amelia moved to take it, amazed the elderly butler wasn't out of breath after climbing the stairs. "You shouldn't have come all the way up here, Fernsby. It could have waited until I returned to the drawing room."

"It is no bother." He dipped his head. "And exercise is good for the soul."

"You are a prime example of that," Amelia said with a smile, even as a glance at the envelope caused her smile to fade. "Hmmm. Another message from Mrs. Nettle. I can't say that I'm anxious to hear what she has to say."

An all-too-familiar unease filled her as she opened the letter.

Mrs. Greystone,

I have received a message from the spirits that you will find of interest. If you would like to know more, please call at your earliest convenience.

Sincerely,

Mary Nettle

"Oh, dear." Dread took a firm hold on Amelia. Not again.

"I do hope it's not bad news," Fernsby said, too polite to ask directly, though he was clearly curious.

Amelia cast her gaze back at the letter. "That is unclear as of yet. The medium only says that she has a message from the spirits she thinks I would find interesting."

"A rather vague note."

"It is. If only she had shared what she learned." Amelia glanced out the window, debating how to respond, aware of the servants waiting to see what she intended to do. "It could have something to do with the King's Cross murders."

After a moment's pause, Fernsby nodded. "It could. Yet she contacted you rather than Inspector Field."

"Excellent point," Amelia agreed, her unease increasing. "Unless she wrote to both of us. Does that mean it has something to do with me personally instead?" Had Lily somehow reached out to Mrs. Nettle again? The medium had never mentioned her, yet Amelia couldn't dismiss the feeling she'd had after the séance.

"Or she prefers to speak with you rather than the Inspector," Fernsby offered.

Amelia released a quiet sigh. After her last visit she'd nearly given up on writing the article, given the strangeness of the situation. "I suppose I have no choice but to call on her. My curiosity demands nothing less." Besides, she would do whatever she could to help Henry with the investigation, and that meant following up on every potential clue. "Please order a hansom cab for me."

"Of course, madam." Fernsby turned to go.

Amelia hesitated. "Yvette, may I pull you away from your duties to accompany me?"

"I'd be happy to." Yvette gathered her cleaning things. "I'll put these away. Did you wish to change before we go, madam?"

Amelia glanced at her simple gray gown. "No need. This is not a social call." Reluctance gripped her, but she pushed it aside. She had two very good reasons to go: Henry and Lily. She held the thought close as she and Yvette readied themselves for the outing and soon departed.

"The weather almost feels like spring today, doesn't it?" Yvette asked as they stepped into the cab Fernsby had hailed.

Amelia forced herself to look out the window and nodded, appreciating the maid's attempt to distract her from her thoughts. "More so than yesterday. Perhaps we will have a break from the rain for a time."

"More flowers will soon be coming up in the garden," Yvette murmured. "It's a joy to see them again."

"It is."

"Would you prefer I remain with you at the Nettle residence, or should I see what the servants have to say?"

The question made Amelia smile, pleased she could rely on Yvette's assistance once again. "With me, to start. Then we will see what the medium says and proceed with caution."

"Caution." Her stalwart maid nodded. "Right." She sent Amelia a wary look out of the corner of her eye. "Does that mean we should expect danger?"

"Possibly." Amelia shook her head, trying to push aside the worry. "But doubtful. Mrs. Nettle doesn't use her ability to speak to the spirit world to harm others, and she is hardly strong enough to overpower the both of us." Yet even as she said the words, doubt returned. Exactly why, she didn't know. "All the same, we will keep a careful watch for one another during the brief time we're there."

Brief. The word brought comfort and strength. They need only suffer the oddness of the situation for a short duration to learn all they could. Directly afterward, Amelia would send word to Henry with what she'd discovered.

It was a solid plan, even if it would take a little courage to execute.

They soon arrived at the medium's home, Mrs. Nettle's maid greeting them with a little more warmth than she'd shown the previous day, though she was still far from friendly.

"Mrs. Nettle was hoping you would come," the maid advised Amelia before looking pointedly at Yvette. "You are welcome to wait below stairs."

Yvette looked to Amelia for approval, and she reluctantly nodded. Already their plan had altered.

"This way, please, Mrs. Greystone." The maid led the way upstairs, surprising Amelia when she continued past the drawing room to the small sitting room where the séance had been held.

Amelia's steps slowed as dread filled her. *No.*

The maid knocked on the door and opened it to reveal Mrs. Nettle at the table with three unlit candles, a white rose, and the sheet of paper before her. The room was dark except for a single candle burning on the nearby side table.

It was a scene all too familiar.

"Good morning, Mrs. Greystone. I'm pleased you're here." Mrs. Nettle rose and gestured to the single chair beside her.

Amelia entered the room, the sound of the door closing behind her causing her to startle. "What is this?" she asked the medium as she glanced around the room.

The medium followed Amelia's gaze, biting her lip even as her hands adjusted the items on the table. "It has become clear to me that you are particularly open to the spirits. In an effort to help with your...research for the article, we—rather, I—thought it might be helpful to hold a séance for the loved ones you've lost."

Shivers ran along Amelia's skin, leaving her chilled to the bone. The urge to turn around and walk out the door took hold, yet she couldn't bring herself to leave. Not yet. "H-How do you know about them?" That question had bothered her since their first meeting, the words slipping out before she could stop them.

Mrs. Nettle smiled, yet the expression was anything but reassuring, a strange light gleaming in her eyes. "As I told you the day we met, the shadows of your past whisper to me. The time has come to give them their say."

Chapter Twenty-Nine

"MR. NETTLE IS AN excellent employee. Those who work under him often sing his praises." Mr. Curtis adjusted his silver-framed spectacles, his mannerisms and appearance professional as one would expect of the vice president at an investment firm.

Hollingford and Company was a prestigious establishment that had been in business for over a decade. The classic décor suggested success without being lavish. It spoke well of Edward Nettle to be employed there, as the company's reputation was impressive.

"How long has he worked here?" Henry asked, notebook at the ready.

His vigil at the Nettle residence the previous evening hadn't resulted in anything of interest, but he couldn't move past his growing suspicion of Mr. Nettle. Why that was he would be hard-pressed to explain—though Amelia had not liked him, and her opinion mattered. He'd finally allowed hunches to have room in his mind, and this one seemed determined to take over his thoughts.

"Five years." The man offered an amused look with the answer. At Henry's raised brow, he waved a hand in dismissal.

"Forgive me. It's just that the last time Mrs. Nettle assisted the police, we received a similar round of questions from one officer or another."

"I'm sure you can understand why," Henry suggested, unbidden anger stirring. "It's not every day that someone directs us to the exact location of a body yet supposedly has nothing to do with the crime."

"Yes, yes, of course." Mr. Curtis folded his hands on his spotless desk, almost making Henry wince at the thought of his own piled high with case files. "We're always happy to answer any questions and support the police as they investigate these matters."

Henry glanced over his notes to see what else he wanted to ask. None of Mr. Curtis's answers had confirmed any suspicions. Thus far, the interview had only been frustrating.

Clearly the time had come to speak with Mr. Nettle himself to gain a better understanding of the man.

"Mr. Nettle is quite proud of his wife, you know," the man confided. "Not every man would be. It cannot be easy to be married to someone who claims to channel spirits."

"Claims to? Do you question her ability?" Henry did his best to keep his own doubt from coloring his tone.

Mr. Curtis shifted in his chair. "Well, of course, logic suggests there must be something to what she sees, based on her insights. From what I know most of her clients are pleased with their results."

Henry refrained from responding, waiting to see what more the man might say.

After an uncomfortable moment of silence, Mr. Curtis lifted one shoulder in a half-shrug. "Still, such things are difficult to accept, aren't they? I suppose one needs to experience it first-hand to truly believe it."

"And have you?" The question was perhaps a little direct.

The man bristled. "I have no need of a spirit's guidance."

Right. He should not have been so personal. "Is there anything else I should know about Mr. Nettle?" Henry asked, hoping the open-ended question might bring an interesting answer.

"No. We're happy he's with us, pleased with his work, and look forward to his future with the firm."

The unsettling Mr. Nettle was sounding less and less like a potential suspect. Henry thanked Mr. Curtis for his time and was soon shown into Mr. Nettle's office, a much smaller version of his superior's, his desk not quite as tidy. A news sheet near the top of a pile of papers caught Henry's eye.

It came as no surprise that it was folded to the article Director Reynolds had shown him earlier; it reported that the medium was working with the police on two recent murder investigations. Henry couldn't help but wonder if Mrs. Nettle or her husband had provided the information to the reporter.

"Inspector Field." Edward Nettle stood, nodding a greeting but not offering his hand to shake. "I thought we might meet eventually, given your recent visits to my home."

"Thank you for taking the time to speak with me," Henry said politely.

"I assume you have questions for me?" Mr. Nettle gestured toward the chair before his desk as he sat, confident in both mannerisms and speech, even as he eyed Henry with wariness.

He couldn't be much older than Henry, with neatly combed pale hair that brushed his collar. His polished appearance included a gray woolen suit, a fussily knotted tie, and a clean-shaven face. His hazel eyes were rather unusual, more golden than brown, and there was a smirk playing on his lips.

Henry already didn't like him.

Still, he offered what he hoped was a polite smile. "I do. Let us start with the important ones. Where were you the nights of the two murders your wife informed us of?"

The other man frowned, eyes positively chilly as he glared at Henry. "I don't believe she told you about any murder, but merely the location of the bodies. Isn't that correct?"

Irritating Mr. Nettle was precisely what Henry was hoping for. He well remembered Amelia's dislike of the man, and now he had his own to add to that. Stirring Mr. Nettle's emotions seemed the best way to put him off balance, so he would say more than he'd intended. That might be easier than Henry had expected.

"Right. The location." Henry nodded as he pulled out his notebook. "And the fact there were *dead bodies* at the location." Bodies implied murder in this circumstance.

Mr. Nettle nodded, seemingly oblivious to Henry's point.

That was all right. He would catch on soon enough.

"Your whereabouts, sir?" Henry asked again.

"At home, as I'm sure my wife told you yesterday." His face tightened with displeasure. "One of your men also came by earlier this morning to speak with our maid to verify the same."

"Oh?" Henry had spoken with the constable earlier and heard as much, but wasn't certain the maid could be trusted, given her obvious loyalty to her employer. "Do you have other servants?"

"A man comes each morning to help with the heavier tasks, and a day maid." Mr. Nettle sent him a pointed look. "As the constable learned when he asked the same question."

"I see." Henry neither confirmed nor denied that. "Your wife's ability to speak with spirits is interesting."

Mr. Nettle's lips twisted. "She doesn't speak with them like you and I are talking. They communicate messages to her using images and sometimes words. Occasionally they speak through her, during a séance."

"How amazing that must be."

"It is." Mr. Nettle straightened, his gratification tangible. "I am quite proud of her. The gift has often been a burden, but she manages it well."

Henry offered a friendly nod. "Doesn't hurt that such things bring some additional money to the household, eh?"

The man didn't take the bait. "It only makes sense that Mary should be compensated for her efforts. After all, few can do what she does, and it is difficult for her."

"How so?" The longer Mr. Nettle talked, the more likely he was to allow something helpful to slip out.

"It's exhausting for one thing. I've suggested she work on strengthening her mind and body, but..." The man's expression suggested the idea hadn't been well received.

"Why not perform for a larger audience like other mediums? That seems like it would be of greater benefit to all involved." Henry tended to agree with Amelia that the Nettles had hoped for some free publicity by having her write an article about the medium—publicity, and the coin that came with it. "I have seen such things advertised in concert halls."

"Mary doesn't want to. She insists it's too much for her."

"But you think with the proper training, she could?" Henry asked, assuming Mr. Nettle would approve of such an endeavor.

The man inclined his head. "It has crossed my mind. However, she might also gain the respect due her by only taking select clientele. Those who are affluent enough to truly appreciate her talent."

And who could pay more, but Henry didn't say that. "Can't hurt for them to hear the police have worked with her." He tipped his head toward the news sheet.

Mr. Nettle's face turned ruddy as he adjusted the papers, covering the article. "Any time her name is mentioned in the news sheets, it can be helpful."

"But it's not as if dead bodies show up daily."

"No." Mr. Nettle's eyes narrowed. "Did you have additional questions?" He gestured toward his desk. "I'm rather busy at the moment."

"Of course."

Mr. Nettle's alibi was questionable as far as Henry was concerned, but he did have one, if the servants could be believed. Henry needed more to pursue him as a potential suspect; something other than a feeling that all was not as the man had presented it.

However, it didn't look as if Henry would learn more in this interview.

"Do you and your wife entertain?" At Mr. Nettle's puzzled look, Henry added, "Do you often have friends visiting, for dinner, that sort of thing?"

"Rarely. Mary never knows when the spirits might communicate with her. It can make for awkward dinner parties."

"I suppose it might. So she doesn't have many friends?"

"No."

Someone had to know more about the couple, and Henry needed to speak with them. "What of relatives? Do you or Mrs. Nettle have any who live nearby?"

"Mary has a sister north of London."

That could be useful. "She doesn't share the same talent as your wife?"

"No."

"Can you provide her name and address?" Perhaps speaking to the sister could be helpful.

"Surely you don't intend to bother her." Mr. Nettle's look of disapproval couldn't be denied.

"I hope not, but I wouldn't want to have to return to your office again for it." Henry glanced out the open door toward the employees working at their desks, several of whom shot them curious looks. "No doubt rumors are already spreading about why a Scotland Yard inspector is speaking with you."

Mr. Nettle glared at Henry as he pulled a piece of paper from a drawer. "Allow me to provide her information for you."

"Thank you."

Henry departed with the address, deciding to keep an eye on Edward Nettle. To that end, he crossed the street and found an alleyway from which to watch.

He was swiftly rewarded. Only a quarter of an hour later, Mr. Nettle emerged, looked both ways, then walked at a brisk pace down the street, Henry close on his heels.

Chapter Thirty

Amelia sank into the chair Mrs. Nettle pointed to, body stiff and mind blank. A voice inside her head suggested she should leave as fast as her feet could carry her, yet she couldn't bring herself to do so.

Not when there was a chance to learn more.

But what was she willing to risk in order to help Henry? She didn't know the answer.

"What do you have in mind?" Amelia asked as briskly as she could manage.

The odd smile remained on the medium's face, making Amelia even more uneasy. "I will call on the spirits to see what their message is for you."

"Just the two of us?" Amelia asked as she glanced around the empty room. "I thought more people were needed. I'd be happy to ask my maid to join us."

Yes, that was it—Yvette. She needed an ally—

"No need when the presence of the spirits is this strong."

That was less than reassuring.

"You remember how it's done?" Mrs. Nettle asked as she reached for the matches.

Amelia drew a slow breath and placed her gloved hands on the table, vaguely wondering if the soft leather would offer protection from what was to come. For some reason, she had the sense she might need a shield of sorts. "I believe so."

"Your feet should be firmly on the floor. Your mind clear," the medium directed calmly. "We shall see who answers our call."

Amelia did as requested, worry forming a knot in her stomach. Was this a good idea?

"Today, we call on the spirits for Mrs. Amelia Greystone." Mrs. Nettle struck a match and lit the shortest candle, her hand trembling slightly. "For her daughter, Lily. For her husband, Matthew."

Amelia's breath caught at the precious names. How did Mrs. Nettle know them? Memories of them raced through her mind, more vivid than they'd been in a long while, making her heart ache.

Was she about to hear their voices again?

Mrs. Nettle struck a second match to light the middle candle. "Spirits of the departed, we call you forth with only good intentions." She hummed the same single note as before, lighting the final candle before blowing out the match and setting it down, placing her hands on the table and closing her eyes.

Emotions flooded Amelia as the medium completed each step. How she longed to see Lily and Matthew again. She missed them so very much. Sorrow for all she'd lost swept over her, and tears threatened until she could hardly breathe.

Yet a rational part of her mind, a quiet still voice, insisted the séance couldn't change the past. Communicating with them again so briefly and through the medium—if she even could—it wouldn't truly help them or her.

And despite all that rationality, Amelia closed her eyes, sending the two her love and wishing them well.

The person she wanted to help most was Henry. To help him find the murderer and bring justice to the victims' families. The thought had her opening her eyes.

Could whatever spirits Mrs. Nettle was supposedly channeling help with that? A glance at the medium showed her swaying slightly, eyes still closed.

There was no time like the present to try. "Who killed Clarissa Digby and Eleanor Tisdale?" Amelia whispered into the quiet.

Cold air swept through the room, the candle flames dancing wildly in response.

Mrs. Nettle's eyes flew open, and she stared across the room. "*He* did." Her voice did not sound like her own.

"Who?" Amelia pressed. The medium's strange tone sent fear racing along her spine, but Amelia was determined to learn more.

"Edward."

Amelia stilled, not daring to breathe. Only one man with that name came to mind. "Edward...Nettle?"

The medium nodded, gaze still holding across the room. "As was noted on the drawing." She spoke slowly, her voice low. "Leave Edward. Danger."

Amelia could only blink as the image of the drawing came to mind. L E had been repeated, as had the letter D. *Dear heaven.*

Mrs. Nettle huffed out a sigh and blinked several times, her breath coming quickly as she glanced about the room before her gaze fastened on Amelia. "Did they come through? Your loved ones?"

Amelia stared at her, uncertain what to say or how to explain what she'd revealed, but knowing she had to try. She licked her dry lips. "Mrs. Nettle, there's something I must—"

A quiet knock on the sitting room door interrupted her. "Mrs. Greystone?"

"Yvette?" Amelia stiffened in surprise.

Another muffled voice could be heard, the two arguing in the hall, then the door swung open to reveal Yvette along with Mrs. Nettle's maid.

"I'm sorry, ma'am," the Nettles' maid said, red faced. "I couldn't stop her—"

"I've warned you against interrupting, Ida." The medium glared at her maid.

"Mrs. Greystone," Yvette continued before the other maid could respond, "I am not feeling well. I'm sorry, but we must leave." The urgency in her tone and expression was clear, but Amelia felt certain it had nothing to do with the maid feeling ill. Then what was it?

Something was wrong. Had Yvette somehow learned Edward Nettle was the killer?

"Of course. We will go, this moment." Amelia turned back to the medium when the woman placed her hand over Amelia's.

"Wait. We must close the connection—"

"There's no time for that," Amelia said, pulling her hand free to pat the other woman's arm to reassure her as a thought struck her. "In fact, I need you to come with us."

Mrs. Nettle stared at Amelia as if she'd lost her senses. "Whatever for?"

"There's something at my house I want to show you. The—the spirits demanded it." It would be too hard to explain, let alone convince the woman that her husband was a murderer.

Yet one glance at the maid, Ida, suggested she already knew the truth. The anger glittering in the servant's eyes would have been enough to give anyone pause, but not Amelia.

Not today.

"Madam?" The worry in Yvette's demeanor was enough to have Amelia pushing to her feet.

"Yes, we must go. I wouldn't want you to be ill all over Mrs. Nettle's nice rug." Amelia reached for the medium's arm to draw her to her feet, mind racing. "I am quite desperate to show you the laboratory at my home. I think you will find it fascinating, the spirits said so." It was the only way she could think to give to convince the woman to come with them.

But it did not appear to work. Mrs. Nettle pulled her arm free, brow furrowing. "I'm sorry, but I cannot leave with you. I am expecting my husband soon."

Oh, no. That was precisely what Amelia feared. "We will return you home before then, I assure you." She was willing to promise Mrs. Nettle anything as long as she left with them. She turned to Ida. "Please get Mrs. Nettle's cloak. It's rather chilly today," she added, hoping to remove the maid from the room.

Yvette hurried forward to take Mrs. Nettle's other arm, seeming to understand why they must take their hostess with them, and sensing the urgency in her mistress's words. "Yes, we should go."

"Please hurry, Ida," Amelia ordered in as calm a voice as she could muster.

The maid eased backward out of the room, clearly torn between following the order and staying with her mistress. Amelia would settle for that. At least she wasn't blocking the doorway anymore.

With a nod at Yvette to confirm they were of the same opinion about departing quickly, Amelia moved forward, drawing the medium along with her. "My laboratory is the perfect place for us to complete the questions I have for the article on your skills for *London Life*." Amelia smiled at the maid. "I will bring her back as soon as we're done. It shouldn't take long—"

"But Mrs. Nettle, I don't think you should go," Ida protested.

"The article is very important, Ida." Yet still the medium hesitated before taking another step. "You know that."

Amelia kept walking, pulling her along, relieved to start down the hallway, the stairs now in sight. "My cab is just outside."

The medium glanced over her shoulder at Ida, even as she continued forward. "I will finish the interview and return home. Please tell my husband where I am."

Amelia shuddered at the thought of Mr. Nettle turning up at her home. Luckily her destination would not be home, but Scotland Yard to find Henry.

How they could prove Edward Nettle was guilty of murder remained unclear, but she had complete faith in Henry's abilities. She need only alert him to the situation. He might not believe it at first, given his doubt in divination, but—

"Mary?" a male voice called out from below, followed by the sound of the front door slamming shut. "Mary. Where are you?"

"Oh, good." Mrs. Nettle nodded, sending Amelia an uneasy smile. "He's here. I can tell him where I'm going myself."

Amelia halted as Edward Nettle climbed the stairs, pausing when he caught sight of them.

"Well, well, well. What do we have here?" he asked, a glint in his eyes Amelia didn't care for.

She tightened her grip on the medium's arm, thoughts racing as to how to escape. If only she'd told Henry where she was going.

Fear caught in her throat. Somehow, she had to save not only herself but Yvette and Mrs. Nettle, then find Henry to tell him what she'd learned.

But how when a murderer stood before her?

Chapter Thirty-One

HENRY SLOWED HIS PACE as he watched Edward Nettle enter his home after fifteen minutes of walking. *Damn.* He'd hoped the man would lead him somewhere of interest. Waiting outside the Nettle residence again was unlikely to prove helpful.

In truth, Henry had nothing other than a hunch that the man was in any way involved in the murders. No evidence had emerged to support the feeling, plus he had an alibi, albeit a questionable one. Granted, his hunch might only stem from his unfounded dislike of Mr. Nettle, something he didn't care to admit. Rarely had he allowed emotions to color his judgment in the past, and it didn't sit well with him now.

And still he stood here, staring at a closed door.

Perhaps he should return to Scotland Yard and find Fletcher. They could review the details of the jewels Clarissa Digby had stolen and sold. Or interview Eleanor's gentlemen friends that her friend had named to see if that led anywhere. Either path could lead to justice for both women.

As Henry paused to consider the options, his gaze swept over the street, halting at the sight of a hansom cab just down from the Nettle's door.

Chances were it had nothing to do with the medium or her husband, but still, Henry found himself walking toward it to ask the cabbie what his business there was. He frowned as he neared, staring in surprise at the familiar driver—the same man who'd driven him and Amelia the night they'd found Eleanor's body.

"Inspector." The cabbie tugged on the brim of his hat. "Fancy meetin' you 'ere."

"What brings you to this street?" Henry asked, fear forming as cold as ice in the pit of his stomach.

Please don't let the driver's presence have anything to do with—

"Mrs. Greystone and her maid are visitin' that house just there." He gestured toward the Nettles' home. "Said 'ow I was to wait fer 'em."

Amelia. Just as he'd feared.

"Thought they'd 'ave returned by now," the cabbie added with a disgruntled look.

Henry didn't bother to respond but turned to run toward the house, leaping over the short fence that lined the garden. He tried to tell himself there was no reason to worry—Amelia might have had a few questions for the article.

Yet that didn't ring true. He didn't think she'd intended to proceed with it after their last strange meeting with the medium. Which meant she could be in danger.

He lifted a hand to knock, only to hesitate at the sound of raised voices coming from within. He tested the door, more than relieved to find it unlocked. Still, years of habit forced him to follow procedure and knock before opening the door. "Police!"

"Henry!" Amelia's cry had him turning to look up the stairs, where she stood two steps above Edward Nettle, her maid, Mrs. Nettle, and the Nettle maid behind her.

He had one foot on the first step when Edward Nettle shouted, "Stay where you are!"

The knife in the man's hand had Henry doing precisely that. *No.*

"Put that down, Nettle," Henry ordered in as calm a voice as he could manage.

The man shook his head, glancing between the ladies standing above him and Henry below. "This—this is all wrong. It's not how it's supposed to go."

"How do you mean?" Henry asked, climbing another stair, his gaze switching to Amelia and the fear glittering in her eyes. Yet she stood forward, one hand stretched out as if to shield Mrs. Nettle, Yvette, and the Nettles' maid. Equal parts admiration and frustration filled him at the way she protected the other women. "Tell me about how it should go."

"None of you should be here." Nettle shifted his focus to his wife. "Mary, why is Mrs. Greystone here?"

"I thought to h-help her finish her article. To better show her my-my ability. Isn't that what you wanted?"

Henry took another step.

"Stop!" Nettle glared at Henry, the knife swinging around. "That's far enough."

"Henry," Amelia began, "he's the one—"

There was no doubt in Henry's mind as to what she meant.

"Shut up!" Nettle thrust the knife toward Amelia and she jerked back as the blade came near her. Nettle's attention remained on Henry, seeming to sense that the way to control him was by threatening Amelia.

Damn if he wasn't right.

Henry remained in place, weighing his options. No Fletcher on the way—no one at the Yard even knew where he was. A rush up the stairs might put Amelia in more danger. She couldn't move out of the way with the others so close behind her. The idea of retreating was abhorrent.

Then what could he do?

Nettle's mouth tightened as he glared at Henry. "My wife told you I was here the nights of the murders, and Ida verified it. I have an alibi."

"Your wife often retires early," Amelia said firmly, even as her voice quivered. "How would she know whether or not you stepped out at night?"

"That's not true." Nettle scowled at his wife. "Is it, my dear?"

"N-No. Of course not." The medium was less than convincing.

"Henry, Mr. Nettle murdered Eleanor and Clarissa," Amelia continued, bracing herself as if expecting the man to swing the knife yet again. "She told me—"

"Mary, what have you done?" Nettle demanded in a harsh voice.

Henry stared. It didn't seem likely that the medium would accuse her husband, but Amelia wouldn't lie.

His wife's mouth gaped as she stared in confusion. "Nothing. I never said that!"

"You didn't," Amelia confirmed. "But the spirits did."

Mrs. Nettle's eyes went wide. "What? What are you talking about?"

"It's true," Amelia continued, though Henry wished she wouldn't, given how she was upsetting Nettle.

Who knew what he would do if pressed? Worse, Amelia was the nearest target.

Henry eased up another step, then another. The least he could do was make use of the distraction Amelia was providing.

"Ida is mending a cloak in the kitchen," Yvette added, her voice trembling. "A man's gray one. A-And I think it matches the sample in your microscope, Mrs. Greystone."

"*Why*?" Amelia asked Nettle, her tone full of outrage as she confronted the man. "Why did you kill those women? You didn't even know them, did you?"

"I didn't realize the first one was a woman until Mary told me. You don't understand, no one does." His attention returned to his wife. "Except for Mary. She is special, and it's time the world sees it."

"Edward?" The horror in his wife's voice was undeniable. "What have you done?"

Henry watched as Nettle's mouth twisted. "What had to be done. A sacrifice, of sorts. A step to lift you up—you were never going to get there on your own. You'd be nowhere without me." He shook his head, his frustration obvious. "I've told you and told you that you need to be stronger to truly let your gift shine. But you wouldn't listen, so I had to act. You left me no choice."

"Oh, Edward." Mrs. Nettle stared in disbelief at her husband. "How could you?"

"I did it for us." The man seemed desperate to convince her. "You and I have always had a connection, certainly more than the one you claimed to feel with Mrs. Greystone. And the only predictions you've had of late were regarding bodies, so I knew that if I sacrificed those two and hid them, the spirits would tell you about them. You could help the police again. You'll soon be famous. I've made sure of it."

Henry eased toward Nettle, but Amelia was even closer and still within reach of the man and his blasted knife. A scratch on Nettle's neck drew his eye. Had that come from Eleanor? The thought enraged Henry.

"How could you?" Mrs. Nettle shoved away Amelia's arm and moved down a step, anger making her movements jerky. "And now you're saying it's *my* fault? You always make it my fault."

"Because you're not as strong as you should be!"

Mrs. Nettle reached out and shoved him back.

"No!" Ida screamed. "Don't hurt him!" The maid tugged her mistress's arm to stop her, but it was too late.

Nettle stumbled, nearly losing his footing on the stairs, and the maid screamed—Amelia stepped forward to push him again, the sudden move enough to allow Henry to race up the last few steps and grab the man's flailing arms, the blade grazing Henry's cheek before he was able to gain control of Nettle's hand.

"Drop it," Henry ordered, cheek stinging and blood boiling, as he pressed his thumb into the man's wrist, only to lose his grip on the waving limb.

"You don't understand!" Nettle fought like a wild thing, the awkward position on the stairs thwarting Henry's attempt to constrain him. "None of you do!"

The blade glinted in the light as Nettle thrust it at Amelia. She cried out and the sound sent Henry's heart hammering.

He couldn't lose her–not when he'd only just found her.

Henry shoved his shoulder into Nettle's side and pushed him into the wall, hoping like hell Amelia hadn't been badly hurt.

Anger lent him strength: anger for Amelia, for Eleanor, for Clarissa Digby, for all the defenseless victims and unsolved murders he'd seen over the years.

Life wasn't fair, as he'd thought so many times before, and men like Nettle were part of the reason that was true.

Henry drew back to punch the man squarely in the jaw, relishing the sense of justice that flowed through him. Then he did it again for good measure, shaking his throbbing fist.

The man slumped against the wall and slid to the step, motionless, eyes half closed.

Henry moved back, not feeling bad in the least when Nettle continued down two more steps. He reached for the knife that had fallen to the floor, then immediately looked to Amelia. "Where are you hurt?"

"I'm not." She gestured toward a cut in her cloak. "N-Nothing a bit of needle and thread can't fix." Her eyes darkened as she drew closer. "But your cheek is bleeding."

He wiped it with the back of his hand and it came away with blood. "Nothing serious." He couldn't resist reaching to squeeze her arm, more relieved than he could say that she hadn't been hurt. "Everyone else is well?" A glance at the others suggested they were all right, though Mrs. Nettle looked terribly upset.

The medium hurried down a few stairs to where her husband slouched, eyes now closed. “Darling, are you all right?” She touched his cheek but received no response.

That was fine as far as Henry was concerned, at least until his temper cooled. “Yvette, could you bring me the cloak with the hole in it?”

“Of course, Inspector.” She smiled as she moved past them, glaring at Ida who stood wringing her hands with tears in her eyes. “I’d be pleased to.”

“Thank you.” He kept an eye on Nettle as he assisted Amelia around the couple and down a few stairs until she was at eye level. “You are certain you’re well?”

“Yes.” She shook her head, her expression befuddled. “But Henry—how did you come to be here right when we needed you?”

Henry tried to let out some of the tension tugging at his shoulder blades. “I interviewed Nettle at his work and didn’t care for some of his answers. I watched outside his office for a brief time, and when he left, I followed. He led me here. Then I saw the cabbie, outside—”

“Oh!” Amelia’s eyes widened. “I nearly forgot he was waiting for us.”

“Would you be so kind as to ask him to find the nearest constable?” Henry glared at the Nettles, noting Ida now sat several steps behind them, pressing her hands to her face. “We are going to need a wagon to take the two of them to the Yard.”

"Both of them?" Amelia asked as she followed his gaze, concern in her eyes.

Henry nodded solemnly. "Mr. Nettle will be arrested for murder, and his wife questioned to determine the level of her involvement."

Amelia nodded and leaned forward to press a kiss on his uninjured cheek, sending his thoughts swirling. "Thank you for saving me yet again. You seem to be making a habit of it," she added with a wry smile.

"Once again, I am to blame for you being in danger in the first place." He frowned, detesting the thought. Was this to be their courtship: danger and then relief?

"As long as I'm with you, I can't bring myself to mind." She grinned, kissed his cheek again, then continued down the stairs. "I will return directly."

Henry blinked to clear his thoughts. He truly cared for Amelia. In fact, from the way his heart pounded, and his thoughts had muddled, it might be...love.

He gave himself a mental shake. Now was not the time for such things. He had work to do.

Henry shifted Mrs. Nettle to one side and reached for her husband, knowing he would take great pleasure in seeing the man taken away in handcuffs.

The remainder of the afternoon was spent sorting through the details of the case at Scotland Yard.

If not for Edward Nettle's confession, the murders would've been challenging to categorically prove. Amelia might have been witness to the 'spirits' claim—channeled through the medium—but that would be difficult to convince Director Reynolds of, let alone a judge and jury.

The initials on the drawing were much the same; helpful, but not conclusive. The bit of torn fabric Eleanor had held was the best piece of evidence, especially when it matched Nettle's cloak, and the hair matched his as well.

Nettle told them he'd selected King's Cross station after taking the train for a work meeting one day not long ago. The numerous people who passed through there, not to mention that it was located far enough away from his home not to rouse suspicion, made it an obvious choice. He'd followed Miss Digby through the broken fence and into the railyard. Nettle acted quite proud of himself for using the abandoned tunnel, sharing that he'd forced Eleanor into it when he'd come upon her nearby. He'd planned to take a third life, if necessary. Thank goodness they'd caught him before that.

"I'm sorry, the wife told Mrs. Greystone that her husband murdered those women?" Fletcher asked with a puzzled look as they watched a constable hauling Edward Nettle out the door, headed for custody. Mary Nettle would remain in custody for the time being as well. The maid was still being questioned.

"Not exactly." Henry shifted in his chair, still uncomfortable about what Amelia had shared. "I'm told that during a séance, Mrs. Greystone asked her who had killed the victims. In a voice that wasn't her own, the medium was quite clear—Edward Nettle."

Fletcher scratched his head. "Huh. That's a new one, eh?"

"Yes, and one I hope we don't encounter again." Henry couldn't claim he truly believed in such things, but he believed in Amelia. She was right. Not all they witnessed could be explained, and perhaps they didn't need to always have answers, even if he felt less than satisfied without them.

"I nearly forgot to mention that Mrs. Digby stopped by earlier to inquire about the status of her daughter's investigation," Fletcher added.

"Oh?" Henry nodded. "I'm pleased we will be able to share the news that we have made an arrest."

"I couldn't help but ask about the reason her daughter had posed as a man," his sergeant admitted with a rueful look.

"And?" Henry was pleased he had as he was curious too.

"She had difficulty finding employment when she moved to London, and noted how many more positions were open for men with far better wages as well. And it was also as you thought—she felt safer pretending to be a male."

"I'm sorry it didn't keep her safe in the end." Henry stood and reached for his hat. "I'm going to call on the Tisdales to advise them of the arrest, then my father, followed by Mrs. Greystone to make certain she hasn't experienced any ill effects from the events of the day."

He was anxious to share the news with his father, but less so to update the Tisdales. They would have more questions than he could answer. However, seeing Amelia again to reassure himself that she was well gave him something to look forward to. If given the chance, he intended to tell her just how much she had come to mean to him.

The sergeant grinned. "Excellent idea, sir. Please give your father and Mrs. Greystone my best."

"I will." Before he could take more than a step, commotion sounded near the entrance.

Sergeant Johnson approached with a nicely dressed young man at his side. "Inspector Field, this is the gentleman who stopped by before. He wants a word with you."

Henry didn't know him, but he was clearly distraught, his face pale, a bead of sweat on his brow. "Is something amiss, sir?" Henry asked politely.

"Y-yes." He removed his hat and moped his brow. "I want to speak to you regarding Eleanor Tisdale."

Henry stilled, sharing a concerned look with Fletcher. "Why don't we step into an interview room?" He led the way to an empty one with Fletcher and the stranger, gesturing toward a chair on one side of the table. "What do you have to tell us?"

The young man blinked rapidly as he sat, shoulders slumped. For a moment, Henry thought he might weep, but he seemed to gather himself and straighten. Still, he didn't speak.

"You knew Miss Tisdale?" Henry prompted, more than anxious to hear what he might say.

"I-I did." He rubbed his hands on his thighs before placing them carefully on the table. "I'm the reason she was killed. I'm to blame. Arrest me if you must."

Henry frowned, given the fact that he knew beyond a doubt they already had the guilty one. But clearly something was on the man's mind. "Explain yourself."

"We were to meet that night. At King's Cross." He sniffed, as if his emotions might overcome him. "We intended to spend the evening together at Covent Garden. It was supposed to be a bit of a lark. That was all. Some time to ourselves. So we could come to know one another better."

With a weary sigh, Henry glanced at Fletcher, who scowled at the stranger.

"Why did you not come forward before now?" the sergeant demanded.

"I didn't know she'd been killed." The man's face crumpled. "*Murdered.*" He shook his head as if still unable to believe it. "When she didn't arrive at our meeting place, I assumed she changed her mind. That her parents discovered our plan or something." He shook his head. "Charge me if you must, though I didn't kill her. But I certainly should've searched for her."

Though it was on the tip of Henry's tongue to agree, he held back. The harsh lesson seemed to be one the young man had already learned. He took out his notebook. "Tell us everything you can."

He hoped the details would give Mr. and Mrs. Tisdale some comfort in their grief. And while he was disappointed to delay calling on Amelia, she would want to know the man's story as well. Besides, he and Amelia had all the time they needed. Their future was only beginning. The thought eased more of his tension as he returned his attention to the young man. All the time in the world.

Epilogue

Two weeks later

AMELIA LISTENED IN FASCINATION as Arthur Taylor described a particularly interesting examination he'd recently performed. While the subject itself was rather gruesome, the surgeon treated it with respect and left out the unpleasant details few wanted to hear, including Amelia. She tended to think the watchful eye of his wife contributed to his restraint.

Henry smiled in amusement at the story, catching Amelia's gaze on numerous occasions, making her heart patter far quicker than any postmortem description. Who could blame her for feeling rather breathless by the time the waiter in a black jacket and crisp white apron served dessert?

The restaurant where they dined was located near the theater district, and popular based on the number of people dining there. The modest décor was comprised of pressed cotton tablecloths, pendant gaslights that cast a soft glow, and patterned wallpaper above dark wood wainscoting. Most importantly, their food was delicious.

Luckily, the tables were far enough apart that Amelia's eager questions only drew a few eyes when the other diners overheard a sentence or two.

Mrs. Taylor was lovely, not to mention positive and kind. She clearly adored her husband and seemed like the kind of person with whom Amelia could imagine becoming friends. Mr. Taylor's regard for his wife was also apparent. He was intelligent and well-spoken, making it easy to see why he and Henry had become friends.

Henry had been quite busy the past two weeks as he sorted through the final details of the murder investigation, but he'd kept her apprised when possible. Mrs. Nettle had professed to know nothing of her husband's activities, despite what the spirits had said through her. After much questioning, she had finally been cleared. She'd promptly fired the maid, who it seemed had been quite 'friendly' with Mr. Nettle, and gone to live with her sister, stating her divination ability had come to an end. What that meant, Amelia didn't know, but thought it was understandable, as Fleet Street had published numerous articles about the couple and the cursed divinations, none of them flattering. Ida, the maid, had been charged with knowingly providing a false alibi. The police had not been able to locate the male servant who had done the same.

Amelia couldn't help but wonder if Lily or Matthew might have reached through the veil during that last séance if Amelia hadn't interrupted Mrs. Nettle to ask about the murder victims. She'd made that choice in the heat of the moment but didn't regret it. A sense of peace had come over her later that day, as if her loved ones were pleased she was moving on. They would forever be a part of her, as would her love for them, but the future now beckoned.

Finally, Amelia and Henry could put the investigation behind them and focus on enjoying their courtship.

She shared another glance with him, her heart filling with joy at the admiration in his eyes. When he'd called on her the evening after he'd arrested Edward Nettle, she'd thought for a moment that he might profess his...feelings for her. He'd made it clear how much he cared, but by the end of the evening, there had been no direct declaration of love.

That was all right, she reassured herself. There was plenty of time for such things. Besides, that would give her the chance to work up the courage to tell him the same, when the moment arrived.

The thought alone was enough to send her pulse fluttering.

"...at Hollowgate Heights," Mr. Taylor continued, the name bringing Amelia back to the conversation.

"I'm sorry," she said curiously. "What were you saying?"

"My most recent case involved a man diagnosed with cancer who died in mysterious circumstances while being treated at Hollowgate Heights." The surgeon frowned. "It's a puzzling situation, and I'm tempted to ask Henry to look into the matter."

"Hollowgate Heights, the new sanatorium?" Amelia asked, worry taking hold.

"Yes. Are you familiar with it?" Mr. Taylor asked politely.

"In a way. A friend of mine is there now for treatment," Amelia said, an image of the desperate Louisa Elmcroft filling her mind. "When she mentioned hydropathy and fasting, I admit to being concerned, though she insisted many patients have seen success. She considered their work transformative."

Mr. Taylor leaned forward, his gaze shifting between Amelia and Henry. "I share your worry. I hope your friend has someone to ensure her wellbeing."

Unease crawled down Amelia's spine as her gaze met Henry's. "I believe I will take it upon myself to do so. How terrible to think a place meant for good health might cause harm."

"It's difficult to say whether the disease caused the death or the treatment in this case." Mr. Taylor shook his head. "But from what little I know, the matter should be looked into."

Amelia looked to Henry, her concern growing. "I don't suppose you would consider accompanying me to the sanatorium one day soon, would you?"

"It would be my pleasure." Henry nodded with a smile, taking her hand momentarily and giving it a squeeze before respectfully releasing it. "With luck, we will find your friend much improved."

Yes, with any luck.

So why was it that Amelia feared that wouldn't be the case?

Ready for more of the Field & Greystone series? Look for ***The Sinister Deception***!

A fashionable new sanatorium is attracting London's elite with the promise of curing many ills but whispers

soon emerge of questionable practices. Do they offer miracle treatments...or something far more sinister?

Amelia Greystone is alarmed by the rumors as a friend currently resides within the sanatorium's walls. She turns to Scotland Yard Inspector Henry Field, and together they begin to track down patients and scrutinize supposed cures.

Before they can press further, disaster strikes. A bomb detonates at Scotland Yard, and Henry is caught in the blast, leaving Amelia shaken. Seeing Henry injured stirs the grief she's tried to put behind her after the deaths of her husband and daughter. She can't bear the thought of losing another loved one. And she detests that science has been twisted into a weapon against the man who's become so dear to her.

Henry is unaccustomed to being the victim of a crime, and he struggles knowing his growing affection for Amelia has placed her in danger yet again.

As ominous truths about both the sanatorium and the bombing emerge, Henry and Amelia must rely on each other to expose a sinister deception.

Order your copy of *The Sinister Deception* today!

Author's Notes

I hope you enjoyed Henry and Amelia's latest adventure in *The Cursed Divination*. If you are curious to peek behind the scenes at some of the research involved in the story, here are a few of my notes that you might find of interest.

Divination of all types was of great interest to the Victorians, whether it was with séances, crystal balls, or tarot cards. The idea of spirits communicating with the living through mediums fascinated people from different social classes, including Queen Victoria.

King's Cross received its name from a statue of King George IV that stood at the crossroads outside the rail station. The monument, erected in 1836, was demolished in 1845, though the area kept the name. A smallpox hospital once stood where the station was eventually built.

Dowsing, water divination, or water witching, as it is sometimes called has been used since ancient times. It has also been used in an attempt to locate minerals, ores, gemstones, and oil. Dowsing or divining rods made of twigs or L-shaped rods are normally used.

The Knowledge of London test was started in 1865, reportedly after the Great Exhibition, to ensure cab drivers had a thorough knowledge of London streets as visitors to the city were less than impressed by some drivers' knowledge, or lack thereof. The examination includes 25,000 streets within a six-mile radius of Charing Cross. Drivers are tested on the standard 320 runs (or routes) and must know them backwards and forwards.

To this day, passing the Knowledge confirms that a licensed taxi driver has a thorough understanding of the roads, the routes, and the landmarks. The Knowledge is considered one of the most grueling taxi tests in the world, takes three to four years to pass, and, according to a team of neuroscientists at University College London, changes the brain of those drivers able to memorize the information by making their hippocampus larger than the average person.

Thank you for reading the story, and if you have a moment to leave a brief review, authors and other readers both appreciate them! Watch for the next book in the Field & Greystone series, *The Sinister Deception*.

Other Books by Lana Williams

The Field & Greystone Series

The Ravenkeeper's Daughter, Book 1 Also available in Audio
The Mudlark Murders, Book 2 Also available in Audio
The Gravesend Murder, Book 3 Also available in Audio
The Rookery Killer, Book 4
The Cursed Divination, Book 5
The Sinister Deception, Book 6

The Mayfair Literary League

A Matter of Convenience, Book 1
A Pretend Betrothal, Book 2
A Mistaken Identity, Book 3
A Simple Favor, Book 4
A Christmastide Kiss, Book 5
A Perilous Desire, Book 6
A Sweet Obsession, Book 7
The Wallflower Wager, a novella connected to The Mayfair Literary League and the Revenge of the Wallflowers series

A Secret Seduction, Book 8

The Wicked Widows Collection

To Bargain with a Rogue, a novella

The Duke's Lost Treasures:

Once Upon a Duke's Wish, Book 1
A Kiss from the Marquess, Book 2
If Not for the Duke, Book 3

The Seven Curses of London Series

Trusting the Wolfe, a Novella, Book .5
Loving the Hawke, Book I
Charming the Scholar, Book II
Rescuing the Earl, Book III
Dancing Under the Mistletoe, a Novella, Book IV
Tempting the Scoundrel, a Novella, Book V
Romancing the Rogue, A Regency Prequel
Falling For the Viscount, Book VI
Daring the Duke, Book VII
Wishing Upon A Christmas Star, a Novella, Book VIII
Ruby's Gamble, a Novella
Gambling for the Governess, Book IX
Redeeming the Lady, Book X
Enchanting the Duke, Book XI

The Seven Curses of London Boxset (Books 1-3)

The Secret Trilogy

Unraveling Secrets, Book I

Passionate Secrets, Book II

Shattered Secrets, Book III

The Secret Trilogy Boxset (Books 1-3)

The Rogue Chronicles

Romancing the Rogue, Book 1

A Rogue's Reputation, a Novella, Book 2

A Rogue No More, Book 3

A Rogue to the Rescue, Book 4

A Rogue and Some Mistletoe, a Novella, Book 5

To Dare A Rogue, Book 6

A Rogue Meets His Match, Book 7

The Rogue's Autumn Bride, Book 8

A Rogue's Christmas Kiss, a Novella, Book 9

A Rogue's Redemption, a short story, Book 10

A Match Made in the Highlands, a Novella

Falling for A Knight Series

A Knight's Christmas Wish, Novella, Book .5

A Knight's Quest, Book 1 (Also available in Audio)
A Knight's Temptation, Book 2 (Also available in Audio)
A Knight's Captive, Book 3 (Also available in Audio)

The Vengeance Trilogy

A Vow To Keep, Book I
A Knight's Kiss, Novella, Book 1.5
Trust In Me, Book II
Believe In Me, Book III

Contemporary Romances

Yours for the Weekend, a Novella

If you enjoyed this story, I invite you to sign up to my newsletter at lanawilliams.net to find out when the next one is released. And I'd be honored if you'd consider writing a review!

About the Author

Lana Williams is a USA Today Bestselling Author with over 55 historical fiction novels filled with mystery, romance, adventure, and sometimes, a pinch of paranormal to stir things up. Her latest venture is writing historical mysteries.

She spends her days in Victorian, Regency, and Medieval times, depending on her mood and current deadline. Lana calls the Rocky Mountains of Colorado home where she lives with her husband and a spoiled rescue dog named Sadie. Connect with her at https://lanawilliams.net/.

Printed in Dunstable, United Kingdom

74106765R00204